THOSE WE LEFT BEHIND

THOSE
WE
LEFT
BEHIND

a novel by

MILREE LATIMER

LUMINARE PRESS

WWW.LUMINAREPRESS.COM

Those We Left Behind
©2018 Milree Latimer

Printed in the United States of America

Cover Design: Claire Flint Last

Luminare Press
438 Charnelton St., Suite 101
Eugene, OR 97401
www.luminarepress.com

LCCN: 2017961197
ISBN: 978-1-944733-51-3

To Jerry,

who brought me to a writer's dream,
to a home in the country, the best writing retreat
any author might desire.

You have given me my best adventure ever.
And you are there.

When we speak of loss, we also speak of love
The ribbons tie again and the dots connect.

Loss finds its voice as memory take its cue
How we came to this theater is the miracle.

—**JOHN BASS**, "Sister"

Prologue

She wondered that hope
was so much harder than despair.

—**PATRICIA BRIGGS**, *Cry Wolf*

September 1962

Casey climbed the stairs to the second floor of the Home for Unwed Mothers and turned toward the distressed cry of a newborn. The wailing stopped. She waited outside the room from which the crying had come. A woman holding a babe bundled in white flannel blankets soon emerged, hurrying past Casey toward the stairwell. The baby lay quietly in the nurse's arms. Casey caught a glimpse of a tiny red face, eyes squeezed shut.

"Can I go in there?" Casey asked as the nurse slipped by.

"Not right now. The doctor gave her a sedative a few hours ago. She was very agitated."

The nurse continued walking and then stopped. "Wait, are you Helena's social worker?"

Casey nodded.

"Then yes, take a gown from the outer room and go in. You need to be with her."

"And the baby, may I …?"

But the nurse had already disappeared down the stairs. Casey crept into the room where Helena had given birth early that morning. The lights were dimmed; a faint antiseptic smell wafted through the air.

The young girl lay sleeping in the hospital bed in the middle of the room. Dark, black curls flared across the white pillow. Her skin was crystalline. A woman sat in a chair by the bed, watching her. She looked up at Casey as she approached the bed.

"Casey, I'm glad you're here. It was a very difficult birth. One of the worst I've seen here at the Home."

"I decided to come back, Janet. I'm grateful to you for taking over for me when I left. Helena and I had a terrible scene. Not professional—not even compassionate. But I'll stay with her for a while now. Then I must leave. Her aunt will be here soon."

After the nurse left and Casey was alone in the room with the sleeping girl, her mind returned to their last encounter, earlier that week when Casey had called in to see Helena. Her baby was due any day and Casey had wanted to say goodbye, to wish her well. But, as she'd told the nurse, it hadn't gone well. At all.

Working with Helena over the previous two months had not been easy, but nothing had prepared Casey for that day. Helena's mercurial temperament often left the social worker feeling off balance, never knowing how the girl might be on a particular day.

They had stood facing one another in Helena's room, as Casey explained she would no longer be seeing her. "The nurses and the doctor will take care of you now. You'll be in good hands, and your aunt will be here soon to take you back to England. You've been very brave through it all. I admire you."

Helena's face fell. "But, why are you leaving me?" she wailed. Suddenly her eyes flared, and she brought her arm up as though to strike Casey. "You have no idea how I am. Godammit! I was raped. Raped by my father! And you … you just walk away. You're just a damn social worker. You don't even care."

"Enough!" Casey had yelled, shocking both of them. Frustrated, wanting to stay, knowing she had to go. She threw her arms into the air, let them drop. Resigned. "Enough," she said quietly, as her mind registered Helena's torment. *Helena, you're a young seventeen-year-old girl about to deliver a baby … Of course you're angry. You're scared. You're alone. And all I can do is stand here, saying I have to leave.* Casey felt ill.

She had tried to reach for the girl at that point, to take her hand. But Helena stepped back, stopping any contact.

"After …" Casey looked at the floor. The words "the baby" stuck in her throat. "You'll be leaving, going back to England. Your aunt will take care of you. She's wealthy and can take you anywhere in the world. You might even stay here in Canada. You can begin all over again." Casey attempted to reach for Helena's hand but she couldn't penetrate the girl's wall of fury.

"I'm not going back to England." Helena mumbled through tight lips.

"What did you say?"

"I'm not going back!" Helena shrieked.

"Okay, Helena. You need to sit down, in this state you're going to …"

"Oh right, like you care?" Helena shook her head from side to side. "You're just like all of them, you all pretend. You are pathetic."

Casey felt lost. She'd asked for this assignment in this Home for Unwed Mothers, thinking she knew what to expect. She hadn't expected to find young, wealthy girls whose families had abandoned them. Young girls like Helena, thousands of miles from home. Enraged and bitter.

"No, you're wrong, Helena. I care—I care very much. I even imagined at one time that you and I might become friends ..." Casey's voice trailed off.

Another Helena appeared: a sarcastic, sullen Helena.

"Oh for God's sake, Casey. Grow up. What are you—twenty-seven, twenty-eight? Old enough to know the world is a rotten, horrid place. Just go play your nice games somewhere else."

Everything Casey had thought she might do to help Helena was cracking apart. All she could see now in front of her was a confused, angry, possibly even psychotic girl.

Helena stood, one hand over her eyes, the other pressed against her swollen belly.

"I think it's best if I just go, at least for now." Casey said and starting walking toward the door. "But this is not how I hoped we'd say goodbye."

She grasped the doorknob and waited a moment for some reaction. "Helena?"

But no reply came, only cold silence.

CASE NOTES

Helena Stafford
October 10, 1962
Casey MacMillan
Social worker—Toronto Central Agency

Seventeen-year-old girl from Dorset, England. Raped by father, pregnant. Baby delivered on

September 26, 1962, at Sally's Place, Home for
Unwed Mothers, Toronto Ontario.
Description of Helena: A spirited young woman
who is lost ...

Casey reached for the correction fluid and crossed out
her last sentence. Typing over the blank, she wrote:

Helena Stafford, presented as a disturbed and
abused young woman. Traumatized by being con-
tinually sexually abused by her father in Dorset,
England. Her baby, a boy, has been placed at this
time with a couple in their mid-thirties and proce-
dures for adoption have begun. The Children's Aid
Society has taken over the case.
Helena has been released from care at Sally's
Place and is under the guardianship of her aunt,
now living in Toronto. It was her aunt in whom
Helena confided about the horrendous life she
was living with her father. Helena's mother chose
to avoid and ignore what was going on. At this
time I recommend that Helena receive immediate
psychiatric care.
I am at present bringing this case to closure on this
10th day of October, 1962.

Casey sat back from her desk, her fingers resting on the
typewriter keys. Her head bowed. She felt empty.

Chapter One

If you don't receive love
from the ones who are meant to love you,
you will never stop looking for it.

—ROBERT GOOLRICK

January 1982

She used concentration like a drug. When life delivered the unexpected, when the unpredictable reared up, she went to her desk and mentally bulldozed confusion and consternation. Heady ideas veiled the real world.

Casey MacMillan, Chair of Humanities at City University, disavowed the life of emotion. She learned this art as a very little girl the day her parents were killed in a car accident and she survived. The expert in the Humanities Department on Love, Loss and the Human Condition, usually kept herself in a regulated state of cognitive control. But not today. Not this morning. Not since Galean's call late last night.

Four o'clock in the morning, Casey sat in her kitchen. Weary and sleep-deprived. Brain chatter had interrupted her occasional naps throughout the night. A sense that felt like an emotional buzz.

Finally, at 3:55 a.m. she'd given up and walked to the kitchen, where a soft light from a lamp and a boiling kettle for tea soothed her for a few moments, but only a few. Still the chatter whirled in her brain. Her mind was filled with excited images of possibilities, which was not at all normal for Casey. And all of it gathered around a man. As many times as she'd think, *Ridiculous! He's my friend. What am I thinking?* The anticipation kept bouncing back.

A budding prospect.

ACROSS TOWN AT THAT EARLY HOUR, GALEAN WAS AT HIS desk, writing. A late-night emergency at the hospital had left him exhausted, yet a tingling excitement stirred him. He filled the silent spaces with unreserved energy. So much was happening; so much to consider. Galean, methodical Galean, was teetering on the threshold of a life-changing decision.

Unable to focus on writing, he unfolded his lanky body from the chair and wandered over to the television, flipping on the early morning news. The newscaster went through the main stories of the day. The possibility of a Constitution for Canada, a Charter of Rights. Poland paralyzed by sanctions; American economic restrictions against Poland. Ireland, and more shootings.

None of the world's troubles could hold Galean's attention this morning. Grabbing the remote, he switched off the television, walked back to his desk and stood staring down at what he'd written earlier. The inexplicable combination of titillation and turmoil in his body and his mind pushed against the weariness. Picking up one page of the draft, he dropped into a chair by the fireplace, perched his glasses on the end of his nose and read.

FIRST DRAFT CHAPTER 1

Suffering the Gift of Love
by Casey MacMillan and Galean Laihy

Sometimes in what we think are our predictable lives, we are catapulted off our chosen path by an unexpected collision with fate. We have seen and experienced life unfold in dramatic, unanticipated ways—illnesses, accidents that change lives forever. We are all sufferers. Grief and vulnerability are born into our humanness.

Life can assault us in myriad ways when we are not looking, or even when we are paying close attention. Life is capable of taking from us those we love and whom we treasure.

Yet. There are encounters in our lives—fateful ones—that might feel almost magical and unbelievable. It may be when we are sure we know about life, about ourselves and what's possible, that we are blindsided by love. A kind of love that we may not have experienced. In essence we lose our footing and fall headlong. Any idea of loss is incongruous.

Resting his head on the back of the chair, Galean let the paper fall to his lap. He closed his eyes and remembered when he and Casey had written that particular piece. They'd sat here together in his den only a few weeks ago, talking and writing, sharing what they knew about the vagaries of life and loss and love.

"Remarkable, isn't it?" Casey had said. "We've been friends

all these years, right from grad school. We go our separate ways, and here we are ending up at the same university on the same faculty. And now, we're writing a book together! Who knew? Isn't that what is called serendipity?"

He smiled. Serendipity indeed. Casey was the person who'd made the case to the dean to bring Galean on to the Faculty.

Tomorrow he'd see her.

CASEY WOKE WITH A START. SHE'D FALLEN ASLEEP, HER HEAD resting on her arms on the kitchen table. She sat up and shook her head, trying to remember why she was here in her kitchen, asleep at the table.

Galean's call—that was it. He's coming over this morning. I've got to get moving!

She remembered his words, clearly, distinctly: "Case, I wonder if you are free for coffee. At your house as usual. There's something I want to talk over with you. It's important."

Leaning back against the chair, arms folded across her chest she wondered, what was afoot? Why the mystery?

Lately Galean had been acting unlike Galean. He was asking her unusual things when they worked together: "Case, do you think people need to know one another for long before talking about love … or marriage?" Or, he'd arrive unexpectedly at her office. "Do you have a minute?" He'd rush in, shutting the door like a man pursued. "When is it too late to consider marriage?" Or she'd find notes on her car windshield: "Casey. Alfred North Whitehead wrote once that, 'It is the business of the future to be dangerous.'

He was talking about science, but what about relationships?"

She felt puzzled and off her mark this morning. Her sense of anticipation crowding out doubt.

Yesterday she had walked around to Anne Morgan's office across the quadrangle on campus, just to see how it sounded if she dared say what she was thinking. Anne was a good friend, a colleague Casey depended on for truth, whether it be about a journal article, a student issue or life's conundrums.

She'd started right in, the moment she arrived, immediately after the hellos. "I've known Galean for almost ten years, Anne. We have been good friends to each other." And then she blurted: "I think he wants marriage."

When Casey repeated her reasons for her suspicions, telling Anne about all Galean's comments, Anne laughed. "Casey, Galean's a middle-aged man. What is he, fifty-four, fifty-five? Sounds like he's having a later-than-usual mid-life crisis."

Now today, after a sleepless night, Casey wondered, *Is Anne right? Am I imagining things? What's changed? How did I land here?* She, who could be merciless with herself, distrusted moments when optimism showed its rainbow colors. Yet, here she was. Anticipating. *Why?* she asked herself. *Why do I want this?*

Closing her eyes, Casey remembered the beginnings of the friendship she and Galean had fallen into ten years ago.

1972 SEPTEMBER

"Anybody sitting here?" He asked, pointing to the chair beside her.

No response.

Casey, with her head down over her thesis chapter and her pencil moving from line to line, was either oblivious to his presence or ignoring him. (Years later, she told Galean it was a bit of both).

He tried again, this time pulling the chair back toward him, "Excuse me, mind if I sit here?"

Without looking or turning, Casey shook her head and murmured, "Go ahead."

He sat.

People, other grad students, walked into the room with casual nonchalance. Casey, in her spot by the professor's chair, appeared to be the only person there with fervid intent—the description Galean liked to use when he would later describe their first meeting.

Putting his briefcase on the table, Galean pulled out his thesis manuscript. He set it down and flipped pages and stood them in bunches, making sure the papers were all neatly aligned. He took great care to square up each bunch, hitting the table, jogging them this way and that, straightening and stacking, straightening and stacking.

"Could you please not do that?" Casey asked, annoyance plain in her voice. "I'm really trying to concentrate on this chapter before Professor Kingwood comes." She had not lifted her head, so she appeared to be talking to her pencil.

Galean leaned down and spoke into her pencil.

"Sorry. Can I help?"

Silence. A poised pencil and a sound like a repressed chortle.

Casey sat back, turned to Galean and, with somewhere between a smile and a grimace, nodded to him. "I'm defending my thesis in a month and I'm very tense," she said. "I'm here because I need help with revisions and Dr. Kingwood is my advisor. He suggested I come to this class while I'm revising. And, I'm tutoring students. Anything else?"

Galean leaned back in his chair and folded his arms.

"I could also use some help with my revisions, and added to that I have patients at the hospital. So … who wins here? Who's most tense?" He grinned.

Moments when a friendship can take flight or ground into the dirt are sometimes built on one or two comments. This was one of those moments. A bit of silence, a fraction of time to swallow, a second to decide and …

Casey laughed. "I really am, aren't I? Very tense."

"Oh yes," he replied. "If you were a patient of mine I'd prescribe a long walk, a cup of tea or a beer." (When the story is told later, Galean insists he didn't include beer in this list.)

"It's just that …" Casey turned her chair and sat facing Galean. "I'm on a leave from my work to finish my doctoral program—I defend just before Christmas. I'm also tutoring undergrad students. And I'm about to fire my advisor, who is a lovely, intelligent man. Put all that together with, I'm not even sure today why I'm here. So don't even ask!"

By this time (as Galean told her later), he wasn't sure whether to become her doctor or offer his friendship. He decided on friendship.

From then on, the two met regularly, sometimes for a coffee over breakfast before seminar classes; a glass of wine occasionally at The White Horse Inn & Tavern. Conversation always stayed in the safe realms of research and breakthroughs in their writing. There were no personal revelations, no questions about the course of their lives; only matters of higher thought, rarified wonderings. Anything approaching real feeling was always couched in humor or speculation. Safe ground for both.

One evening when they met for supper at the Inn, Galean seemed more pensive than usual. "Casey," he began. "Is real love attainable without all the pain? Or is what most people hope for just too lofty?"

At this point in time, both of them had been working seven days a week. Galean faithful to his time at the hospital and working on his research about medical ethics. Casey writing, not sleeping, worrying about her relationship with her advisor, as her defense approached.

Casey cast him one of her steely gazes, which were famous among her students.

"Is real love attainable, without the pain? Are you kidding me? You just blew my thesis out of the water!" Her words snapped like a whip.

"Whoa, whoa, whoa! Hold on!" Galean held up his palms open toward Casey.

"I'm wondering, just wondering. You're the one who's always telling me to be more reflective, to think deep thoughts"

"So, you want me to answer that question?" Casey parried and tried another sidestep. "Maybe I'll hand it back to you. Have you ever dared to love someone?"

The air between them iced over for a microsecond, long enough for Casey to realize she'd infiltrated forbidden territory. She imagined some fledgling spirit in Galean scurrying for cover.

"Galean, I'm sorry. You don't have to say anything."

Leaning into the table, intertwining his fingers around the empty glass, he looked over at Casey. He shook his head, "No. You shouldn't be sorry. But it was a real question."

When the waiter returned to the table with their food

and wine, the conversation dwindled. The subject remained closed for many years thereafter.

THINKING BACK TO THAT CONVERSATION NOW, CASEY SAW it in a new light. Maybe all those years ago Galean had wanted to say something to her. And maybe now, the time had finally arrived. Getting up from her kitchen table, Casey stretched a tall, delicious sweep toward the ceiling. As she turned she caught a glance of herself reflected in the glass doors on the kitchen cupboards.

"What a mess you are!" she said out loud.

Galean could arrive at her door in less than an hour. Did she want him to see her looking so disarrayed, disheveled and scraggly? No!

Chapter Two

*Our hope to circumvent heartbreak in
adulthood is beautifully and ironically child-like;
heartbreak is as inescapable and inevitable as breathing.*

—DAVID WHYTE

Casey's past was something that, in her present, she kept
bound and tied, away from the light. Galean's past was
like an abandoned house, still and silent, waiting for
someone to pierce the hollowness. Neither accepted that
avoiding the past or accepting the emptiness, was like living
half-lives. Both realized and acknowledged the spirited
aliveness that passed between them. Which made their
ultimate sorrow even more poignant.

Standing at the open closet door in her bedroom, Casey
stared at a row of pants and skirts, assessing her options. It
was an unusual moment for Casey, who spent little time in
her life thinking about what to wear. This Saturday morning, with her anticipation of Galean's arrival and her sense
that he seemed on the verge of something momentous, she
reached for her only pair of flared wool pants and her lone
cashmere sweater. Beige and grey and elegant.

Half an hour later, she surveyed herself in the full-length
mirror. *Dressed for a celebration,* she thought, giving herself
a boost of courage.

She'd taken time to pin back her hair, which was usually left to curl around her neck. Laughing at herself she said to the mirror, "Galean will wonder what's going on." And in fact he would.

Downstairs, Casey opened the front door and saw that the wind had blown drifts of snow across the driveway and up onto the front porch. For a fraction of a minute she thought about going out into the elements and clearing the drive. But looking down at her wool pants, feeling her tentative curls preparing to collapse, she decided no. Galean could make his own way. He'd find a path.

As she walked back down the hall toward the kitchen, Casey put her hand up to her neck and pulled out from under her sweater a thin gold chain. It was the gift that Galean had given her upon receiving her PhD—a surprise because theirs was not a gift-giving relationship. Oh, a book here and there: "Found this book about loss in the used bin in the bookstore. Thought it might come in handy for your thesis," Galean might say to Casey, handing it to her over coffee. "Here's a book on the history of medical ethics. It was on the remainder shelf at the library," Casey said as she handed a book to Galean one day at seminar, shortly after they became friends. But the gold chain was something different and, if she admitted it to herself, she treasured it. She wore it almost every day hidden under her blouses and sweaters.

On this morning she let it rest on her neck, over her sweater. A token of possibility. A yes to showing up.

Chapter Three

The wound is the place where the Light enters you.

—RUMI

Sitting on the side of his bed, Galean squeezed his eyes shut, trying to erase the picture in his mind of the recurring nightmare that had woken him. It had arrived in the early morning hours, sliding in on the edge of wakefulness. Holding his head in his hands, Galean let his breath go free, as though waiting for the horror to release itself. When he looked over at the bright numbers of the digital clock beside his bed, he felt a sense of relief. 5:15. He could get up and start his day. There would be no more nightmare for now.

The haunting dream appeared at least once a week and, some weeks, more often. It began the same way each time: *He sat on a beach where a storm roiled in the sky over dark water. He searched the waves but couldn't see her. He tried to call her name, but his throat closed and wouldn't let sound escape. His legs felt rubbery, wouldn't hold him when he tried to stand. And then he saw her rising from the water, kelpies and tiny squid-like creatures dripping from her hair, ropes wrapped around her naked body. He tried to scream out for her, but only a strangled argh emerged.*

The nightmare was relentless, occurring again and again

over a space of months. When it started to seem like it would never stop, Galean chose to talk with a good friend, a psychologist who worked at the hospital with him. His name was John Anthony.

"I need you to tell me that I'm not crazy." He said to John as they were slowing to a stop after running together one afternoon in July. Sitting on a bench by Lake Ontario, on the edge of the city, Galean told him his story.

"She was ... what do the romantics say—the love of my life. And I was, to use that word, *crazy* about her. Her name was Kate. We were in med school together back in the mid–nineteen fifties. I was twenty-seven, old enough to know better. She was off-the-charts smart. And beautiful. I couldn't believe she'd landed in my world. She wanted to intern in Neurology, when most people hadn't even heard of it. A mysterious woman. She wondered about things like the human soul and if she might be a good enough scientist to prove its existence. Let's just say, in my life, she was like someone from another universe."

"Believe it or not," Galean continued, "I asked her to marry me, and I should have known then because she kind of laughed and said, 'Let's wait and see, let's enjoy the feelings. Let's not go there just yet. We've got lots of life to live and time to live it.'"

Before going on, Galean paused, compressing his lips as though holding back the rest of the story.

"But, it turned out she'd already decided she liked her pharmacology professor better, for a lot of reasons. Access to drugs, wild parties. 'He's fun,' she told me. This coming from a woman who believed in the human soul. The professor, him? Charming and evil, I knew that, I knew that." Galean shook his head back and forth. "And I couldn't save her. From him or from herself. She died of an allergic reaction to coke." Galean paused for a moment, staring out at the lake. "And he left the university shortly after. I think if ever I were to run into him, I'd kill him."

He paused for a moment, more an exclamation mark than a comma. Looking out over the lake, he seemed to be marking and following the course of three sailboats catching a land breeze, immersed in his own world of thought and memory. John waited for his friend to continue.

"And now, something has happened, something strange … a woman. It's almost frightening how much she resembles Kate, as though she's returning after a long disappearance."

The psychologist watched his friend's face become a mask, only his eyes reflecting the pain and confusion he was experiencing. His professional intuition told him that the pain he was witnessing in Galean was deep; deeper than loss of a future, deeper than loving and losing. He saw a man grieving, and he saw a man seeking comfort.

"This is big." He told Galean. "You and I need to talk this through. The nightmare? That's your wake-up call and your way out of the anguish I see in you. There's more going on here than Kate and whoever the woman is you speak of. They could both be triggering something you've pushed away for a very long time." He stopped and waited, wondering if Galean was going to respond to his invitation. But the reaction he got was not at all what he was expecting.

Galean responded swiftly and dramatically. "This was a mistake, John. Truly a mistake." He stood and moved away from the bench. "I shouldn't have involved you—at all. I'll deal with the nightmares. Now that I know I'm not crazy, I can do that on my own. I really have to get to the hospital.

Thanks for listening." He gathered up his running jacket and walked away.

Stunned, John watched his friend pick up on his run and head around the bend in the lake.

CASEY STOOD AT THE KITCHEN COUNTER, BEATING EGGS for an omelet, sunflower apron protecting her cashmere sweater and wool slacks. She was humming.

There came a loud knock at the back door, followed by Galean loudly calling, "Get out of bed, I'm here!"

"Get in here before you wake up the neighborhood," Casey said as she let him in.

Galean followed her into the kitchen and stood there as she poured the beaten eggs into a pan and turned on the stove.

"Come sit," she told him. "Put the bread in the toaster. Make yourself useful."

For a moment she stood with her back to him; hesitant or self-conscious, she wasn't sure. She focused on preparing the omelet as Galean made his way toward the table set for two, where the toaster was waiting. The two of them assumed their places in the kitchen like actors taking spots on a stage waiting for the curtain to rise.

Realizing he had yet to take off his parka, Galean rose from the table just as Casey turned around to put some juice on the table. He cocked his head. Grinned.

"Before I go and hang up my cheesy wet parka, let me say you look dressed to the nines for an early morning breakfast. Something going on today? Did I miss an invitation?"

Casey felt her face heat up and her cheeks redden. "I

just decided to dress in honor of the occasion. You know …our book."

Galean slid over her words and her self-consciousness with barely a glance as he went to hang up his parka. Casey poured coffee into her favorite yellow-and-blue striped mugs and placed them on the table, then took a seat. All without looking up at him.

"I finished part of the chapter I was working on for our book." Galean said as he pulled his briefcase from the floor onto the empty chair between them.

"Toast." Casey pointed to the bread. Anything to calm her heart's pounding. Galean slid the bread into the slots of the toaster and sat down.

"Bad storm going on out there, Case. If you have to go anywhere, take it easy." Galean chattered on. "Bit of a breakfast feast for me. Thanks. You know how I often go for rounds at the hospital after only eating a bit of dry toast."

Amazed at how jittery she felt, Casey inhaled a long slow breath and then let it out with a sigh. Feeling a little more relaxed, she found herself smiling as she said, "Well, somebody needs to look after you. I mean … you know … sometimes you don't take care of yourself." She wanted to shove the words back into her mouth. It all felt too personal, as if she'd taken on the job of "mother" or worse, wife. But Galean kept eating as though he hadn't heard the meaning of what she'd said.

She watched him, this fifty-five-year-old man with graying hair. He pushed the egg around his plate, picked up a small piece on his fork and absent-mindedly put it into his mouth. He was silent for several minutes.

Okay, Galean, what's in that head of yours right now? She wondered.

Suddenly he broke the silence, his voice a crisp unexpected sound as though he'd come out of a trance and realized where he was. "Casey ..." he began.

She dropped her fork letting it rattle onto her plate. "God, Galean, you almost startled me."

"Casey," he started again. "I have something to tell you; something I haven't shared with anyone yet."

She picked up her coffee mug, holding it still so she might be still. "Yes?" She waited.

"And I need you to be perfectly honest, tell me what you think."

Still wanting to stretch out time and anticipation, Casey sipped on her coffee then placed the mug very carefully and quietly back onto the table. "I will be honest," she said to him. "Just tell me what's on your mind."

"There's someone I've met and we've been seeing one another for a while now."

Something cold wrapped itself around Casey's chest, in a vise-like grip. She swallowed just to see if she could. Inhaled, just to see if she could. She felt rigid. She thought she might be sick. Swallowing again, she put both hands flat onto the table, feeling the smooth texture of the cloth. A small sound escaped, and she realized it was her own voice. "I'm not sure what you're telling me, Galean. Or maybe, why?"

"I'm turning my life on its head, Case. Aren't you the one who said we are each responsible for resuscitating our own lives? Well, I'm breathing life back into mine. And it's you, my friend, who has buoyed me up, reassured me, given me courage to do what I'm about to do—ask the lady to marry me."

Casey felt pinned to her chair. *I need an exit line. Give me an exit line.*

"You've never said a word about anyone you've been seeing, and now … you're …?" her voice cracked. *Careful, Casey, careful … take it slow.* Voices began to warn her, old voices; the ones that can tell when there's danger in the room. Except this time the danger was coming from within—her own searing humiliation. "My God, Galean. What! What are you saying? Marrying! You're getting married?"

Walking away from him could not have stunned him any more than her words did. And now he watched her clench her hands into fists. He wondered for a second if she were going to hit him. Somebody looking like Casey sat opposite him, but she felt like a stranger to him in that moment.

Very cautiously, as though approaching a wounded animal, Galean reached over to put his hand over Casey's fist. "What just happened here?" he asked her.

She sat straight in her chair and closed her eyes for a moment, drawing her hand away from Galean's. They sat neither moving, nor speaking, until Casey regained her composure.

"What's her name? Who is she?" Casey's voice was quiet, controlled. She grabbed back pieces of herself, in just the way she had all her life; rescuing herself from despair, removing herself from old hurt.

Sitting back, Galean relaxed, letting his own tension ease. A master of learned denial, skilled at dodging dissension, he deflected Casey's shock and dropped the other shoe.

"She's someone I met at the hospital. Her name's Helena Stafford."

Chapter Four

Why didst thou promise such a beauteous day,
And make me travel forth without my cloak,
To let base clouds o'ertake me in my way.

—WILLIAM SHAKESPEARE, *Sonnet 34*

Casey sat immobile. Frozen. Her throat felt closed, her breath locked.

"Casey? Are you all right?" Galean started to get up, to move to her.

She waved him away. "No, stay there."

He sat back in his chair, confused. "What just happened? You look like I've just told you your best friend died. What's going on? I came here to tell you to see what you think. I guess I've truly misread us and our friendship. I thought you might be happy for me." He spoke almost hesitantly, like a tightrope walker missing a step.

When she gave no response, he threw his arms into the air then brought them down and placed his hands, fingers intertwined, to the back of his head—Galean's default move whenever a confounding medical case or a baffling problem reared up in his path. "I'm mystified. No—I'm dumbfounded," he said, shaking his head. His forehead already creased, became a furrowed frown, his black eyebrows almost meeting.

Casey stiffened her spine even more and leaned back in her chair like a displeased teacher waiting for some clear answers. She inhaled one short breath and, on the exhale, finally spoke, each word delineated with a crisp emphasis. "I knew Helena Stafford. I knew her very well."

"What do you mean you knew her?" Galean asked, even more confused. "You say that as though she's some kind of pariah." He shook his head. "What the hell is going on? I've never seen you like this."

There were times when Casey could leave her body and stand watching herself. She wished this were one of those times. Instead her body hung from her shoulders like a heavy cloak, her throat still tight. The shock and resentment were leaking through her skin, leaving her empty. When she spoke, her voice sounded hollow.

"Galean, you and I have never talked about our personal lives. What's ironic is, I tried a few times and you always just shut the conversation down. And about knowing her? Yes, I knew her, probably better than you might. When I knew her she was pretty much a mess, maybe even kind of fierce. That's all I'm saying. Just be careful."

She swallowed. *Go no further, Casey MacMillan,* came the voice—that familiar warning voice, cold and stern.

Seeing his friend now so distressed and unsure, Galean wanted to reach over and take Casey's hand the way he might if she'd brought a faculty problem or a rejected journal article to him. But this was unfamiliar territory. A man–woman relationship place they had consciously sidestepped. Now, Casey unbeknownst to Galean, was sitting in a morass of her own humiliation combined with genuine fear for him.

He tried again, his voice quiet. "I really need to go, but I have to know what's happened. I hate not being able to talk to you, Casey … talk to me. I'm your friend. Remember me?" His intuitive way of reeling Casey in when she disappeared into her own troubled world was the linchpin in their friendship. His had an uncanny way of rescuing her from dark places. But not today.

Outside, winds whipped up fresh snow creating whirls like phantoms jigging and twirling and rattling windows. Inside, silence held court. Casey cut through it like an axe breaking ice.

"You have to go, Galean. You have patients to see. It's getting worse out there, so let's leave it all for now and catch up later, maybe on Sunday." Her voice, a depressive shade of gray.

Galean stood up. He walked out to the mudroom and grabbed his parka then came back into the kitchen. "You know, Casey, there's a whole lot I don't understand about what just happened. But I do know one thing: this conversation is not over." He put his hands on the back of the chair he'd just left and leaned in. "Case?"

"Well …" she started, knowing she shouldn't continue but unable to stop herself. "I can tell you one thing. If you decide to do this, marry Helena, it'll be the worst decision you've made in a long time."

Bitter thoughts flowed out of her embarrassment. *What was I thinking? Foolish, silly woman!* the demon Shame shouted at her. Self-judgement danced in company with her irritation at Galean's capricious and, in her eyes, adolescent behavior. She wanted to say to him, *What in God's name are you thinking?* She felt her face flushing, her throat tightening again. Escape. All she wanted was to escape. *Go, Galean. Dammit, just go.*

"Okay. This is serious." Galean picked up his gloves,

wrapped his wool scarf around his neck. Walking over to the door, he pulled on his gloves, snapping the leather against his wrists. He turned back to look at her, shaking his head, "I've always thought you were one of the most level-headed, reasoned persons I'd ever met. But today, at this moment, I don't even know who you are."

"Oh my God! We're having a lover's quarrel." Casey shot back. The words were out of her mouth before she could stop them.

Bewildered, Galean sent a returning volley across the bow. "Casey MacMillan, you are jealous! Open-minded, rational Dr. MacMillan is jealous. I don't believe it!" Digging himself further into an unfortunate hole, he laughed.

"You know what, Galean? You are an idiot! Just go!"

The wind caught the outside door and slammed it behind him as he left. The exclamation point. The final word.

DR. CASEY MACMILLAN WAS KNOWN AS THE "LOVE EXPERT" on campus—one of the reasons for the lengthy waitlist of students wanting to take her classes. The irony was, she knew much more about the subject of loss than the substance of love. Something she didn't hold back from her students.

Her late twenties had witnessed a short marriage, one that ended in a blizzard on a country road. Her husband, "who shall remain nameless," she'd say when she told the story to her students, was killed in his red-and-white Austin Mini. "Nothing much was left of the front of the car," she'd tell them.

Every year she shared her stories with the new crop of students and each time of telling, she separated herself even further from that young woman. "Guess I got lucky, which is why I'm here telling you this story. The woman in the passenger seat wasn't me. It was Marge Longstreet, our neighbor in apartment four. She was naked." Casey liked to shock her students.

Possibly time does heal wounds; but it also sows resolve. An accumulation of losses can do that. Casey chose to keep the casualties of her life locked away, only revealing them in the pages of her journals or using them as material for her students. She'd learned to separate herself from her life experiences so well that now when she related some of the stories, she felt was talking about a stranger.

Love became an elusive image, there to be explored and analyzed by Professor MacMillan. Losses became experiences to polish and refine her staunch spirit; they were the impetus to her being strong, independent and determined. No more fairy stories, no more romantic idealistic images. A vow she had made many years ago. But with Galean, Casey had foolishly dropped her cloak of self-protection and walked into images of happily ever after.

Well, never again. Never again.

———————

AFTER GALEAN WALKED OUT THE DOOR, CASEY STAYED seated, letting the humiliation wash over her. But not for long. She was determined not to stay like that, whimpering and licking her wounds. She would do something about this. Down the hall in her den lay answers. Answers chronicled in her journals.

Standing in the den, she scanned the shelves until she found what she was looking for. Pulling one particular journal from the shelf, she walked to her desk and dropped into her chair, already thumbing the pages. Written in Casey's bold hand were all the reasons Galean must not marry Helena.

GALEAN, STILL STINGING FROM CASEY'S WORDS, DROVE through the storm with renewed intent back to the hospital, back to meet Helena. He was a man confused, annoyed and enraptured. A man who bore little resemblance to the Galean who Casey thought she knew.

Hospitals are sexually charged places. Living and dying partner with one another every hour, a physicality of truth that pervades the blood and the body, particularly of the people who spend their days saving lives in company with one another.

Helena and Galean were two of those people. They'd met during a long, intensive heart surgery. She, head operating nurse, he in the gallery mesmerized, watching how she moved. Her deftness, her take-control aura reached somewhere into a lost part of his soul and his body.

It had been months ago when the inexplicable happened between the two of them and, from that moment in time, for Galean being with her became like a drug. For a reason he could not explain, he'd told nothing to Casey. Until now.

Chapter Five

To be wise, and love, exceeds man's might.

—**SHAKESPEARE**, *Troilus and Cressida*

ooking through her personal journals, Casey became immersed in a tide of memories as she read the accounts she had written after leaving the young, troubled girl at the end of the day. Casey was exhausted on those nights, but still she came back to her room in the Home, wanting to write about Helena and what was becoming increasingly clear: that her charge, a young seventeen-year-old, might be drifting into a kind of madness.

Day 15, September 24, 1962

Helena believes, somewhere within herself, that she is Helena of Midsummer Night's Dream. A chaotic family and a sense of disconnection from the real world provide fertile ground for Helena Stafford's illusory thoughts.

Yesterday afternoon while we sat in the sunroom, Helena, large and awkward in her advanced pregnancy, said to me, "I think Helena in Midsummer Night's Dream is me, or I'm her. Because she talked a lot about love, probably because she wasn't loved very much by anybody. Kind of like me."

Now, reading through her notes, Casey felt a chill. She took a long, slow sip of coffee, set the cup on the side table, and went on reading.

> Helena is a 17-year-old young woman who lives her life with a kind of defiance that at times seems manic and at other times seems deeply sorrowful. She will sit and talk about "her situation" with me but refuses to talk to a psychiatrist or a medical doctor, although she receives care for her pregnancy. She is in robust health, yet fantasizes about dying.

Casey put the journal aside. She remembered that it was soon after she wrote these entries that her placement at the Home finished. Even though she had asked for an extension and the possibility of staying on, her supervisor didn't approve it.

"Possibly too involved," he'd said, assuring Casey that Helena's case would be reviewed by the board at the Home and that Casey's notes would be made available.

How then, could it be that Helena was here in the same city and working at the same hospital with Galean? It all just seemed bizarre.

Flipping back through the pages of her journals, Casey hunted for a conversation she remembered having with Helena. She found it, back among her earlier notes.

September 22, 1962

> Tonight Helena was both determined and despairing. I wanted to just sit with her and listen, but she left the room and would not come back. She told me to "let her go."

She talked about wanting to go to nursing school, in this city. I'm worried that she may be delusional about what's possible. Then again, she is remarkably determined. But still, I fear for her.

Recalling all of this now, Casey tried to understand Galean's fascination for Helena. Was it the rescuer in him? The doctor? Or maybe there was something mysterious about Helena. *What is the attraction? He's acting like a moth to the flame.*

Putting her journal down on the floor, Casey leaned back into the armchair. The volume of chatter and self-questioning in her head was relentless. It felt like static.

How could I have been so harebrained? What was I thinking? Galean and me? What stupid story did I create?

Helena. Helena Stafford. It's been her all along. But now, I need to do something. She's dangerous.

Head back, eyes closed, Casey considered her options: *Call Galean and leave a message? What could I say that wouldn't sound senseless to him? Wait till morning and go to his office? I can't wait. Maybe I can try to explain in a letter.*

Casey went over to her desk and opened the side drawer, pulling out several sheets of paper. Sitting on the edge of her chair, she grabbed a pen from those sitting in neat parallel rows and began to write:

Dear Galean:
First things first. I am so sorry I made such an ass of myself today. I'll try to explain.
Maybe you were right, maybe I did feel a stab of jealousy. Maybe I crossed a line.

Elbow on the desk, left hand propping up her chin, pen in mid-air, Casey stopped for a second. *What line did I cross?*

she wondered. But she let the thought remain on the page and continued to write.

That's my mea culpa. What I really need to explain to you is my reaction when you told me her name. I do know Helena Stafford—or rather, I knew her. I'm sure she's the same one. How many Helena Staffords might there be with an English accent? She and I lost contact a good 20 years ago. But I remember her well.

When I was a social worker in this area, I was sent to work at a home for unwed mothers. I know, it sounds very medieval doesn't it? However, there I was. The young woman I was asked to counsel while there was Helena Stafford. Again I ask, how many Helena Staffords can there be? She told astounding stories about her life, some of which were true ... I think. She was from England, raised in a wealthy home. Some of what happened to her, I'd rather not put in this letter. I'm just hoping you and I can talk soon. Friend to friend, professional to professional.

When I look back, Galean, I think of her and remember her as a lost soul. Someone searching for a place where she might belong, yet railing against a world that she said had abandoned her. I watched how clever she could be when, with a kind of calculated intensity, she drew people into her space rather like a spider weaving a web. Including me. I thought she was extraordinary. Smart, funny, and yes, brave. After I stopped working at the Home I went back to see her, but she was gone. I tried to find her, but she just disappeared. Knowing that she dreamed of going into nursing, I'm even more convinced that you and I are talking about the same Helena.

Rest assured I'm calmer now (sort of), but I worry for you. It's all so sudden. At least it feels that way for me.

*And please believe me, this isn't envy or jealousy talking.
It's because I care.*
*Might you think about getting together with me to talk
more about what's happening? I promise to be quiet
and listen. What are you doing on Sunday morning?
Please, give me a call.*
Casey

Putting the letter into a blank envelope, Casey sealed
it and wrote Dr. G. Laihy across the front. Throwing on a
red wool coat, pulling a toque over her head down almost
to her eyes and grabbing her gloves off the counter, she
strode to the mudroom, stuffed her feet into her boots,
grabbed her keys and strode out the door—a woman on
a mission.

BEAUTIFUL, INTELLIGENT HELENA WAS DETERMINED TO MAKE
her own way, refusing to depend on the traditional roads of
marriage and men. But in the darkness of her mind raged
a demon, gasping for air.

It was that Helena Stafford, head surgical nurse at City
Hospital, who'd just gotten off work and now stood outside
the front entrance, sheltered from the snow, waiting for
Galean to pick her up. He had said he wanted to take her
to dinner because there was "something he needed to say."

When he pulled up and beckoned to Helena, she ran
across the snow-covered driveway toward his car.

"I was worried you weren't coming," she said, clamber-
ing in beside him. He leaned over and kissed her with an
un-Galean-like intensity. He smiled.

God, she's wonderful, he thought. Her black curls spilling from her woolen toque; her eyes brilliant; her face shining.

"Oh, why rebuke you him that loves you so?" He asked her.

Helena laughed. "Oh Demetrius, you *do* love me."

Were Casey nearby she might have shivered, feeling a chill run up her neck. Galean was quoting lines from *A Midsummer Night's Dream*.

A SHORT WHILE LATER, GALEAN AND HELENA WERE SITTING in their favorite restaurant. It was small, intimate. Ten tables covered with crisp white tablecloths. Candlelight shimmering. Day slipped into evening, new-fallen snow glistened under street lights.

Sitting beside Helena, Galean felt a quiver, an old remembered feeling, one unlike his determined, rational self. *The insanity of falling in love,* he smiled to himself. *Something Casey might say.*

"You're smiling," Helena said. "What are you thinking about?"

"Just enjoying," Galean replied, reaching his hand across the table to Helena's.

For an instant her eyes clouded. And just as quickly, they cleared. She drew away, pulling her hand from his. "Enjoying? Enjoying what?" she asked him.

"You, this feeling."

Helena laughed, "Are you sure it's not the wine?"

It was Galean's turn to cloud over. His euphoria, for a second, punctured.

"No, not the wine, it's you. You've cast a spell. I'm a man about to throw himself into the fire."

Galean could not believe what he was saying. Truth was, he felt bewitched. *Beware of feeling out of control.* Casey again, interrupting this moment.

He sat back against the seat, trying to gain equilibrium. He stared at Helena. *My God, she's beautiful.* Another voice intruded: *Beautiful and young. Am I just being an old fifty-five year old man, yearning after my youth?*

"Galean. You're acting strange and you're frowning. Where's that brilliant, everything-has-an-answer man I'm getting to know. How long have we been seeing one another? A few weeks, a couple of months? I haven't seen this side of you. I think I like it."

The eroticism of power aroused her. Her dark eyes fixed on his, strands of black hair fell around her face. She moved easily, leaning into him across the table. Her fingers like delicate flames found his hands.

"I like it a lot," she whispered. Her warmth beckoned.

"Marry me," he said, freeing his breath, letting warmth flow through him.

Helena smiled. "I think that might be lovely."

A strange reply, Galean thought. Reaching across the table to her, he enfolded her hands and brought her fingers to his lips.

————

AT FIVE O'CLOCK THE NEXT MORNING, GALEAN LEFT HIS house and a sleeping Helena. The night before blurry in his mind; a fog of love-making and passion he'd not experienced for a very long time.

Driving through the silent streets, he let himself feel the euphoria. Letting himself into his office, he stood for a moment in the darkness. Something on the floor caught his eye. A stark white envelope addressed to him, written in Casey's distinctive handwriting.

Chapter Six

We must all, in order to make reality more tolerable,
keep alive in us a few little follies.

—MARCEL PROUST

Sleepless nights were familiar to Casey, but tonight was relentless. The wind wailed against her windows, crying out heartbreak.

The clock by her bed mocked her: 3:40 a.m. Minutes moved at a snail's pace, almost hypnotically. Finally Casey gave in, rose from under the warmth of the down comforter and walked to the closet. Struggling to pull her yellow fleece sweatshirt over her head and over her blue-checked pajamas, she slipped her bare feet into a pair of dilapidated slippers. Superstition was one of Casey's closet habits. Whenever she woke like this, wondering and worrying, she needed to put on that particular yellow sweatshirt and her ratty, worn slippers before padding down the hall to her typewriter.

Along the way to her writing room, thoughts bounced around Casey's mind. *I wonder if Galean has found my letter. Maybe I'll give him an early call. I know he gets up to run.*

Switching on the lamp by the phone, a diffused light spread across her desk. Casey stood for a moment just looking at the phone. Doubts and misgivings transformed into incredulity. Wanting to call Galean felt like a brick on her chest. *This is not happening. And if it is, why do I care so much if he isn't who I thought he was?*

Times when she'd called him before in the dark hours of the morning had been exceptional moments: the day of an important interview; the celebratory moment when she'd put the final period on her first book. But it had never been for something like this. The Galean who exuded quiet confidence, who offered reliable friendship, was receding from view and someone unknown to Casey was emerging.

She moved away from her desk, but as she turned she noticed the notes sitting ready for tomorrow's early class, now only four hours away. Picking up the papers, she wandered to a chair that beckoned to her. Cheerful with its yellow and white stripes and a large sunflower pillow propped against its rising back, the chair promised warmth, offered contemplation. She dropped into it.

The group on early Friday mornings was a favorite of Casey's, a small group of nine people on the final road to their dissertations. Some were close to her in age, and they were often the ones who asked the deeper questions, the ones with whom Casey felt a kinship. Thus she often shared her deepest reflections and personal experiences with this class. "We are all seekers together," Casey liked to tell them.

Sitting now in the comfy chair, her papers on her lap, she read over what she had written in preparation for that day's class. It was a poem called "When We Two Parted" by Lord Byron. She began reading it but stopped midway with a shocked "Oh my God!" She stood up and started pacing from one side of the room to the other, reading aloud to herself as she walked.

When we two parted
In silence and tears,
Half broken-hearted
to sever for years.
Pale grew thy cheek and cold
Colder thy kiss;
Truly that hour foretold
Sorrow to this.

Casey had chosen this poem a few weeks ago, but now it felt all too close to the bone. The wind wailing at her window as she read over the lines of the poem, heart thumping. *Silence and tears ... half broken-hearted.*

The clock on her desk chimed 5:45 a.m.

"Truly that hour foretold, sorrow to this." Casey spoke aloud as the chime subsided, her mind recollecting something she couldn't quite put her finger on.

I remember where I heard that quote. It was in a class, a literature class. When was that? It feels like a while ago ...

She drew herself over to the bookcases that lined her office, where suddenly thoughts of Galean and Helena dwindled. Casey stood still, eyes closed. An old image wavered, like a hazy memory: a man half sitting, half leaning on a desk, one leg stretched forward balancing himself. A thought penetrated the air ... *Sometimes the universe intervenes, tonight might be one of those times.* Pulling a book from the shelf, her hand reaching as though guided. *The Love Poems of Lord Byron.* How long had it sat there? Years.

Flipping to the inside front page, Casey saw the quote. She remembered when he'd written it.

"All farewells should be sudden."
Lord Byron wrote that, but I don't believe he meant it.
I know I didn't mean our farewell to be so sudden.
Andy, 1972

Ten years ago, he'd been her doctoral advisor. It was the time in Casey's life when she had set out upon her academic journey, keen to leave behind the world of social work. She was driven by a need to separate herself from the past, to uncover the possibilities of her mind and to try and fathom the worlds of love and loss. Andy Kingwood became brother, friend and mentor. He encouraged Casey to mine what he called her "luxuriant intellect" and to delve into the wealth of insights and ideas that she possessed.

For some reason his spirit drifted into her room on this early morning. She had not thought about him for years. Why now, why this poem? For a few moments she let herself remember.

ANDY'S CLASSES ON THE ROMANTICS, BYRON IN PARTICULAR, were works of art to Casey. He had a way of standing by a table or a desk, quoting whole poems, asking each person in the room to absorb the words and create meaning for themselves. When she asked him if he might be her advisor for her thesis, his decision was quick. Oh how she remembered that conversation. How brave she felt that day after class, all those years ago.

"Dr. Kingwood. I wonder if I could make an appointment to talk with you about my doctoral thesis. It's really become clear to me, in your classes, what I want to explore and what I want to write about."

"And?" was all he had said.

"I want to figure out what it is that moves us—we humans—to put ourselves in the path of the sadness and sorrow that often accompany love."

Casey still felt pride in the fact that she'd been able to articulate what she wanted to explore and that she'd done it so succinctly. She realized now that she had looked upon this man with awe. But that's what Casey did consistently: bestowed illusory attributes on those whom she admired and who admired her. She created stories around people.

"Admirable quest, totally unrealistic." He'd said in response to her idea, and then he smiled. "But very intriguing. Let's talk and see where it goes."

Thus their work together began. It was intensive. Some days their conversations were lofty, other days fervid and edgy. Casey's world revolved around poets like Yeats, Byron and Elizabeth Bishop, who wrote about love and loss, and real-life characters like Héloïse and Abélard who loved and lost and whose hearts had been broken. She luxuriated in a world of ideas and broken hearts. Eventually their meetings adjourned to the White Horse Inn & Tavern. There they sat, Casey defending her latest chapter, Andy, secretly glorying in her unfolding passions.

Casey began to see changes and possibilities within herself she never had imagined. It was Galean who'd raised the warning flag. "Casey, you talk about him more like he's your lover than your professor." She'd walked away from Galean, not looking back. She knew her face was flushed. Later that month she told Dr. Kingwood, who was Andy to her now.

"I have to find another advisor."

Andy Kingwood, distinguished faculty member, married man, father, told Casey he was in love with her extraordinary mind and her passion for life. Galean was right.

On that day Casey told her advisor she no longer wished to work with him. A book of Byron's poetry left in her mailbox at the university was their last connection.

"IT WAS A KIND OF MADNESS," SHE BREATHED QUIETLY TO herself now. How hard she had worked to become detached from caring too deeply. And yet here she was caught once again in someone else's story.

Sitting there in her writing room, the book still on her lap, she searched through it as if she were looking for something to explain her unrest, her disillusionment about Galean. She thumbed the pages, one after the other, stopping every so often to follow a line of poetry.

A folded paper fell to the floor. Casey picked it up, and read the words:

Casey: I don't understand what happened, but I honor your decision."
I'll turn your files over to Dr. Olden today. You are a remarkable young woman with an extraordinary mind and I will miss our meetings. Please don't ever hesitate if you need a reference or, more importantly, if you need an ear.
Remember, there's always Ireland.
Wishing you a good life,
As ever,
Andy

Behind her the clock chimed six-thirty.

"Oh shit! I need to get moving." She jumped up to go down the hall to get ready for class, the note still in her hand. She paused, flipping it over. There, in her own handwriting, was a phone number and an address for Dr. Andy Kingwood where he was now teaching in a college in Cork, Ireland.

I think the universe just spoke to me again. She smiled for the first time that morning.

CASEY'S LETTER LAY OPEN ON GALEAN'S DESK. HE WHO never allowed himself to feel confused or helpless was frozen. Bewilderment was something unfamiliar to him.

Reaching across the desk, he picked up the phone and dialed Casey's office number. It rang once. Shaking his head, he put the receiver back down and hung up. "A note is better," he said to the walls.

He took a pen from the holder on his desk and grabbed a piece of clean white paper, which had been part of a neat stack on the side table at his elbow. Across the top of the paper was embossed, Galean P. Laihy MD.

Galean's office
Friday, January 8, 1982
6:30 a.m.
Dear Casey:
I just read your letter. You started with a mea culpa, maybe I should follow your lead.
We've been friends for almost ten years. Good friends, I've always thought. Now I'm wondering if all along I have given you the wrong idea.

Remember how we talked about how unusual we thought we were, not letting the man–woman thing interfere with a remarkable friendship? Maybe I should have checked back with you on that, because it seems you presumed some things had changed.

Galean stopped writing, grasped his forehead as though he might squeeze the words from his brain onto the page. "God, this is hard," he said out loud to himself. "Casey's the one who usually helps me with the 'feeling' stuff!" The walls stared back blankly at his outburst. Galean continued writing.

We have a great friendship. You are probably one of the best friends I've ever had. Your letter and what you tell me about Helena has disturbed me. We can't even be sure we're talking about the same woman.
I can have coffee with you on Sunday, but I think I need to show your letter to Helena. If it is her, I can't, no—I won't be talking behind her back. And if it isn't her, problem solved.
I'll call you.
Galean
P.S. What happened to that chapter you were going to show me? We're still professional colleagues, aren't we?

GALEAN SLIPPED THE LETTER INTO ONE OF HIS SIGNATURE envelopes—he was the only professor in the department who had his own embossed letterhead. He walked through his office, down the hall. Alice, secretary to several professors but staunchly loyal to Casey, met Galean at the door to her office.

"Good morning, Dr. Laihy. Can I help you?'

"Hopefully," he said with a wry grin. "Could you please give this letter to Casey when she comes in?"

"I will do that. I'm not sure if she's coming to the office first, she has an eight o'clock seminar group. But I'll put it on her desk."

Galean smiled, nodded and backed away. The last person he wanted to run into at this moment was Casey. Her letter, now sitting in the pocket of his jacket, was to be the first thread that could unravel their friendship. His letter, the second.

Chapter Seven

If we will be quiet and ready enough,
we shall find compensation in every disappointment.

—HENRY DAVID THOREAU

"Dr. MacMillan?"

Rob, one of Casey's advisees, announced his entrance into her morning class. He dropped his briefcase onto the table and stood leaning forward, his hands on the table supporting him, his head down.

"Rob? Are you all right?" Casey asked.

Two other students who'd been talking at the other end of the room looked up.

"You seem perturbed," Casey prodded gently, knowing from past experience how unsettled many students become near the beginning of her course on love and loss. She waited.

Still standing, Rob lifted his head. "I began reading some of the articles and poetry you suggested. I was awake most of the night." When he spoke he looked beyond Casey and out the window. Snow sparkled in a new sun-filled morning.

Before continuing, Rob sat, moved his briefcase aside and folded his hands. Almost in supplication. "You said the other day, this is not a course in therapy but one where we reflect and link our experiences with the material."

Was this a question? A confrontation? Casey waited.

Gradually other students were making their way into the seminar room. Their chatter dwindled as they tuned into Rob and his apparent angst. Professor MacMillan taught the theories and literature of love and loss and encouraged her students to link their own experiences with what they were learning. It seemed that Rob, self-deprecating, droll Rob, had questions.

"I think everyone has arrived," Casey said. "Why don't we begin, and Rob, why don't you tell us more about what kept you awake last night."

The rustle of papers, the snapping of pens, the scraping of chairs: these familiar sounds brought comfort to Casey. This was her world. A place of words, thoughts and questions, all of which stirred and invigorated her, keeping away her demons for a while.

The other students, now poised, turned to face Rob, who was sitting across the table from Casey. He stalled for a moment. He picked up his pen and tapped it on his notebook, marking time. He let the pen fall and caught it rolling off the table.

"Would you rather wait for another time, Rob? Am I asking too soon?" Casey leaned on the table folding one hand over the other.

"No, no. I read Byron's poem 'So We'll Go No More a Roving' last night." Rob stopped, hesitated. "I'm an English teacher by trade and a romantic by nature."

Gentle laughter drifted across the room.

Rob grinned, "Guess I never really admitted that to a room full of people."

Casey smiled. "Not a bad admission, Rob. And not a bad place for all of us to begin this morning. Takes a particular kind of bravery to admit to being a romantic, I think."

Casey's intuition was to let Rob flow. Her sense of what he needed was in full sail. She realized she hadn't thought about Galean, or what to do, since Rob began speaking. She felt moments like this in her soul, when someone's learning became deeply personal, undisguised and witnessed.

"Why don't you read the poem for us, Rob," she suggested.

Several people nodded.

Reaching down beside his chair, Rob pulled a book from his briefcase. "I just happen to have a book of Lord Byron's poems with me," he said with a grin. Taking a moment, he held the book in his hand, the other hand placed across the cover in what seemed to be a loving gesture. All was quiet. Rob began to read.

So we'll go no more a roving
So late into the night,
Though the heart be still as loving,
And the moon be still as bright.

Casey felt a great silence enveloping the room. Rob's voice and Byron's poem were the only sounds that mattered. The winds of yesterday's storm had died away; the world stilled.

For the sword outwears its sheath,
And the soul wears out the breast,
And the heart must pause to breathe,
And love itself have rest.
Though the night was made for loving,
And the day returns too soon,
Yet we'll go no more a roving,
By the light of the moon.

Rob sat back, stared out the window. Quiet prevailed. No one moved; not a pen, not a breath. Casey waited.

A young woman named Anya, who was sitting at the end of table, spoke: "I was thinking of not coming back to this class for personal reasons. Now I feel as though I'm supposed to be here."

Casey gave air and space to her words. She believed that spoken thoughts and responses needed time to establish their own significance rather than being run over by too-hasty support or, worse, ill-considered questions. "We are often invisible and without sound in this world. Let's listen to one another carefully, and let's see one another," was something Casey often said. Anyone who spent any time with her experienced uncommon moments of being heard.

After a moment an older man, Stephen, who sat across the table from Rob, turned to Casey. "Do you want us to comment on what Rob has brought here this morning?"

"Possibly Anya has already begun to comment," Casey responded, turning toward Anya and sliding her hand and arm down the dark wood, almost as an invitation. "Anya?"

Anya's pale features assumed a pink tinge. She coughed, put her hand across her mouth. "I'm not sure I want …" she began but trailed off, looking down while absently flipping pages of her notebook.

"It's all right, Anya. I just wondered if you wanted to say anything more about how you feel about the poem." Casey needed to assure Anya that this was not a moment to reveal her own stories, only an invitation to respond to Rob.

Anya shook her head no.

Casey moved the discussion along. "Stephen? You wanted to comment?"

"I'm probably the oldest person in the room," he began, smiling.

Casey waited, wondering what might follow.

"And here I am learning about love and loss." He paused.

Others looked across and down the length of the table, possibly intrigued or wondering if he might get to the point.

"Maybe what I'm saying is, I find that particular poem very poignant, because I know a lot about loss and I may even know a little about love."

These were the moments in class that Casey held up to the light, the moments when the philosophy and the lore of being human took on life. Beyond here, beyond this room, she lived in her own bubble of protection. Very carefully and slowly, she turned to Stephen.

"Where do you feel the poignancy in Byron's poem, Stephen?"

"You know ..." He shifted his chair, moving back from the table. "I may be a little over my head at this moment. This is a new place for me, talking about feelings and personal truth."

"You've come to the right class then," came the clear and confident voice of a woman sitting by Anya. "This is my third class with Professor MacMillan." Turning to Casey, the woman smiled. "You terrified me initially, and now here I am back for the third time." She turned back to Stephen, telling him, "Thinking about this as a new place might be very true."

Casey leaned forward, thinking *Maybe I need to rein this in a bit.* She started to interrupt, then stopped herself. Often it was the students who nailed the issue of the day.

"So, Joanna? A new place?"

"I remember a course I took with you, Dr. MacMillan a couple of years ago. I'd just started the courses for my doctoral work and I was pretty much a mess, coming out of a divorce, fighting a custody battle."

Outside by the window, some branches on a tree laden with heavy snow shifted in a slight wind, dropping mounds of white like a heavy cloak, landing with an unexpected thud. The silence in the classroom that had been surrounding Joanna's story dissolved into a startled murmur.

Joanna, undaunted, finished her thought. "You talked about Nietzsche and his ideas of self-overcoming and the free spirit. I walked away from that course feeling confident and transformed. Maybe that's what I mean," she said to Stephen, "by a new place. Here is where you get a chance to shift the image of helplessness that we take on sometimes."

He nodded. "I wonder if we all live out images of ourselves that somebody else created for us."

Casey recognized that Stephen and Joanna were gradually moving into a conversation that could exclude others around the table. She sensed the disquiet but got carried off by her own thoughts. *Self-overcoming. Free spirit. How could she have been so fraudulent? The taste of mortification was vile. Galean asking her to marry him! What a stupid, stupid assumption...*

"Dr. MacMillan? What do you think?"

Casey heard her name but had no idea to what the question was referring. Who had even spoken?

"Sorry, I drifted there for a moment. What was the question?" she asked the class.

"Is getting through loss a kind of self-overcoming, I wonder?" Rob asked, for the second time.

"You know, I may have an answer, Rob, but I don't think we're here on this Friday morning to listen to pronouncements. We are all well beyond that. I believe it's time we wrote for a while. What responses are we having to everything that's happened thus far? What about the poem Rob chose to read? Is it about loss? If so, what kind?" Her words tumbled, urging the people around the table, "Make room for your own wisdom. It's there, waiting."

If only I believed that, thought Casey to herself. Words that Rob had quoted floated back to her, and something shifted in her—like a ship correcting its course. *And the heart must pause to breathe.*

Chapter Eight

No excellent soul is exempt from a mixture of madness.

—ARISTOTLE

Galean's home welcomed Helena. Lamplight gleamed from the front windows and a porch light shone across the steps, lending radiance to Helena's spirit and to the snow covering the walkway.

It had been a difficult day. The death of a patient had left her feeling distraught and anxious. Being in the profession for many years had not lessened the effect of watching a life end. Today was especially disturbing. The surgeon had been late for that operation. Helena felt he'd been wielding his power making everyone wait. And a person had died. The thought of folding herself into Galean's arms, maybe talking about their future, helped to jettison the darkness of the day.

Climbing from the car, she jumped over the snowbanks and walked up the front steps, which had already been cleared of snow. She stood at the entrance searching for the keys Galean had given her, but before she could find them the door swung open. Galean stood, arms open, inviting her into the comfort of his home. Helena experienced a gratifying moment of being received—not a customary feeling for her. He had been home expecting her, anticipating her. It was the image of home she yearned for.

Lamps gave gentle light to high ceilings, dark wood and plush beige carpets, all signaling Galean's need for beauty. Paintings graced the walls; soft colors lent to a monochromatic room. To Helena, this house, this place, represented safety. Her sanctuary.

"Welcome home," Galean greeted her warmly. "Give me your wet things. I have a fire on, and wine is poured."

For a moment Helena stood still, the cold wind on her back, the light beckoning her in. "Galean. You are everything I need right at this moment."

"Get yourself in here," he laughed and took her hand, shutting the door before drawing her into the hallway.

Helena stood before the hall closet, wet snow melting onto the black and white tile. Galean took a sleeve of her coat.

"So, are you staying?" He smiled.

"Oh yes." She reached out, letting her coat drop to the floor. "Just hold on to me for a bit right now, I've had a terrible day."

Two people unfamiliar with revealing themselves stood holding one another, both terrified.

Later, fire crackling in the fireplace, lights dimmed, they sat on the couch, Helena wrapped in a red wool shawl, legs covered with a yellow throw. She laughed: "I look like a crazy striped lollipop." Her bare feet rested on Galean's lap. More luxurious feelings flowed as he rubbed her ankles, almost absentmindedly, while he talked.

"It's all happened very fast, you and I, but I'm not feeling like waiting around, are you?" He looked over at Helena and saw her eyes were closed. He tapped her foot gently.

"I'm not sleeping," she murmured, eyes still closed. "I agree. We're grown-ups."

"But we do need to talk about something, before we start making plans." Galean said. He held on to her foot as though afraid she might run.

"What might that be?" Helena opened one eye, peering at Galean. She was curious but not alarmed. That would come later.

"I want to show you something," Galean slid out from under Helena's legs and stood up. When he turned back to her, she was sitting on the edge of the couch, her hands cupping her chin, elbows resting on her knees. She looked like a woman expecting a surprise, sure of what it might be. A smile flickered.

"Wait here," Galean said and walked down the hall, disappearing into a room and emerging with a paper in hand. His expression was taut. Helena's smile began to fade.

"What's that?" She pointed to the paper.

"Something we need to talk about." Galean sat down beside Helena and unfolded Casey's letter.

"I'm not feeling … good about this, Galean. You're scaring me."

Helena had a gift for discerning trouble, and the feeling of foreboding was a familiar one in her childhood. The capacity to feel a shift in someone's energy was one of her strengths as a nurse; however, in her personal life it was an affliction, an alert that made her want to escape and disappear. Because of this, Helena's relationships and friendships often ended abruptly, leaving the other person puzzled and hurt.

Galean moved closer to Helena, placed Casey's letter in her hand. No one stirred, no one spoke; only the dying fire sizzling created sound.

"What is this?" A faint inflection, suspicion, a warning voice from somewhere within Helena.

"Read it, Helena. It's important because it may be about you, and about some things you possibly haven't told me ... and it might be about us."

Galean sat silent and without moving while Helena began to read.

She gripped the page, thumbs and fingers holding it still. She hovered over the words. Her lips tight, her brow creased. When she finished reading she crumpled the letter, crushing the words, the accusations, into a tight wad of paper. Turning to Galean, she dropped it into his lap.

"Galean. I want to go."

When she started to rise from the couch, Galean reached up and clutched her wrist, his fingers wrapped around the thin bones like a handcuff. The crumpled letter dropped from his lap to the floor. He watched in shock as another Helena materialized in his living room.

Helena knew physical terror. So many times she had lain under her bed, hardly daring to breathe, listening to the heavy steps of her drunken father approaching her bedroom. Whenever she felt scared and threatened, as she did now, those memories of brutality came racing back, sending her into high alert.

She flung herself away from Galean, using a force extraordinary for her slight body. Her surprising strength caught Galean off guard and sent him tumbling from the couch. For a moment, Helena now standing, stared down at him, a strange smile floating for a brief second at the edges of her lips. Then, as though witnessing a frightening scene, she stepped back, hand to her mouth, her eyes wide.

Galean stood slowly, cautiously, making sure his knees were solid. He stood at full height watching Helena as he might a wild cat who was stalking him, ready to pounce.

Suddenly, Helena staggered, looking bewildered, as though she'd lost her bearings. Her eyes now were lit with terror.

Galean made a measured decision, arising from two sources: his own life experiences and his medical training. Demons lurked. And he knew he'd unleashed Helena's.

"Helena," he said, speaking with the gentleness of protection.

Carefully he reached out and took her hand. She showed no resistance but let him lead her back to the couch. She followed submissively, all her angst and air deflated. The tears came. She wept, fists balled, rubbing her eyes, the way she might have as a young child. Like a protective father, Galean gathered her into his arms, soothing her, stroking her back.

A subconscious, guileful part of Helena knew at that very moment she held power. She'd learned those lessons well. Power is everything.

"What do you want to do about this letter?" Galean asked, still holding her against his chest.

"Sorry I crumpled it," she said into his chest. "Gut reaction." She leaned back putting her hand on his cheek. Her fear now gone, her actions became calculated. She transformed into a cunning woman. "Give it back to me, Galean," she told him. "I want to read it again, then decide what to do." Helena already knew what she wanted to do, she just needed to think it through carefully.

With care, Galean leaned away from her, reaching down to where the letter had fallen and handing it to her. She moved back onto the pillowed couch, drew up her legs and crossed them. Her eyes were bright, her hair tousled in mad curls and she was smiling as though a secret pleased her. She transformed herself before his eyes.

"Kleenex, please, Galean," she asked sweetly. "I'm afraid I might weep again. Or even better, hand me a glass of that pinot gris."

He did as she asked and then watched her uncrumple the letter, waiting for another outburst. Instead she smiled up at him.

"I remember Casey MacMillan," she began. "I remember an unhappy, manipulative woman." Helena stopped for a moment, calculating how much mythology about her own life she might safely manufacture. "Tonight, I came here to tell you about my past."

"Then you *are* the Helena she thinks you are. You met in a home for unwed mothers?" Galean wavered with the question.

A decisive, dangerous moment.

She leaned into him, kissing him softly. Putting her mouth to his ear, she whispered, "I have a checkered past, my love. But then, don't we all?" Her fingers fondled his cheek.

Galean closed his eyes. Captivated in a mysteriously dark way, he felt submerged in a pleasurable weakness. He surrendered to an unknown presence: Helena's sexual machinations; her calculated revenge for Casey's tampering with her life. For the first time in Galean's adult life, he felt out of control.

Helena moved away from Galean, placed the wrinkled letter on her knee. Smoothing the page with an easy stroking motion, she was aware that he sat silent, watching her. Aware too of his quickening breath. She experienced the familiar rushing in her body that blighted her as a young girl when profaned by her father, a feeling that had transformed into a twisted sense of her own power, a rejection of her powerlessness. Casey's letter and the now hateful image of her spurred on Helena's provocative advances. The woman would pay for her intrusion.

"Galean?" Helena reached for his hand, drew her finger across his palm.

"We don't have to do this tonight." He bent down to reach for Casey's letter. "It'll wait. Let's enjoy what's happening here now."

A smile played at the corners of Helena's mouth. Her hand still outstretched.

Galean—doctor, professor, man of reason—experienced a sort of madness. "I'll be right back. Don't go away." He turned, inhaled a long slow breath and walked down the hall to the kitchen. There, the familiar scent of beef stew slowed his heart, which was banging against his chest.

"Galean Laihy. What have you done?" He said quietly to himself as he extracted another pinot gris from the fridge.

Back in the living room, Helena folded Casey's letter and placed it on the coffee table. *What a surprise she'll have.* The thought made Helena smile.

GALEAN LAY BESIDE HELENA, LISTENING TO HER BREATHE. She slept with a childlike peacefulness. Just an hour ago, in a sea of wildness, she was movement, sound and frenzy. Now lying on her stomach, her head was turned away, black hair tousled and plummeting across the pillow.

Slowly, quietly, he eased himself up from the bed, one foot on the floor, two feet on the floor. Helena uttered no sound, nor did she stir. She slept the sleep of the satiated.

Without looking back, Galean walked to the bedroom

door, stepped out, and closed it soundlessly. Standing for a moment in the dim hallway, he felt overwhelmed by Helena's energy, her sensuality and the intimacy she offered him. She inflamed some longing in him that felt old; a fierce desire for something yanked away from him long ago.

Entering his den, Galean shut the door and flipped the switch on the wall beside him. A brass lamp cast a circular glow across his desk. A leather folder lay precisely in the middle of his desk, a pen in a gold holder sat as if in anticipation beside it. A small pile of cream-bond paper embossed with his name lay in a dark mahogany box at the top of his desk. He sat, resting his elbows on the desk, his hands over his eyes, cupping his forehead.

Galean, head in hands, body pulsating from his last few hours with Helena. He felt a ripping like a physical tear within. Old wounds. Soul wounds. Dangerous territory awaited. He wanted to love Helena but fear penetrated.

Chapter Nine

In ancient Roman religion and mythology,
Janus is the god of beginnings and transitions,
thence also of gates, doors, doorways, endings and time.
He is usually a two-faced god since he looks to the
future and the past.

—CRYTRALINKS.COM/JANUS

The month of January offered a gift. The god Janus, the god of beginnings and transitions, recommended that Casey wrap herself in the warmth of an old, threadbare, well-loved kimono and spend the Saturday morning in bed marking papers, rather than at her desk. All was still with the silence of snow-covered streets, a gray darkness beckoning dawn.

Sitting up in her bed, pillows soft at her back, books scattered across the woolen coverlet, Casey felt sadness stretching out upon the bed before her. Galean's note lay on the floor next to the bed, left where she had dropped it the night before.

Beginnings and endings … the phrase drifted into her mind and became a thought. *Beginnings and endings waver and merge.* She leaned over to pick up the note and read it one more time. "Time to stop the self-pity," she said aloud to herself. She held the note in one hand as she reached for the mug of coffee on her bedside table. A coffee gone cold from lack of attention. She sipped the bitter cool liquid as she read Galean's words.

You started your letter with a mea culpa, maybe I should follow your lead. We've been friends for almost ten years. Good friends, I've always thought.

Casey inhaled a long, uninterrupted breath and exhaled. Perplexity worried her brow. She read with apparent detachment, as she might peruse a student paper.

Remember how we talked about how unusual we thought we were, not letting the man–woman thing interfere with a remarkable friendship? Maybe I should have checked back with you on that, because it seems you presumed some things had changed.

"What the hell does that mean, Galean! *I* presumed?"

The walls stared back, silent. Casey flicked her finger at the paper, almost ripping it. Exasperation felt stronger than sadness. Energy flowed from exasperation. Any of her attempts at detachment were slowly replaced with a grating aggravation that felt cleansing, like a controlled burn clearing a field of weeds and brambles. Casey's smoldering indignation ignited. *I think I need to show your letter to Helena,* he'd written.

"Seriously? Seriously! *Why?*" Casey said aloud as she threw the note into the air, letting it float down to the end of the bed. Humiliation over the past two days had felt like a spreading gray stain throughout her body. A stain that was now being replaced by a red ribbon of anger.

Casey kicked back the bed covers, throwing books and student papers onto the floor. She strode across the room, arms swinging, toes digging into the wooly shag of the rug. Mirrored closet doors reflected her tousled hair, the kimono dragging on the floor as she withdrew one arm then the other. As it landed on the floor, she slid the doors back with a force that rattled the mirror.

Sometimes one person's well-intended action—or what he sees as well-intended—instigates the unexpected. Galean miscalculated with great exactness. First, thinking he should show the letter to Helena and, next, telling Casey he wanted Helena to read it. He was about to regret the results of his supposed well-intentioned actions.

MORNING DARKNESS IN JANUARY DOES NOT SUCCUMB easily to light.

Casey drove slowly, following a snowplow, its yellow light blinking atop the cabin. Snow flew from the plow's blades, creating a mist on her car's windshield, the wipers laboring to cast off fine ice. The orange wool toque she'd yanked onto her head, the multi-colored scarf wrapped around her neck, her face eerie green in the reflection of the dashboard, all seemed to transform her into some mystical creature's sister. Her jaw was tight, her cheeks felt cool, even though the heater blasted warm air.

All her life Casey possessed a survival spirit, an energy that inspired and emboldened her through a dark child-hood. Often at the worst times, she imagined herself a child of the universe, one able to transform cruelty into mercy, meanness into kindness, bewilderment into composure. She felt now that a test lay before her.

As she left the protection of the plow and turned onto University Avenue and toward her office, a calming sense of self-possession washed over her. Helena, the university, Galean, everything that was happening around her, it was all peripheral to what she needed to do. She began to write two letters in her head. One to Galean, the other to Andy Kingwood in Ireland.

SUNLIGHT SLIPPED THROUGH THE PATTERNED CURTAINS and across the floor of the bedroom, marking squares and lines in the carpet, a playful game to awaken Helena. Or so she liked to think.

She lay, one arm across her eyes, waiting for a troubling dream to fade, waiting to return to the world of reality. Visions of the night with Galean flickered behind her eyelids like a silent movie, her body holding the memory of his passion. She smiled, wondering at this freedom to feel the true sensuality of her own body and this unaccustomed sense of receiving love.

The dream began to creep back into the edges of Helena's conscious self. Unfolding the covers, she rolled to the edge of the bed and gradually pushed herself up till she sat with her hands on the edge balancing her. The squares and shapes of sunlight dancing along the carpet, fading in and out, mesmerized her.

Shaking her head, she stood, walked to the bedroom door, opened it and peered down the hall. A light shone from Galean's den. Still experiencing a kind of ineffable bodily warmth, she padded down the hall toward her Demetrius.

ENGLAND, 1959

Alone, sitting in the school library long after school had

ended for the day, not wanting to go home, fifteen-year-old Helena did not pause to look up from her book when Mrs. Dearcroft, her English teacher, entered the room.

"Helena, dear. It's almost five o'clock. What on earth are you doing still here? You didn't have a detention did you? Surely not you?"

"No, ma'am. I'm reading the play we're studying. I'm reading *Midsummer Night's Dream*. I like being here in the library where it's quiet." Helena turned away for a moment, not wanting Mrs. Dearcroft to see the wretchedness that consumed her. The wickedness.

"Do you mind if I sit with you for a while?" Mrs. Dearcroft was a rather round, little woman. Some of the less generous students called her "Shorty." But to Helena she was a hero; someone who spoke gently, who brought to mind mothering, or Helena's image of what Mother might be.

"We could talk about some of the characters, if you'd like. Sometimes that's a very good way to understand a story, by finding out which characters speak to us." Mrs. Dearcroft offered.

Helena felt as though she might cry from the sheer relief of being visible to another human being and not feeling slatternly, a word she had learned from her mother, the Countess.

They began to talk, the teacher and the young girl. Five o'clock became five-thirty and then six o'clock.

"Oh my, Helena. Look at the time. What a pleasure it is to sit with you and see what a bright young woman you are becoming. You really need, though, to get on your way. As must I. But before we go, I have to tell you how you remind me of Helena in the play, remarkably so, even the way you look. Have you ever imagined what Helena looks like?"

"Oh, yes!" Helena leaned across the glass top of the library table. Excitement lit her eyes. "I really think I *am* Helena!"

"Well, my dear, let me tell you. With your lovely dark curls and your winsome smile, you could play Helena any day."

Mrs. Dearcroft stood, picked up the books she'd come for and walked around the table. She stopped and looked down at Helena, who was gathering her things, gradually, slowly.

"You have given me a great deal of pleasure this late afternoon, Helena. I thank you," she told the girl sincerely. "Please think about all I've said in the last while. Think about how wonderful it is to have such a fine mind as you have. Think about all that is possible in your life. On that note I will leave. See you in class tomorrow." And she was gone.

Helena could scarcely absorb the fact that someone like her English teacher thought she, Helena Stafford, might be smart or worthy of a conversation like they'd just had. She only felt the strained silence in her own household, a huge rambling draughty estate house where people avoided one another. Except when her father chose to find her.

On that day at school, Helena decided to join forces with Helena of *Midsummer Night's Dream*; to merge her own life with a fantasy character, and enter her own contrived world of madness. It made her young life tolerable to alter her being and become another person.

HELENA MADE HER WAY DOWN THE HALL, FOLLOWING THE shaft of light shining through the door to Galean's den.

She moved to push against the partly ajar door but stopped when she saw Galean. He was sitting with his back to her, his head in his hands, murmuring as though in pain. The moment felt intimate, almost restrictive, so Helena backed away quietly and walked to the kitchen. Whatever was happening there in Galean's den, she felt it did not bear interruption. Was he agonizing about her, about last night, or was he lost in the past? A story of tragedy and loss? Only once had he mentioned that there had been someone.

In the kitchen Helena leaned against the counter and looked around at the shining wood floors, the glass and whiteness, stainless steel and chrome. She felt shoddy standing in the midst of such shine and gleam. *What is his obsession with perfection?* she wondered. *What is he doing thinking of marrying me—damaged goods? I need to run. Now. I need to leave ...*

"Helena, look at you, standing there. You bring beauty with you everywhere you go. Even in the kitchen." Galean stood at the entrance to the kitchen, smiling now, transformed from the man she had just witnessed a few moments ago.

"Galean?" she was surprised to see him there, and so changed.

"I thought I heard you up and around, and I needed to find you, to tell you ... how magical you are." He paused and lifted his hand, beckoning to her.

The room whirled white, shining. Helena moved toward Galean and let herself be encircled in his embrace. Her Demetrius. Her future.

THE LINE OF CARS AT THE DRIVE-THROUGH OF THE LOCAL doughnut shop stretched out onto the street, appearing like phantoms in the blizzard-like conditions that were draping the city in another mantle of virginal snow. Casey, her mission still firm in her mind, chose to park and go inside to get her usual bran muffin and coffee with cream rather than wait in the long line of cars. Back in her car, she read the letter she'd written to Galean one more time before placing it back in the envelope. She would go to his house now to deliver it to him, place it in his hand.

The letter to Andy in Ireland she had left unfinished on her desk at her office. That one needed a bit more thought and planning, because that letter was her transformation, her metamorphosis. She'd been too long in the chrysalis—it was time now to take flight.

Driving along Galean's street, peering through gusts of driven snow, Casey crept forward, searching for the familiar brown-brick bungalow with the front porch light he never turned off. Spotting it, she turned into his driveway and stopped. So unlike Galean, snow had piled over yesterday's car tracks. He'd not been out to plough his lane, and an unfamiliar car sat in front of his garage.

Apprehension assaulted her confidence. Cutting the engine, Casey grabbed the envelope from the passenger seat and licked the seal. The door handle moved down easily at her touch. Without even shutting the car door completely behind her, she trudged through the snow, up the porch steps, and started to push the letter through the slot in the door. It swung open.

"Hello, Casey. Why don't you come in?" Helena smiled.

Arctic wind blew across Casey's back as she stepped inside.

Chapter Ten

There it was again, the prickling sense of standing on a precipice.

—LAUREN MYRACLE, *Let It Snow*

Helena was a master of confrontation and a wizard at masking her truth. But on this cold Saturday morning, she underestimated Casey's sixth sense. An intuitive wisdom had become honed within Casey when she had worked with the young Helena at the Home for Unwed Mothers, all those years ago. And so almost immediately, Casey absorbed the reality of the situation. She feared she may be too late to save Galean.

Helena, still smiling, offered her hand. "Casey MacMillan, I wondered what had happened to you. Will you come in?" Her greeting spoke volumes. Standing in her housecoat, bare feet on the indoor mat, she threw down the gauntlet.

"Helena," Casey responded carefully. "Well, it has been a while." For a moment, the two women stood enclosed in the memories of one another.

Then Helena stepped back, sweeping her arm up, beckoning Casey to come inside. Brushing the snow from her coat, stamping her feet, Casey put her gloved hand in one pocket and pulled out an envelope. Her letter to Galean.

"Don't worry," she told Helena. "I just came by to pick up a manuscript Galean was reviewing, and I have something for him."

"Another letter?" Helena's smile slipped into a disdainful grin.

Casey's experience with Helena's chicanery rose to the moment. She felt her face flushing, her chest tightening. Words erupted. "Galean is a good friend; I won't see him hurt."

Helena stepped back into the shadows of the hallway, as though gathering breath to retaliate. Before she could respond, a cool voice came from behind her.

"Maybe I can look after myself." Galean strolled around the corner and stood by the archway into the living room. "Hello, Case. Why don't you come have a cup of coffee? Seems we all might need a moment to clear the air."

"Probably a good idea." Casey replied, knowing this could be the last time she'd have a chance to say what she felt needed saying.

Walking down the hall and into the kitchen, they were an odd-looking group: Galean leading the way as though taking troops into battle, Casey following him, envelope in hand, and Helena wrapping the dressing gown more tightly around her nakedness. At the door into the kitchen, she paused.

"You two go ahead," she told them. "I need to go and put on something a little more decent." She smiled, knowing how her body felt, knowing Casey might be wondering or imagining. Turning, she let her gown loosen as she walked away from them.

In the kitchen Galean stood by the window. Silent. Casey leaned against the threshold; her arms folded, her head bowed. Both stood in foreign territory, immersed in emotions and confusion. Throughout their friendship they had always discouraged real feelings, only allowing dissension as something to be examined critically, theoretically. Cool and separate.

Galean reached for the coffeepot and turned to Casey, breaking the silence. "Would you like …?"

"No, no, thank you. I think I just want to say what I came to say, give you this letter and I'll be on my way." She moved to hand the envelope to him, but Galean appeared not to notice.

He put the coffeepot on the warmer, looked out the window and seemed to be absorbed in the miniature drifts of snow accumulating on the sill outside. Ice crystals moved across the windowpane as though in slow motion. "Casey," he began. "I'm … it's hard to … explain."

"Wait, Galean. Let me say something, before Helena comes back." Moving into the kitchen, watching him struggle, Casey thought, *He needs my friendship more than my judgment*. She felt like the wise person in the room who thought she knew about love and the blindness and pain that could accompany it. She also felt an indescribable sadness—all the sorrow she'd hoarded throughout years of self-denial.

Galean turned, leaned back against the counter, folded his arms across his chest and crossed his ankles. "Okay," he said. "I'm listening."

Casey placed a hand on her hip and leaned into that hip, with her other hand folded under her chin like Rodin's *The Thinker*.

"Oh, no." Galean interrupted, recognizing what that pose meant. "Not Professor MacMillan—no. I'd like Casey here in the room. No more lectures."

Dropping her hands, she slipped into a chair and folded her arms. "Helena may be back."

Galean shook his head no. He stood watching his friend, her chin resting on her chest, her legs stretched out under the table, arms crossed. She looked defeated. "No, Case," he said to her. "I think she'll give us time. Say what needs airing. I'm listening."

Chair legs scraped across the tile floor as Casey straightened and readied herself to speak her piece.

DOWN THE HALL, HELENA STEPPED INTO THE SHOWER, turned the faucet and let the warm water flow across her body. She stood with her head down, her hands flat against the shower tiles. Water streamed in rivulets onto her shoulders, weeping down her body. Eyes closed, Helena let herself feel. A way of being that she normally avoided.

She turned and leaned back against the glass wall enfolding herself in an embrace. Her demons chattered and wailed, yelling at her, calling her cowardly and fraudulent. Telling her how stupid she was for believing, hoping … The chatter in her head poured over her like the shower of water drops beating against her body.

She worked daily, hourly, keeping the inner jabber at bay. The muttering, the murmuring that would not cease. She wanted the life that Galean offered her; she craved the enchantment of being loved, even though she knew *I'm not loveable* because the jabbering said so. With Galean, sometimes she felt visible, as though he could reach into her soul.

Turning off the flow of water, Helena stepped from the shower, toweled off her dripping hair, then wrapped herself in a soft, fleecy white kimono. A bold sureness began to creep over her, an old voice capable of quieting the jabbering ones. *You are Helena, you can break the rules. You can make him love you. She can't. She has lost.*

Slipping into wool slacks, she watched her face changing before her in the mirror. She saw her eyes brighten, a smile began at the edges of her lips. She knew how desirable that look could be. It was her power.

The distance from the bedroom to the kitchen was very short, hardly more than a few steps. Helena ran her fingers through her hair as she walked, letting damp, thick curls fall in wild disarray. Her face glistened. The conversation became discernible as she made her appearance in the kitchen.

Galean sat holding a paper, his forehead etched into a frown. "Are you serious?" he asked Casey. "Why Ireland? Why now? You've just established yourself here. This is ridiculous."

"Oh." Helena stopped at the threshold. "Bad timing?"

"Not at all, Helena." Casey stood and made her way toward the doorway. "I just gave Galean what I thought was great news, but obviously he doesn't agree." Closing in on Helena, she stopped in front of her. "Maybe you and I need to share our connection with Galean, and maybe we all just need to be honest."

A crackling at the window issued warning of a sleet storm, the sounds of nature seeming to comment on the glacial air in the kitchen.

For a moment, Helena's expression was inscrutable, then something flickered in her eyes. Anger. Cruelty. "Casey, I saw that other letter you wrote to Galean. I know what you are trying to do. You left me helpless, now you can't stand that my life is good." She flicked her hand toward Galean. "And this, seeing us together, turns your stomach, doesn't it?"

Throughout this exchange, Galean stood, saying nothing, arms still folded. Protecting himself?

Casey snapped her head forward, her face inches from Helena's, and, looking directly into her eyes, she said, "Helena, I care about Galean, and I know your games. I've been at the other end of them."

By now, Galean, losing patience with what he saw as melodrama, let his arms drop, his hands slapping his legs. "Casey, whatever it is that you think is wrong here, maybe none of it is your business. I'm very sure I can't fix that. I think we all need to disentangle ourselves and get on with our lives." He turned, dropped his cup into the sink and watched it break into pieces.

No one said a word. In some moments life shifts ever so slightly and no one is ever the same.

"All right, Galean. Could I please get my manuscript from you, and then I'll go." Casey grabbed her coat from where she'd flung it across a chair.

"Whoa, whoa, whoa." Helena, suddenly the peacemaker, stood in the middle of the kitchen, hand in the air, like one directing traffic. "I'm feeling that we all need to take a breath. Sit down, Casey." She pulled out a chair and pointed.

Casey remembered moments like this with Helena, when she had shifted characters, becoming another person before her eyes. "Helena, I'm not sitting down. I gave up on your not-so-subtle abuse years ago; now it's Galean's turn to be your punching bag." She felt a new ascendancy rising in her chest. Chaos becoming order. "It's extraordinary that I know both your stories, and it appears to me that neither of you knows who the other is at all. I didn't come here to lecture; nevertheless, here it is: Both of you are headed for catastrophe, because you have never ever—either one of you—taken a moment to understand or face up to your past. You're like two cripples hanging on to one another. I began thinking I was wrong to come here, yet I did. I think I finally get it. "

"Get what?" Galean spoke, his lips almost disappearing. His mouth tight.

"I probably know too much about each of you, and I'm in territory where I don't belong. I was trying to rescue both of you. No more." Her declaration degenerated into silence, an impermeable silence. She stood by the kitchen door, putting one arm into her coat, then stuffing her other arm into the empty sleeve. Her preparation to leave needed no language. *We are done here* echoed throughout the room. She pulled on her gloves one distinct finger at a time. As though creating a space of time for something more. Some resolution.

"You know what I think is really going on here, Case?" Galean began as he walked around the table. "I think you're pulling the 'I'm smarter than all of you card' and walking away. You do that walking away thing very well. Doesn't she, Helena?"

Now it was Helena's turn. She'd been watching the drama unfold, like another character observing the play from the wings. It was time for her entrance. She walked to Galean and placed a hand on his shoulder. The final humiliating act.

"I agree with Galean, Casey. You're creating all kinds of suggested stories about us, but now, I don't even know why you're here or, maybe more importantly, what business you have with either of us."

They were like three warriors circling a fire, none able to turn away. All required to stay till the truth was told. Casey's letter to Galean lay on the table. She pointed to it.

"Read the letter, Helena. I understand you've seen the other one. You might as well get the whole picture. Oh yes, you're in this one too."

As Casey opened the door leading to outside, a blizzard-like wind blustered into the kitchen, swinging the overhead lamp and blowing the letter to the floor. She left.

Galean ran to shut the door tight as Helena picked the letter from the floor and sat down. Outside Casey plodded through the snowbanks to her car, already invisible in the swirling of snow.

When Galean looked over at Helena, she was smoothing the letter on the table as she read, like she'd done with Casey's previous letter. A kind of repetitive motion—like a child rocking and soothing herself.

"Helena, I don't think you need to read any more letters."

Without looking up at him, Helena stopped reading, never ceasing to rub her hand across the letter from top to bottom. She seemed to be trying to erase what Casey had written.

Walking to her, Galean put his hand on her shoulder. "Why don't we just—" he began, but without warning Helena whirled in the chair and shoved his hand away with a force that sent Galean reeling, only catching himself when he grabbed the counter.

"She's evil! She lies!!" Helena shrieked.

To Galean, it was a demon sound that evoked some old memory within him from a long-ago life. "Helena," he spoke softly, carefully putting his hand on her arm. "Helena, it's all okay. Let's sit for a few minutes." He pulled a chair beside her and sat down, putting his hand on her knee. He'd witnessed the edges of radical behavior in Helena before, but never with such ferocity. Taking Helena's hand, now limp in her lap, he watched the bizarre brightness fade from her eyes and become replaced by wet tears. "What do you think Casey is lying about?" he asked her.

"Have you read what she's saying about me?"

"I have. She says you had psychotic episodes when she knew you, that you … Helena, you've told me about what life was like for you. Why does this upset you now? It's all done with and I can take care of you."

Helena grasped his hand as though fearing he might disappear if she let go.

"But what does she mean …" she turned, took the letter, quoting Casey's words, "'Eros and madness are strange bedmates?'"

"That's the professor talking, Lena. That's Casey's way of describing something she doesn't feel or understand. She doesn't know how it feels to love, the way you and I do."

"Look, the sun's coming out," self-assured once again and cunning, another Helena emerged. "How extraordinary. I feel better."

Galean, in his dream-like state, felt only relief watching a sensual Helena reemerge. Whatever concern he had felt was now blocked, by Eros.

Chapter Eleven

My mind is troubled like a fountain stirred.
And I myself see not the bottom of it.

—**SHAKESPEARE**, *Troilus and Cressida*

University campuses are never so beautiful or so bleak as on the day classes are cancelled because of snow warnings. Casey loved both the bleakness and the beauty. This morning, coming directly from Galean's house, she needed the comfort of the familiar.

She climbed from her car and stepped high, swinging one booted leg across a snowbank. Missing her footing, she landed in the middle of the bank, snow filling her boots and her gloves and sticking to her bottom. *How poetically appropriate*, she thought, picking herself up.

Tree limbs bent low, white snow outlining the black curve of branches. Someone had been out to shovel a pathway to the front door of her office building, for which Casey was very thankful. Her boots were already uncomfortably damp from the inside out. Key in hand, she walked to the front door. It bore a brass crest, an outline of some philosopher; she had never quite known who. The threshold was carved with the stone impressions of books and faces of young children. The building itself housed the Education faculty in company with the Humanities, Casey's department.

Some days she entered feeling a sense of pride, a joy in her life's work of teaching and learning. Today, she stepped through the entranceway hardly noticing the carvings, thinking little of what the building represented. She had other things on her mind. Shadows and beams of light played across the floor of the hallway. High clerestory windows gave a feeling of sanctuary, something Casey needed to calm her rattled soul.

As she approached her office, she saw a light glowing through the high window transom over the door to Galean's office. For a second she thought, *Maybe he beat me here and wants to talk*, before she remembered he always left a lamp lit on his desk. He hated coming into a dark office. Casey's desire for all to be well, and her hope that he might have changed his mind, clamored for her attention. But she knew that Galean—her sensible, intelligent friend; her best friend—was caught in Helena's web.

Walking down the echoing hall to her office, Casey shook her head, trying to absorb the perplexity of it all. Today she had come here to complete two tasks: write a letter to the dean about the sabbatical she'd been offered, and finish a letter to Andy Kingwood in Ireland. First though, she wanted to reread the letter she'd written to Galean.

Her office welcomed her. This was the place where she felt whole, where uncertainty and unpredictability were muted for a while. As she walked through the door into her inner office she noticed a light across the way, opposite her window. Anne was working in her office.

"Oh Anne, thank you," Casey said aloud. "I could use your wise counsel about now." Going to her desk, she lifted the phone receiver from its cradle and dialed Anne's office code. One ring, two rings, three.

"Hello?" Anne's voice answered, mildly irritated. Casey recognized the feeling. Anne had come to work, probably to make some progress on her book or maybe to catch up on reading dissertations, which, if they were extraordinary, took long, reflective hours. Interruption broke the concentration.

"Anne. I'm so sorry to trouble you." Casey blurted into the phone. "But ..." she trailed off.

"Casey? What are you doing in the office this morning? I thought ..."

"Don't ask, please. Can I just come over there? I promise I won't stay long, I just need—"

"Case, has this anything to do with Galean?"

For the first time that morning, Casey succumbed to desolation. She swallowed. "It's pretty much a catastrophe, all of it."

"Oh, Case. Come on over. I'll make some tea." With that said, Anne cleared her desk of manuscript papers, shut down her electric typewriter and pulled the box of tissues from the bottom drawer. A bottle of Scotch rested beside the Kleenex; however, Anne thought tea might be better. After all, it was still early Saturday morning. A small knock came at the door.

"Come on in," Anne called to her friend. "It's open."

A bedraggled, rather unkempt Casey walked through the door. Her usually bright eyes were dulled, and her hair was yanked back into a knot.

"Ah, Casey—what happened?" Anne walked to her, arms outstretched.

"Don't be nice to me," Casey managed a weak smile. "I am an idiot. What I need is a smack in the head."

"Come over here and sit down, take off those wet boots. Give me your jacket. Why are you so wet?" Anne assumed her mother role without missing a beat.

"I fell into a bloody snowbank." Casey made a wry face and tossed her head. "I'll sit down, but I really don't need sympathy. What I do need is someone who is thinking clearly—hopefully you—because I need you to read something for me. Then we'll talk. I've made some pretty drastic decisions in the last hour or so."

Casey pulled a copy of the letter she'd given Galean from her coat pocket. It, too, looked rather beaten. "I'll make myself a cup of tea while you read," she said, handing the letter to Anne, who sat down and began to read.

Dear Galean,

I'm feeling as though I have just lost my best friend. And I didn't see this coming at all. It's time for me to shake my head and figure how I have got myself so entangled in your life when, in your words, it's really none of my business what your personal choices are. But … keep reading, because I'm your friend, and friends don't want to see friends get hurt.

I need to explain myself to you, and my behavior. Humiliation reigns. In the last day or so I've betrayed myself, and probably our friendship, because I began to think we'd become more than friends. Stupid, stupid, stupid! I know better. I teach this stuff, for God's sake.

But I have to tell you what I see as being true at this moment. You are the best friend I've ever had. You are probably the first person—man, woman or child—I've let myself care about deeply and it kills me to watch you take your life and toss it away. Why are you doing this? I know you. I know your story. I know all about your father's death, how your mother abandoned you. You are rolling your eyes because you won't admit how alone you are. You think because you've become the

*successful Dr. Laihy, nothing can touch you. That
you've created a life, and you're in control. Well, you
are wrong.*

*I obviously missed all the signs and didn't know you
were involved with anyone, let alone Helena. I have to
ask myself, and you, why you never talked about her. If
you were my brother, I couldn't be closer to you. What
stopped you from telling me?*

*And now, to Helena. As you know, I have lived with
her. I was her resident counselor and we were friends
at one time. I don't know how much you know about
her past except where she and I met; beyond that, it's
her story to tell you. But I can tell you that I've seen
her violent, I've seen her raving and, Galean, I've seen
her weep for herself as though her heart might break.
She is one of the smartest people I've ever met. She's
articulate, she's funny and she's dangerous. She says
she loves you, and in her way no doubt she does. But
she will be relentless. She'll want to possess you. Eros
and madness are strange bedmates.*

*I truly believed at one time that we were good friends,
she and I. However, I recognized something in her, early
on in our work together. She's cunning and she knows
how to get what she wants. Her past taught her to be
shrewd, to take care of herself—whatever it takes. And
so, right now I'm feeling a kind of impotent rage because
I feel helpless. I don't like that feeling. You and I have
taken care of one another, through troubled times and
good moments. But it's time for me to let whatever is
going to happen, happen.*

*Now, to me. You were right when you said once that I'm
a rescuer and a fixer, but now I realize the only person I
can fix is myself. I'm due for some months of sabbatical,
which I've been putting off. So I'm going to apply and*

take up the invitation of my friend and advisor, Andy,
and go to Ireland.
Take care of yourself, Galean.
Casey

Anne put the letter on the couch beside her, said nothing for a moment. Casey sipped on her tea. She sat quietly, only wanting to say what might help her friend in the midst of her turmoil.

"Casey? I'm wondering something." She waited.

"I'm listening."

"I wonder if anything happened between you and Helena all those years ago, that makes you so fearful." Casey started to shake her head.

"No." Anne reached across and took Casey's hand. "Hear me out. Did anything happen before you left or while you were her case worker, that drove a wedge between the two of you?"

"Don't you think I've tried to go back to remember those days, trying to understand why I'm acting like a jilted lover?"

The two women froze in the moment. There it was.

"Oh Casey," Anne lifted her hand and put it on Casey's cheek, a gentle gesture that said I am your friend, your ally, I know why you are hurting.

Sitting, without movement or protest, Casey spoke in almost a whisper.

"I guess I care more about that man, Galean, than I've admitted even to myself and now he's gone. And I'm too proud or something to turn back."

"Have you give the letter to Galean?" Anne asked quietly.

"Yes. And Anne, everything in the letter comes from the truth, except the admission I'm making to you now. So, I guess we move on from here. Anyway, I'm sure Helena is reading it as we speak."

Chapter Twelve

*When something extraordinary shows up in your life in the
middle of the night,
you give it a name and make it the best home you can.*

—BARBARA KINGSOLVER,

High Tide in Tucson: Essays from Now or Never

Two weeks later, another Saturday.

The phone ringing at two o'clock in the morning brought chills to Casey's heart. She had been sitting in her bed, still reading student papers, and she jumped at the jarring sound of the phone beside her bed. Throwing back the comforter she'd wrapped around her shoulders, she grabbed the portable receiver from its stand and took a nervous breath before speaking.

"Hello?"

"Casey, so good to hear your voice," came the response.

"Andy?" she replied, in shock. "Andy, what's wrong?"

"Nothing's wrong. I got your letter yesterday and I'm excited. Really excited!

"Ah, and you didn't think about the time difference, I'm guessing." Casey laughed.

"Oh my God. Oh, I'm really sorry. What time is it there? Damn! It's the middle of the night isn't it?"

"Yes, my dear friend." She smiled, remembering Andy's

impulsivity and his way of throwing himself into a moment without any thought of the time or ramifications. Casey loved his headlong spontaneity, so different from her own trudging approach to life (as she liked to describe it). However, her inclination toward caution had been shifting radically over the past few weeks. She was starting to feel fiercely heroic, as though a new taste for adventure and change was leading the way.

"It's okay, Andy," she assured him. "In fact, I'm very glad to hear your voice too."

"Oh, Casey. I can't believe you're making arrangements to come to Ireland—when I read that I may have given a very un-professor-like whoop for joy."

Casey let out a snort of laughter at the image of Andy, her one-time thesis supervisor, Dr. Kingwood, whooping. "I'd liked to have seen that! But seriously, Andy, I have to create a good reason for asking for a sabbatical now, especially when I turned one down last year. Is it possible we might do some work together over there?"

"Is it possible? Casey, I've been wanting to work with you since, well … for a long time." His voice trailed off.

Casey remembered the conversations they'd shared—inspiring one another, finishing sentences, reaching into the stratosphere of lofty ideas. Until she decided one day to find another advisor because she believed their passion for ideas was becoming dangerously close to his passion for her.

"Andy, how's your family?" Her question was tentative and hung in the air for a moment. She had not corresponded with him over the past seven years—not at all since she'd arrived at City University. Andy wondered at times how their friendship, which had been a bond of passionate interest in the narratives of love and loss, could have ebbed so completely like a gentle tide pulling away from the shore.

"Oh, the kids are good. Peter is teaching young teens at an inner-city school in Manchester and loving it. Gabriella is following her dream of oceanography, which scares the hell out of me, because her letters are full of descriptions of deep-sea diving in some far-off waters no one's ever heard of."

Casey laughed. "She always was an adventuress, your daughter. But you are very proud of her, aren't you?" As she spoke, Casey experienced a blending of illusion and reality. Their conversation felt familiar, as though the two of them had spoken only yesterday. "And Kate?" She asked, waiting, listening to Andy's breath. A moment passed; another breath.

"She left, Casey. A couple of years ago." Another moment. Deeper silence.

"Oh, Andy, I'm so sorry."

"Well, things were not good, and I couldn't figure out whether it was us, me, the move to Ireland, her own restlessness ... and one day, oh you don't want to hear all this. It's all old news. The end of the story is I'm now a roving bachelor."

Casey waited. She detected anguish, a buried heartbreak. "Andy ... what happened?"

She rested back against her headboard, pulled the comforter around her shoulders. "Please. Tell me." Here she was, once again. A woman in her late forties, alone, opening her heart to somebody else's pain. And as often occurred in Casey's life, that somebody else was a man.

After a moment's hesitation, Andy said, "No, Casey, I didn't call to talk about me. Let's just say that Kate and I have been on different roads for a long time, and leave it there. The reason I called was to reconnect, tell you I'm delighted

you might be coming to Ireland, and see if there's anything
I can do to pave the road ahead."

She smiled. "How I've missed that expression of yours,
'pave the road ahead.'"

"How far along are you with your application for sabbatical?" he asked her.

"Everything has happened very fast. I've actually only
made the decision in the past couple of weeks." Much to
Casey's chagrin, her voice broke.

It didn't escape Andy's notice. "Hmm. I think there
may be a story here?" A soft invitation floated across the
airwaves in her direction.

Pushing the comforter away, Casey folded her body,
knees under chin, arms folded around her legs, the phone
resting against her ear. She swallowed the lump in her
throat. *What is wrong with me?* she thought. *I need to pull
this together.*

"Casey? You okay?

"Oh yes, I'm fine, just some stuff rising to the surface.
You know me and my battle with 'stuff.' Being human is
very difficult for me." Casey put one hand over her eyes
and grimaced. *Damn, why did I say that? Dumb, dumb,
dumb.*

Moving to the edge of her bed, she put her feet on the
floor and stood up. She padded barefoot to the bookcase
by the window in her bedroom and, after briefly scanning
the shelves from floor to ceiling, she pulled her bound dissertation from its place on the top shelf.

Andy, silent on the other end across the ocean, knew
about Casey's need sometimes to "take a moment." Many
times throughout their friendship and their work together
he had sat quietly waiting for her "moment" to dissolve,

when she would reveal the thought that had stopped her in mid-sentence. He waited.

"Andy? Still there?" she checked.

"Not going anywhere, Casey."

"I'm holding my dissertation, as I speak, and get this—remember what you wrote on it the day I brought the final bound copy to you … at six in the morning?" Casey laughed, "Even though you were no longer my advisor." She quickly continued, "Remember? I wanted you to be the first to see the final copy."

"Oh, I do, I do. I remember that day very well. I think Kate thought you and I had something going on—you standing at the door in your ratty jeans and yellow sweater, me in my pajamas." He paused, took a breath. "Read to me what I said in my note."

Both were listening to one another's breathing, whispers across the phone line.

Casey took the note that was tucked between the cover and the title page. Andy's distinctive script was scrawled across the paper. She read to him, her finger following along under each line, like a child who has just discovered the wonder of words.

To my friend: a learned student, a keeper of wisdom—to you, Casey.
You are a seeker and a purist. "Love holds the power of transformation, the potency of debasement, but loss purifies." Recognize that line? Your own beautiful words. Some days your brilliance dazzled me, and some days I trembled. In knowing you, I have garnered something incomparable, not to be replicated. My world has been transformed. May you someday realize how extraordinary you are.

My one regret? We didn't complete your "opus" together.
Andy

Silence held Andy and Casey in the moment. He had forgotten the intensity of his words. She remembered the pangs of regret when she'd first read that note—wishing she'd never sent him away. Again, Casey was the one to break the spell.

"Andy, I need to get some sleep," she told him now. "But I do need to talk with you about what the possibilities might be if I come to Ireland. I know I could work on my book, yet I'm serious when I say I want to work with you, in some way. Without getting too far into it, I feel I owe you something."

"No you don't, Casey. You made a good decision all those years ago. Let's just say we'll pick up from where we left off and see what happens. I should go now, appointments await. Take care of yourself, and know I'm thinking about you. I'll be in touch."

Before she could say goodbye, she heard a soft click as he hung up.

Sleep was no longer an option. Casey stood beside her bed, felt the softness of the rug under her feet. She curled her toes into the soft gray pile, an extravagance she had given herself when she moved into this, her first house. There was a sensual pleasure, feeling the softness under her toes; one accompanied by the buzz of the unknown path she was about to take.

She walked out to her den and switched on the desk lamp. Taking a seat in the white leather chair, she took pen in hand, smoothed a blank sheet lying waiting on her desk and began to write.

Dear Dean Atwater,
As you know, I have been at the university for seven
years and Chair of Humanities for three of those years.
Last year I was offered a sabbatical—for the winter,
spring and summer term of 1982. When the oppor-
tunity was offered to me, I felt it was not a good time
to leave my position because of the new construction,
moving offices, new faculty coming on in the depart-
ment. However, I have reconsidered and, furthermore,
I have a chance to work in Ireland for a period of time.
If granted leave to go, I would request time beginning
after this term, in early April, and if possible extend the
leave from April through to the end of December 1982.
Might it be possible for me to make an appointment with
you so we may discuss how I plan to use my time through-
out my sabbatical? I want to work toward the completion
of my book, one chapter of which has been accepted as an
article in the Humanities and Philosophy Journal.
I am willing to suggest someone to replace me for that
period of time—my colleague and good friend, Dr.
Anne Morgan.
I appreciate your consideration of my rather untoward
request.
With regards,
Cassandra MacMillan

THE SKY SPARKLED THAT EVENING, OR SO IT SEEMED TO
Helena. Standing on the steps just outside City Hall, she
watched the cars make a river of white headlights as they
crawled along the crowded street. Late afternoon traffic,
people wending their way home, ordinary life being ordinary.

Today for Helena though, this moment did not feel ordinary. She was waiting for Galean to finish up the final details with the judge who had married them, only a half hour ago. She wanted a couple of moments on her own to absorb the intensity of feelings she was experiencing and the warm flow of something close to triumph. Maybe now the demons might skulk away.

The wind caught the edge of her red woolen coat, lifting it away from the cream of her silk wedding suit. "I wonder if this is real." She said to the chill air of the early evening. "I wonder if I'll just wake up and turn off the alarm and get ready for work."

"Not for a few days, if I have anything to do about it." Galean spoke as he exited the revolving door at the entrance to City Hall. He stood behind her, hands on her shoulders. "Hello, Mrs. Laihy. Let's go home and have some champagne."

She smiled. Helena sensed it could all end—everything good always did. But in the present, here, now, she felt as though she were shining like the headlights reflected on the pavement. And she watched the demons slink away, down the street.

Saturday, January 16, 1982. Helena could rest into her life for a while yet.

DEAN ATWATER FOUND TWO LETTERS SITTING ON HIS DESK, one beside the other, when he arrived in his office on Monday. One was Casey's request for her sabbatical to be reinstated; the other, a request from Galean for three days off following Reading Week, so that he might take his new bride on an extended honeymoon.

The first letter surprised but pleased the dean. He liked his faculty to enhance their learning, and he had been chagrined when Casey had initially asked that her sabbatical be delayed. The other letter surprised and puzzled him. Dr. Laihy, the radical professor, getting married? And in the middle of the term? *Oh well,* thought the dean. *Galean Laihy may be a strange man, but three days added to Reading Week for a honeymoon is doable. Wonder who she is?*

Chapter Thirteen

O, when she's angry, she is keen and shrewd!
She was a vixen when she went to school;
And though she be but little, she is fierce.

—SHAKESPEARE,
A Midsummer Night's Dream

"We held a wedding and nobody came." Galean laughed, the pop of a resistant champagne cork accompanying his comment.

"Only the important people attended," Helena said. The two—the new husband and the new bride—sat, shoes tossed to the floor, feet resting on the glass coffee table.

Galean seemed to have jettisoned his need for perfection and predictability along with his shoes. It was past midnight, moving into a Sunday morning. They intertwined their feet and toasted their mad decision to "run off and get married." Helena liked the unceremonious feel to the phrase, and they rested in the lull of the moment. There would be few such moments down the road of their marriage.

"Galean," Helena's voice was a feathered whisper.

"Lena?" Galen asked, becoming concerned when he saw her eyes were bright, tears brimming at the corners. "What's troubling you?" He reached his arm out to invite her in.

Unwinding her feet from his, Helena folded her legs up

onto the couch and placed her head on Galean's shoulder. She felt serenity and she felt sadness.

"The letter. Casey's letter. I need to talk to you more about that." Her face was pressed into his shoulder, her words muffled.

"I'm sorry, I couldn't make out what you said. Are you talking about Casey's letter?" Galean drew back, put his hand on her damp cheek. "Is that what you said?"

Helena lifted her head and nodded. "I need to tell you how painful it is to be happy, and how terrifying it is. What Casey wrote may be true: Eros and madness can be strange bedmates." Sitting up, she turned to face him. "If I don't brave my demon, she'll win."

The demon, or Casey? Galean wondered.

For a moment silence awash with sad memories filled the room. A woman open and available to her story; a man pushing his own story farther into the shadows.

Galean reached for the champagne bottle, pointed to Helena's glass and asked, "Might this help?"

Helena nodded. She watched as he poured the champagne into her glass, concentrating on the gentle stream of miniscule bubbles accumulating like broken promises. "Casey is prudent," she said. "Always was. And she's insightful; really insightful." Helena offered her glass to Galean in a toast: "Here's to prudence and insightfulness."

He watched her face settle into a small smile as she sipped on her champagne.

"But I was always just a little ahead of her," Helena added.

"Okay. I'm not sure what's happening, but I feel as though I just missed something," Galean said, setting his glass on the coffee table firmly enough to make Helena jump.

She turned to him and spoke, her words piercing the air.

"That letter? She may be right about all that stuff about your past and you not wanting to admit how alone you are, but I don't think she's really worried about you at all. I think she's feeling humiliated because she totally misread you, and—"

Galean stopped her there. "Wait, wait, what do you mean she misread me?"

What was intended to be a celebratory, happy wedding night was, minute by minute, deteriorating into crackling defenses. Galean defending himself and Casey; Helena gathering steam for attack.

"Oh Galean, we talked about this. You have to know that Casey loves you."

"Of course she does, but we're friends; loving friends. Have been for ages." By now Galean was easing over to the other end of the couch.

Gusts of winter wind rattled the windows.

"See, I told you," said Helena. "She's rattling windows now. She's really pissed." She laughed a harsh, guttural laugh.

For a few seconds Galean experienced a visceral alert. "Helena, you're talking in circles. What are you trying to say?"

Slowly, almost cat-like, she unwound her legs and stood up, took a last gulp of the now tepid champagne, placed the glass carefully on the table. "How much time do you have, Galean?" She looked away, out at the snow falling in a blur against the window. "I'm going to get the letter," she said and then was gone, almost disappearing before his eyes.

The hopes that both of them had brought to this day were blurred now, like the snowflakes accumulating against the window. Galean rested his head against the soft wool of the couch and closed his eyes, trying to make sense of it all: Helena's tempestuous reaction to Casey's letter, the fear, the anger and now this. Her calm unnerved him. *Who is she? A little late to be wondering that, Laihy,* he chided himself. Yet he felt an unexpected heat. The foreboding around her unpredictability, her sudden transformations, aroused something physical in him. It was the kind of fear and wonder that excites.

When he stirred, he realized she'd been gone almost ten minutes. "Lena? Where'd you go?" he called out. Sitting up, he moved to stand when she appeared almost as she had left, like some kind of apparition, her wedding suit now replaced by a diaphanous silken robe, her hair in disarray falling across her shoulders. As she walked toward him, the rustle of silk summoned a fervor within him. It felt like surrender.

"Let's forget the letter and Casey for a while." Helena's voice was a sigh like a rustle of silk.

Galean lay back and closed his eyes. He sighed a moan of pleasure.

EARLY MONDAY MORNING, DEAN ATWATER SAT AT HIS DESK, mulling over all that needed to be put in place right away to expedite Casey's sabbatical.

On that same morning, Galean sat in his office at the university staring at the phone. He felt as though he'd been set adrift. *I need to talk with Casey.*

While the two men considered what to do next, Casey sat in her classroom, waiting for three of her doctoral students. In her mind, she was crafting a letter she was planning to write: one more plea to Galean.

Across the city, Helena was at the hospital changing

into her scrubs. She carefully folded the jeans she'd been wearing and then placed them in her locker. Inside one of the pockets was the paper on which she'd written Casey's office address and phone number.

Everyone awaited the next move.

"HI, DR. MACMILLAN. THANKS FOR MEETING WITH US THIS morning."

Rob arrived before the other students, greeted her and swung his briefcase onto the table. "Wait'll you see what I have for you this morning."

For a moment Casey felt a pang of sorrow. She wasn't sure if she'd ever have students quite like this again. The three she was meeting this morning were graduating in the summer, assuming all went well and their committees accepted their theses. Casey was more than confident all three would walk away from their respective defenses with laud and honor flowing like the graduate gowns they'd soon don. But she'd not be there. Provided the dean accepted her letter and her request, she expected to be in Ireland by mid-April.

"Sounds like you had a successful weekend, Rob. What do you have for me? Or do you want to wait till Anya and Stephen arrive?" Sorrow sat more lightly as she took on the cloak of teacher. Life-giving assurance lay in those moments.

"I'd like to go ahead, if that's all right with you," he said.

"You have my undivided attention. Do you mind if I keep some notes?" Casey smoothed her hand across a blank sheet of paper in her writing pad, a gesture she always made as she prepared to write.

"Not at all. Shall I start?"

Casey picked up her pen and nodded.

Rob opened his briefcase, reached in and pulled out a manuscript—the first draft of his thesis. His dark eyes shone with anticipation that he might have uncovered something wondrous within himself, which gladdened Casey to see. Her hope for all her advisees and her grad students was that they discover their own energy of possibility.

"Here's what I really want you to see," Rob said. He leaned forward and slid a page across the smooth mahogany table toward Casey. He seemed rooted in his chair, his gaze fixed on her.

Two people sat together, both hopeful; both anticipating; both setting out on a new path.

Casey sat back, picked up the page. For a moment she paused, noticing that the winds had hushed. A morning sun shone expectantly. Rob did not take his eyes from her while she read. When she finished reading the page, she placed it on the table, slowly, carefully. Resting her chin on her hand, she began.

"It's a radical approach, to tell your own story as your thesis. And saying that, I think you need to do this. It might mean taking a longer time because you now have three other people to convince—your committee members. But knowing them as I do, it's not impossible. Difficult yes, not impossible."

At that moment Casey was swimming in the role of educator/advisor, a safe place for her to be. During these times, she realized the paradox between what she taught and how she lived her life. Rob's forthright story, his own description of love and loss, was a work of beauty; prose as poetry, a clear expression of his own truth. His testament to staying the course through some very difficult times. Casey envied his clarity. What was her truth? Was she living a life in shadows, fleeing from her own story?

"Dr. MacMillan? Are you okay? Are you thinking I may have a problem?" Rob's forehead creased into deep lines, his eyes clouded.

"Oh no, no. You have expressed something beautiful and clear. Academe has the notion that clarity and beauty lie only in the realm of scholarly writing, which says we should never allow ourselves to reveal academically what we think or feel. It's not measureable—so *they* say. But as far as I'm concerned, I think "they" are afraid of losing power in the halls of academic research." Casey inhaled with an audible whoosh of breath. *A little edgy are we?* she thought.

"Is this going to be a problem for you, me taking this curve in the road?" Rob asked.

"Not a bit because I'm ..." She caught herself before revealing her plans that were not yet approved. "I mean, we've chosen your committee very carefully."

Casey held her reservations close to her chest. Maybe a year ago, a month ago even, she might have warned Rob that including in his thesis his story of finding his way back from grief and despair might be discounted as not intellectually rigorous, too personal. Now though, she saw the beauty of his story and the truth that tumbled off the page. The wisdom.

"You've written something courageous, Rob. And the research community is beginning to shift—the conversation is widening and deepening. Numbers are no longer hold-ing court as the arbiter of knowledge. It's your experience that holds the wisdom, and your remarkable clarity. Don't diminish your experience. Write about unraveling your cover story and finding your way back."

Casey lingered, letting her thoughts drift inward. *I've been diminishing my own experience all my life.* Rob's thesis—a story of a plane crash, a family destroyed, a young boy's endeavors to reconstruct a life—was one where he'd searched out his own wisdom, whatever the cost. This moment of Rob's revelation gave Casey pause to consider, with sadness, Galean, and his resistance to untangle his past. And the layers of pain he rejected.

"Stay true to yourself, Rob," she told her student, smiling. "You are creating new paths. For all of us." And to herself, she thought, *Are you paying attention, Casey?*

Rob grinned and stood up. "If you don't mind me leaving before the others arrive, I'm going to go to the library. I'm about to explore the literature on paths of new research."

"Good idea. And remember, someday another student will read your work and have the courage to move forward. Now go," she said with a laugh as she waved him toward the door.

Something shifted within Casey. Sureness began to flow alongside doubt, and she knew what to do next.

Chapter Fourteen

... let's realize we'll not get through
unsmirched or unscathed. The road
will only get darker as we go,
and nothing's pure.

—STEPHEN DUNN,
"Formalities for the Long Road"

Shortly after Rob had left the seminar room, Stephen and Anya arrived, each gripping their briefcases that held the beginning chapters of a year's work. Their meeting with Casey left them like Rob, with renewed intention and a clear sense of the way forward. She had a gift for restoring the confidence of her students when they became fatigued and discouraged. The air in the seminar room that day was charged with resolve. Taking a note from her own counsel, Casey decided to listen to what was nudging her from deep inside: she would go to see Helena.

Sitting there in the silence, Casey opened her folder, took out a sheet of university letterhead and, with pen in hand, she began to write her last appeal.

January 25, 1982
Dear Galean and Helena,
Truth, personal truth, is something that's elusive and
difficult to capture in our world today, yet you, Galean,

and I over the years of friendship have been able to grasp it, express it and honor it.

She raised the pen, tapped it against her cheekbone, wondered, *Am I being preachy?* Deciding no, she continued to write.

And we have been remarkable friends. But now I fear that our shared openness has taken wings and flown into the stratosphere. I wonder where truth goes when it dies.

She could almost feel Galean pushing at her, getting impatient for her to say what she needed to say.

I need to explain myself once again, but I only need to do so because I fear I've tarnished something in me. Both of you need to know, Galean, that I'm wondering how I could have thought you and I might take the friendship we have nurtured and possibly botch it up by marrying one another. You and I have been so clear and comfortable in what, I think, has been a unique friendship. You are the best friend I've ever had, Galean. You are probably the first and maybe only person I've cared about so deeply and, in return, you made me feel such worth and acceptance. And now I can't just stand by and watch you walk into her fire.

Helena, I see you still deeply troubled. All those years ago at the Home, you were filled with hate for your father, and with good reason. But he's dead now. Are you still hating him, still searching for someone to become your father? Remember how you told me you wanted to destroy the demon? Please. Galean is not your father, and he is no demon.

Remember too, Galean, I know your whole story as you know mine.

Another moment, a niggling doubt, before Casey carried on.

Your lone flight from Ireland in company with strangers when you were a very young boy. How abandoned you felt. Your father's murder, your mother's psychosis. I know you believe you've put all that behind you... You have become successful in the world you've chosen, and you've survived. Forgive me, Helena, but letting Galean place his life in your hands shouts to me that he's denying his past.

Casey placed the pen on the paper, leaned her elbows on the shining surface of the oak table and put her hands over her eyes. *Who am I talking to here? Galean? Me? Both of us? Helena?* Uncovering her eyes, she shook her head, trying to clear the questions that bewildered and confused her. She had to stay the course. Picking up the pen, she wrote with reenergized resolve.

Galean, I know that your mother was a sick, psychotic woman. Everything you have shared with me tells that story. Helena, I know that your past haunts you too. I know how angry you have been. I watched your ruthlessness, I lived through your rages, I remember when I could taste your anguish. And yes, we've laughed together till I thought I'd stop breathing. We were friends. I tried to save you in those days when I thought I was everyone's savior. Living there, with you in that Home, I believed I was meant to save you. Now I know the only people we can truly save are ourselves. Yet here I am, back wanting to rescue the two of you. What a trio we are.
I've already begun what I need to do about going to Ireland. And I just have one request for each of you—

that Galean, you revisit your past and, Helena, that
you go to yours. I'll leave with my hope you both will
try. And that then, you are able to show up for one
another, honestly.
Take care, my friends.
Casey

Casey folded the letter, placed it in her leather book
bag, and stood up.

A LATE-JANUARY THAW PROMISED NEW LIFE. ANYTHING
stirring lay buried beneath mounds of snow, which only a
few days ago had been crisp and solid. Icicles hanging from
the eves of the front porch dripped onto Casey's woolen
cap as she pressed the doorbell and waited. After a minute,
she pressed the doorbell again. Finally she heard footsteps
approaching, the click of a lock. The door swung open and
a fatigued, sleepy-eyed Helena stood before her.

"Oh, Helena," said Casey. "I woke you." Some of her
resolve began to crumble.

"Uh … no, I mean yes. I was called into an emergency
early this morning. If you need to see Galean, he's gone to
talk with the dean." She made no move to welcome or invite
Casey across the threshold.

"Well, no. I'm really here to talk with you. May I come in?"

Helena wrapped her silken robe more tightly around
herself and motioned for Casey to enter, saying, "Come
inside then, I'm freezing here in the doorway. Come to the
kitchen, I need some coffee. Would you like a cup?' She
walked ahead, down the hall toward the kitchen, leaving
Casey in her wake.

Following along, Casey was struck by Helena's discernable composure; struck by it—and suspicious. She had witnessed her cunning many times before.

"No, Helena. Thanks, but no coffee for me. I need to say what I came to say and then go."

"Sounds as though we're going to have that old conversation. Don't you think it's a little boring?"

A spoon fell to the floor, jarring the tight silence between the two women. Coffee grounds spilled from the spoon, scattering across the tiles and creating a chaotic design. Appearing to ignore the mess, Helena began pouring water into the coffee maker.

"You and I, Helena, have never been boring," Casey said. "Unceasing maybe, but never boring. Let's do this. Let me say what I came to say." With that, Casey pulled the letter from her book bag.

Helena rolled her eyes. "Oh God, another Casey essay."

Not deterred, Casey paused eyes closed, giving a moment for her heart to slow down. "Do you remember all those years ago, when we had times like this?" Casey put the letter on the counter between them.

Helena took a wet towel and, almost defiantly, bent down to wipe up coffee grains. She looked up at Casey, cocked an eyebrow and smiled. "Maybe?"

"Oh, I'm sure you do." Casey sensed a small churning at the top of her stomach, a sign that her patience was waning. "It would be hard to forget that scene, the way you were screaming."

"You let me down," Helena said as she stood up and shook the coffee grains into the garbage under the sink. She seemed deliberate, almost brazen, tossing the grains into the bin. She brought a fist down onto the edge of the sink.

Casey went on. "And you clearly still think people are pawns, peasants to be provoked and bullied to get your way." Her resolve to remain calm was failing. She wanted to take Helena by the shoulders and shake her.

"Good Hermia, do not be so bitter with me," was Helena's response. Her voice had taken on a soft taunting lilt. She had become *Midsummer's* Helena in an instant before whipping back to herself, present again with hardly an intake of breath.

The two women were like a tableau, stock-still waiting for release from a frozen moment holding them in its cold grip. Casey moved first, picking up her letter from the counter.

Putting the letter back into her book bag, Casey pulled a leather-cushioned stool up to the counter and sat down. She folded her hands, one over the other. "Helena, nothing is going to happen that's any good unless we start talking to one another. I'm party to this craziness. Funny that it's someone like Galean—good-hearted, compulsive Galean—who's thrown you and me together again."

Helena poured herself a cup from the coffeepot, pointed to an empty mug by Casey's hand. "Now?"

Casey nodded yes.

Something shifted in the air in the room. An imperceptible semblance of kinship floated between the two women.

"Aren't you going to show me your letter?" Helena asked. She held her coffee mug with two hands, her eyes peering over the rim. She took a sip.

"You and I know what's in that letter, Helena. I think it's time I stopped dropping off letters when what I need to do is throw some words into the air and see which ones you catch. Let's start with, have you been getting help in the years since I last saw you?"

"You mean since the time I was told by you to see the psychiatrist at that Home? The doctor who gave me drugs for psychosis? No. Not since then. Nor do I intend to." Helena's mug landed on the granite with a firm crack. "He was the last. Remember, I work at a hospital."

"And Galean? Does he know all about you—your past? Us?" Casey pushed back against Helena's thinly veiled derision.

"He knows enough," Helena responded. "Is this what you wanted to talk about, my past?"

Casey leaned her head into her hand; sighed. "No, not just your past—Galean's, too. Do you know anything about him?"

"I'd better," said Helena. "He's my husband!"

"What!" Color faded from Casey's face.

"We got married a week ago Saturday." A sly smile skirted the corners of Helena's mouth. "That's where Galean is right now—talking to the dean. We're going to Barbados during Reading Week. Hasn't he told you? Haven't you two talked?" Helena eyes brightened, her cheeks reddened. Something close to a derisive snort escaped from her lips.

A bad taste of humiliation collected in Casey's throat. How could she ever have thought that her opinion of their lives or what they chose to do mattered to them? She stood, propelling the kitchen stool back with a fierce thrust. Swinging her book bag up from the floor, she strode toward the hallway. She called over her shoulder as she reached the front door, her hand grasping the handle. "I'm done now. Finished. I wish you both … life."

Helena listened to the reverberation of the slamming door and smiled.

Chapter Fifteen

To say the truth, reason and love keep little company together now-a-days.

—SHAKESPEARE,
A Midsummer Night's Dream

Grey morning light blurred the horizon, blending the winter earth with overcast shapeless clouds. The lamp on Galean's office desk cast a yellowish glow, emphasizing the shadows that surrounded him. *February and Reading Week can't come soon enough,* he thought to himself as he unfolded a shiny brochure depicting clear sunlit waters and white sandy beaches. A photo of a yellow cottage with a white-railed veranda partially cheered Galean's melancholy, which was caused not so much by the weather as it was by the feeling that his friendship with Casey was in danger. He considered walking the length of the hallway to her office and barging in but then thought better of it. *Not my style. I just wish I knew ...* and he stopped. *Work—that's what I need right now. Work.*

He stood and walked over to a credenza sitting under the window. It was clear of clutter except for a manuscript sitting in an oak letterbox. He picked it up and walked over to his chair. As he flipped through the type-written pages, he realized the complete manuscript was not there. A moment of panic: *It's sitting on my desk at home. Stupid,*

stupid. Galean's characteristic organization and precise way of being were suffering over the past few weeks. He didn't function well amid unpredictability or uncertainty. The world he had so carefully constructed had become fuzzy and unsettled like the distant horizon out his window. And now, part of a manuscript about the torments of love—the vast experiences of loss that humans suffer—sat open on his desk at home, almost inviting Helena to read it. Her precarious and fitful moods of late alarmed him. Reading what he and Casey had written about the ambivalence of love could be catastrophic.

Turning his attention back to the portion of the manuscript he was holding in his hands, Galean recalled that he and Casey had begun writing it for their book months ago. In the midst of the present tumult, the writing had dwindled, like their friendship. Galean pushed the glittering brochure of beaches and yellow cottages aside and set the manuscript in front of him. The title page read:

> *If love's a sweet passion, why does it torment?*
> *If a bitter, oh tell me, whence comes my content.*

They were lines from Henry Purcell's *Fairy Queen* libretto. Galean shook his head in wonder. *The Fairy Queen* had been adapted from Shakespeare's *A Midsummer Night's Dream.* A chilling thought occurred to him: Helena's obsession with that very play. He and Casey were using the context of madness to explore the vagaries of love and loss. How might Helena react if she discovered the manuscript? She'd gone into Galean's study at times, to look for a book or to polish his desk, which he'd asked her not to do. But still she did it.

Galean felt dread move from vertebrae to vertebrae.

Life and its unexpected paths had brought him to this place because of a mystifying ardor. Was Helena his temptress? His Siren? Was what he felt a temporary madness? Was this how it felt to love someone? He sat, head in hands, wondering at what point his carefully planned life had begun to unravel.

Looking back down at the page, Galean read what he had written when he and Casey had worked together, last December.

How do we discover, in truth, loving relationships in our short lifetime? Are we born searching? How do we know how it feels to love, to truly love? How do we avoid the prosaic? Is there room in our bodies, in our hearts or in our souls for the longings, for the exquisiteness and, ultimately, the loss?
As children, a young boy, a small girl, how could we know what it felt to be loveable when what we knew was chaos? We did not know love.

Galean raised his pencil and looked beyond to the bleak horizon. *I have to talk to Casey.*

DEAN ATWATER'S OFFICE WAS ACROSS THE COURTYARD. Casey's morning appointment with him was teetering close to the scheduled time. Still reeling from humiliation for being the dupe in Galean and Helena's unfolding tale, Casey strode into her office. Not missing a step, she called over her shoulder to her assistant. "Alice, could you call the dean's secretary and let her know I'll be there, but I'll be a few minutes late?"

"Uh, sure." Alice picked up the phone, dialed the dean's

extension, all the time watching Casey disappear behind a closed door. Something she seldom did—close her office door.

A dim light glowed on Casey's desk, casting shadows across a copy of the letter she'd written to the dean. Bookshelves lined a wall, which usually lent Casey the feeling of retreat and comfort, but right now she experienced neither. Windows behind her desk surveyed the bare, bleakness of mid-winter. Her heavy heart reflected the imaginary sorrow of barren trees. This forlorn feeling was not new to Casey; old humiliations crept through her body like an unwelcome virus. How severely the pangs of self-loathing could penetrate. Many years and expansive distances had not lessened the original torments of a lost childhood and growing up in confused silence.

She dropped into her chair and slumped down with her head against the black leather, one elbow propped on the arm of the chair, hand curved across her eyes. Uninvited memories flowed into her thoughts like unwelcome guests. A grinding of metal on metal; screams; darkness; and silence. Then sirens and flashing lights; a series of rooms. Aloneness.

"Dr. MacMillan? Dr. MacMillan!"

Casey dropped her hand from her forehead and started from her chair.

"Are you all right?" Alice was leaning toward her across the desk, one hand on the phone.

"Oh, Alice. Sorry, I didn't hear you come in. I guess I must have nodded off right here in my chair."

"You don't look well, Dr. MacMillan. You're very pale. Do you want to lie down on your couch?" Alice moved to walk around the desk to Casey.

"No, no, I'm fine," she assured Alice. Checking the time,

she said, "I must go." As though pursued, Casey grabbed the copy of her letter to the dean, threw on her wool coat and ran out the door.

———————

"CASEY MACMILLAN," DEAN ATWATER GREETED HER WITH A warm smile. "Come on in." He walked from behind his desk, arm outstretched ready to take her hand. It was a firm handshake, one that welcomed and assured.

Since Casey's arrival in the Humanities Department at the university, James Atwater had been her mentor and advocate. He was one of the reasons that Casey had become Department Chair in a relatively short time. He admired her dedication to her students, her passion for ideas—and her resilience. He had listened with great care when Casey had confided in him, telling him bits and pieces of her child-hood trauma. Thus the Dean became more a father figure to her than her "first among equals." She took his outstretched hand and held it for a brief second longer than usual.

"Your hand," he remarked. "You're freezing. Are you all right?"

Taking her hand from his, Casey smiled. "That's why I'm here." She walked to a chair by his desk and unbuttoned her coat slowly, methodically, before sitting down.

"Trouble? Is there more than your letter is saying?" James Atwater; friend and confidante. Moving back to take his seat behind the desk, he asked her, "What's going on?"

For a moment, Casey was tempted to tell him every-thing: her foolish schoolgirl whimsy about Galean, her fears about Helena. Instead she sat straight-backed on the chair, folded her hands and gave him the on-paper explanation.

"James, I have a wonderful opportunity to go to Ireland to write and work on our book—the one Galean and I have almost finished. He knows, he knows … I'm going." Casey took a breath, feeling words were tumbling. "I want to collaborate with Andy Kingwood at University College Cork, and possibly teach graduate students about suffering and loss." She smiled, adding, "You know how I like to promote the values of grief and loss."

The underlying edge to her voice alarmed the dean. "You want to go to Ireland and teach grad students about grief?"

For the first time in many days, Casey laughed. Then, gathering her coat around her shoulders, she spoke quietly.

"Grief and loss have many faces … I think the masks need to be lowered. I think we need people in all sorts of professions who aren't afraid to talk about grief, loss …" She paused for a second then finished, "And love." She raised one arm and circled it as though encompassing everything beyond. "Our world is afraid. The so-called enlightened halls of learning sadly neglect the depths of what it means to be alive. We neglect, maybe even reject, talking from our hearts. We all want to be theorists and scholars, it's safe there—just ask me. I'm the expert. In fact, in life we should learn to be astonished at what we hold on to, what losses we bear, what we witness, how dauntless and hero-like we can be. That's what I want to teach, James. That's what I want to write about." In the seconds it took to say these words, Casey began to reclaim herself.

Drops of water drizzled down the length of the window. A shout of greeting echoed from the hallway; students were moving from classrooms, generating a cacophony of voices—allusions to lives being lived.

Keeping his voice steady, the dean asked Casey, "Have

you been unhappy here?"

She held out her hands, a gesture of hope for understanding. "No, no—anything but! You've opened doors for me in ways I could never have imagined." She folded her hands to her lips, prayer-like. "You've given me life."

Pretending to brush something from his eye, the dean turned his chair back to his desk and pulled a thick file from several others resting on a side table. He had the reputation of being able to put his hand on whatever file or paper that was needed at the time—and right now Casey needed exactly what he produced. He turned back to her, unfolded the file and handed her the sheaf of papers.

"Last year we talked about you taking a sabbatical and you suggested the time wasn't right. It seems to me, from what you are telling me, the time has arrived. I'll speak to the provost, whom I'm sure will support our request." Dean Atwater paused for a moment before handing the sabbatical proposal papers to Casey. Walking her to the door, his parting words were, "Get yourself to Ireland."

LATER THAT AFTERNOON, CASEY SAT IN SILENCE. HER OFFICE dimming into twilight, the shadows giving a sense of soft endings to a January winter's day. Her meeting with Dean Atwater had given her reason to feel heartened. Yet uncertainties still hovered.

During the early part of the afternoon, she'd sat with Anya, whose proposal for her doctoral thesis Casey found extraordinary. Throughout January, Anya had written the first draft of her proposal and possibly the first chapter of her thesis, one she was bravely taking into the realm of personal experience—a feat almost unheard of in Casey's professorial career, and yet this was now the second of her advisees this year choosing to do this. Anya spoke passionately about her need to honor her sister's death by suicide. Casey had sat beside her, offering a consoling hand on the young woman's shoulder as she spoke.

"Dr. MacMillan, I feel driven to write about the strong connection between living and loving fiercely. There's so much in the literature and in the lives of authors who wrote with fervor and who took their own lives. My sister was an author who experienced psychotic episodes and who mourned the writer within her because demons attacked and she could no longer find the words; her beautiful soul yearned to be peaceful. So you see, I must write about my sister and the authors she idolized: Virginia Woolf, Sylvia Plath, Anne Sexton and Dorothy Parker. All were brilliant, all gave up on life just like her." Anya's sadness then became old tears, dripping onto her cheeks.

Casey had sat quietly, holding her sadness, and for a moment she remembered a young seventeen-year-old Helena weeping, wanting to die.

Her student now gone, Casey sat in the approaching darkness of her office, still moved by the depth of Anya's passion and overwhelmed by the potency of her own reaction. Casey sought asylum from her demons here in her office, but today she felt a fullness in her chest that took her breath away. Grabbing gulps of air, she rose and walked to her book bag, leaned down and picked it up. She flung the bag onto her credenza, flipped the straps and reached in to pull out a manuscript. It was a rough second copy of the book she and Galean had been writing—up until the end of December, that is. Since then they'd written nothing together. Even the writing time she normally gave herself had dwindled and she wondered if Galean had stopped writing too. She felt as though she might be taking his story away from him.

Casey had lost her way, lost her North Star. She'd allowed emotions and old painful memories to slow her down and confuse her. Now with Anya's sorrowful words hanging in the gloom of dusk, Casey took a deep breath and spread pages of the manuscript across her desk. Her thoughts flashed like beacons: *No more, Galean. No more, Helena. I'll no longer take it upon myself to help you. Fix your own lives. I'm saving my own life from now on.*

She grasped a page in her hand almost fiercely and read it aloud:

> *We do not know we are loveable, or even capable of being loved, when we are born. We are born vulnerable, exquisitely delicate; and we may live our lives seeking a place of wholeness. Feeling "less than" we may aspire to be loved in all the wrong places, by all the wrong people, for all the wrong reasons. Until that day when we turn to ourselves and smile.*

The words penetrated like sharpened darts. *When did I write this?*

She looked at the top of the page for the date—it was December 20th, a Sunday. That was the last time she and Galean had been alone together at work, and they'd decided to write that day. She remembered feeling enlivened and energized when she'd read aloud the section from which this passage came. Galean listened with admiring attention, stopping her every so often. "Read that part again" he'd asked her many times.

What had I touched in him? Casey wondered now. *What had I touched in myself?*

Absorbed in her thoughts, she didn't hear someone stepping into her office. When she looked up, she saw Galean standing in the doorway, his hand resting on the knob.

"Might I come in?" he asked.

Chapter Sixteen

But little by little
as you left their voices behind,
the stars began to burn through the sheets of clouds,
and there was a new voice,
which you slowly recognized as your own.

—**MARY OLIVER,** "The Journey"

His heavy khaki coat was open, belt hanging from the loops. The straps on his suede boots flapped carelessly. Galean, who stereotypically craved certainty in his life, stood in the doorway looking like a man lost.

He asked again, "Could I please come in?" Usually self-assured, he seemed unsteady and tentative. He stalled, moving neither in nor out.

Casey stared at him. The moment felt unfamiliar. The silence, the hesitancy but particularly the mistrust gnawed at her soul. *Damn it, Galean. Even your timing is bad now.*

"I'm really tired, Galean. Can't it wait?" Casey walked over to the old oak coatrack by the window, reached up to take her wool jacket from the hook. She could sense Galean's dismay. He hadn't moved from the doorway.

Sighing, she turned to him and moved toward two large cushioned chairs by her desk, the ones her students called the good news/bad news chairs.

"All right then, come in. Come, sit down." She flopped herself into one of the chairs. "Okay? Or are you just going to stand there?"

In a peculiar way, Casey's edginess reassured him. What chilled Galean was when she seemed indifferent.

"Do you want some more light in here?" He headed toward the light switches on the wall opposite the door.

Another deep sigh. "I'm fine with the lights as they are, thanks."

The atmosphere in the room was charged with Casey's irritation. She crossed her legs and threw her arms in the air.

"What? Why are you here, Galean? And why are you just standing there. It's annoying. Sit down, say what you need to say. I don't have a lot of time." *And shouldn't you be home with your wife?* Swallowing her last thought, she jabbed at the empty chair.

Galean, daring to disregard Casey's impatience, strolled over to the empty chair, sat down and pulled a folded page from his inside coat pocket.

Turning full-bodied in the chair, he offered the page to Casey, who remained immobile and expressionless. Her ancient anger blending with her recent humiliation, creating a seething underground fire within her soul.

Galean leaned in and toward her, put the page on the arm of her chair. He rested his hand on the paper, a man appealing to an old friend. He needed a sign that they still had some kinship binding them.

"Please, Case. I have to show you something; something we wrote a while ago. Remember, the book we're writing? I mean … if we still have a book." He sat opposite her, watching; waiting for some flutter of acknowledgment. He received nothing.

Words that were fueled by past outrage strangled Casey, caught her breath and erupted. "What are you doing to your life?" she asked him. "Why aren't you talking to me? Why didn't you come to me?" Casey MacMillan flared, spewing words into the air.

Oxygen leaving the room could not have been more shocking. A silence laden with disbelief settled between them. No one spoke.

Then a voice cut the air. A chilled, knife-like voice: Casey's. Her anger withering into dispassion. "You, Galean, were one person I finally trusted."

"Casey, I'm—" he started but was cut off.

"No. Don't talk. Just listen." Casey turned away, found a place on the wall and fixed her gaze there. She began to talk slowly, one word following another. "I have decided to leave right after the spring term. As far as I can see, my students will be fine without me, the department will survive, and us? Our friendship...?" Her breath caught in mid-sentence as though trying to stop the next words. Placing her hand on her chest and with her eyes closed, Casey exhaled and continued. "I love you, Galean, and that hurts like no pain I've felt since I was a child. I need to go. I need to leave." Her voice broke.

Galean, who'd sat frozen in his chair while Casey spoke, now bent his head and hunched forward, clasping his hands and resting his arms on his knees. He was silent, deflated.

"Most of the people I've been close to have disappointed and betrayed me, and now you, my friend, have joined the contingent. I feel like I've been left out here on a familiar island ... once again abandoned." Casey paused and ran a hand through her hair. Clearing her throat, she turned around to see Galean staring at her, his eyes sad and bleak.

"Casey. What have we done to one another?" Galean looked at her, as though seeing her for the first time.

"Oh, Galean. We haven't done anything to one another." Some fire returned to her voice. "Everything that's happening, and that has happened, we've done to ourselves, you and I, thinking we knew everything about how to be just friends. We've been fooling ourselves all along, because we're both so bloody scared. And have been for a long time."

Galean stood up and walked to the window. He turned back, folded his arms across his chest and leaned against the windowsill. "It's time." The words were almost inaudible, but then he stood straight and, looking directly at Casey, spoke with an energy that startled both of them. "Both of us need to start telling the truth about our feelings and about what's happening here. Damn it, Casey, we've been friends for a long time and, yes, I probably love you, whatever that means in my life. Maybe what it means is I should just get out of your life." He threw his arms in the air, as though wanting to disavow what love and loss meant now. No longer were they just ideas and theories to explore.

Casey recoiled. "My God, Galean! You are a coward, Galean Laihy. A coward!"

She hurled herself from the chair and strode to the door, where she grabbed the knob and pulled. An image of doors flinging open flashed before her: she saw little Cassandra running from another home, another pretend family, another foster family. Turning in mid-stride she marched back to Galean and pressed her finger into his chest.

"I am angry and frustrated with you, Galean, but I think I'm probably just as angry with myself. We've coasted all this time, at least I have, thinking we're so different from the rest of the fools. But you know what? We're not at all. We are just as afraid of being human, of loving, as everybody else in this insane world. You and I are ridiculous right now—dishonest and ridiculous. Everything you've done in the last while is insane. You've married a woman who's a crazy person, for God's sake!"

"That's not fair, Casey. Just because you're angry."

"Oh, you bet I'm angry. I had to find out from Helena that the two of you got married. You call that friendship? Weird kind of friendship from where I stand."

A wind blew, rattling the glass; sleet tacked at the window. The thaw was over, freezing rain was setting in.

"I'm angry from forever! I'm feeling betrayed. I'm feeling deceived. And by the very people who I've tried to stand by, especially Helena. Do you know that her father raped her on a regular basis? Maybe she's getting her revenge because she thinks I walked out on her, but I had to because I couldn't fix her horror. Well, Galean, we all carry horror of some description. You, me, her."

No breath of air, no sound except sleet on windows.

Casey held out her open hands to Galean. "You want me to be glad for you that you've married a woman whose father used to rape her and who has suffered serious psychological damage because of it yet refuses to get proper treatment? I've lived with that girl, I know how broken she is. And that's why it scared the hell out of me when you told me it's her you wanted to marry." She slammed her hand against the arm of the chair. "And yet! You want me to give you my blessing because you and I are such good friends? I'm not your mother, Galean! I'm not here to take care of you. And I'm not hanging around either, because you are so stupid, you can't see what we really might have had." The tears arrived in one guttural gulp.

Galean moved and stood in front of Casey, whose hands were over her face shielding her tears. "Can I speak now?" he asked her.

She said nothing.

"You're right, Casey. You are not my mother. No one chose to be my mother. The woman who gave birth to me decided I was nothing but a nuisance and left me." As Galean talked, his voice emerged from somewhere deep in his past. He spoke as though he were narrating pictures moving in front of his eyes. "I'm a caricature, a cartoon—a baby left on steps outside a building in Ireland." He looked away as he said this, his mind calling forth images of a building, a set of steps, a baby wrapped in flannel blankets, a cardboard box.

He went on. "But, you know what, Casey? Talking about what's past and gone is a waste of energy and time. This is not going to end well." He reached down to where he'd placed the paper he'd brought with him and then handed it to Casey, who could only stare after him. He walked to the door, but before making his exit, he turned back to face her. "By the way, when I say I love you? That's a truth that I won't mess with anymore. We both have really bad timing. You're right; we're both too bloody afraid. I have to go. Read the damn paper. And finish the damn book."

There are times when old sadness imprisons us, when our lives become stuck in and stuck by the past. For Galean and Casey this could have been one of those moments, but life intervened.

As Galean turned to leave, the phone on Casey's desk rang. But she didn't move. She was fixed to the chair, her gaze riveted on Galean, his words hanging everywhere.

Another jarring ring.

Galean stopped in the doorway. "Want to answer that?"

Collecting herself, Casey reached across her desk and picked up the receiver. "Yes?" A pause. "Yes, he's here."

A harsh voice loud enough for Galean to hear echoed into the room. He recognized the strung out, brittle tone. He closed the door and turned back toward Casey, motioning for her to hand the receiver to him. Helena's voice ripped into him before the receiver was even to his ear.

"I thought I'd find you there!" Her words were clipped, a rant. "You bastard!"

"Helena," Galean started to respond but didn't get far. "Helena! I needed to talk to Casey. No. Listen to me. No. Listen!"

A loud click reverberated across the room. Galean stood holding the receiver looking at it, as though it were something evil.

Casey walked to him and took it from his hand, placed it back on the cradle. "All of us are a little crazy right now, Galean," she told him. "Not a time to try and make sense out of anything."

The angst and the fury were now drained from the room. Anger, disappointment, confusion reassembled themselves into caring as though a clearing breeze had passed through.

"Oh, Casey." Galean slumped onto a couch by the credenza, holding his head in his hands. "I've messed up everything."

For a moment Casey stood over him. She felt life shifting, like a ship slowly changing course. A warm and unfamiliar feeling arose in her—a free-floating, unshackled caring that she dared to call love. In that moment she fell to her knees and gathered Galean into her arms. And everything changed.

Chapter Seventeen

Love sorrow. She is yours now, and you must
take care of what has been given

—**MARY OLIVER**, *Red Bird*

A parking lot, empty of cars on a cold, blustery night, can hold an aura of mysticism, particularly if ordinary life has transformed into something unimaginable.

For Galean on that evening in late January 1982, the unimaginable had happened. Casey's arms and warmth had unveiled an old longing he had bottled up most of his life. It was like no feeling he had ever experienced, not with anyone—including Helena. He felt loved. He felt received.

When she had drifted up onto the couch, they lay in one another's arms, daring to say nothing at first, only savoring a mutual yearning of their closeness, even though the thought of lovemaking did enter the room. Casey had looked up into his face at that moment and said, "We may never be lovers, Galean, yet we will always love one another more deeply than we might ever have imagined possible. Tonight I began telling my story, and that, my dear, friend is sacred ground."

Galean smiled. Now *this* was vintage Casey, the storyteller. For her, when people share their deepest, oldest memories with each other, some never spoken to anyone before, it is a communion of souls.

Now Galean sat in his car, cocooned in the warmth of the heater and the surrounding darkness. Washes of multicolored moments like a Monet painting rose and faded: Casey on her knees holding him as no one had ever held him; the warmth of her body lying beside him, her face buried into his chest; the feeling of how much he wanted to protect her, even from himself. Words and images, of old hurts, hers, his, stayed afloat in his head.

How extraordinary the last hours had been. How astonishing that they'd known one another for all these years without revealing their deepest sorrows. How sad it now seemed to Galean as the realization dawned: Casey would leave soon, and he would be without his treasured friend.

He turned the ignition key, flipped the windshield wipers on and watched the mixture of snow and ice begin to fall away. *How do I go forward now?* He had no idea.

Backing his car out of his parking spot, Galean turned toward University Road. As he crawled out of the lot through the icy ruts forming along the roadway and drove down the street, he noticed a car in his rearview mirror swerving and fishtailing as it, too, pulled out of the lot and into the street. Galean sped up, afraid that the car would lose control trying to pass him. The car, still fishtailing, started to gain on him. Galean realized that, whoever it was, intended to run into him.

CASEY SAT ON HER COUCH IN HER OFFICE, ARMS WRAPPED around herself. Years and years of holding the anguish of invisibility transformed into unrelenting tears. She thought she might never stop. Her demons danced around the room until gradually they became paper thin, like balloon dolls losing air, each one representing a piece of her story. Like Galean, she sat remembering the extraordinary moment she had begun to reveal her story. She had taken on a new kind of courage to enter the black abyss of her past. After laying in the safe embrace of Galean's arms, she had felt moved to talk.

Untangling her arms from him and sitting up, she began. "Galean, all my life, I've survived as this person I created, telling myself over and over that I must never depend on anyone, that nothing is certain. I've taught myself how to be alone."

By then, Galean too was sitting and feeling the intensity of what was happening between them. He had moved to the opposite end of the couch while Casey slid over to the other end. They turned toward one another, each resting a hand on the couch as though to be ready to reach out. Without waiting for any words or encouragement from him, Casey plunged into her story. She needed no urging, only to be heard. Galean was silent, letting her share.

She closed her eyes and began; one word following another, one sentence bleeding into another. "My mother and father, along with my aunt, were killed in a horrific car accident. I was in the back seat and my aunt threw herself across me, saving my life. How many times I've wished she hadn't. It was the late 1930s, and I was left with no one. No brothers, no sisters. Not even grandparents—they were all dead. I became a ward of the province, placed in the hands of Child Care. I know they probably wanted to help me, but I was four years old and my world had imploded. Foster families fed and clothed me, but I could not—would not—let them love me."

Casey had paused then. Her anguish and guilt for being alive, accumulated over years, caught the words in her throat. Breathing hurt. Galean reached for her hand and she shook her head no. Instead she stood up went over to her desk, reached in to a side drawer and pulled out a file folder, from which she took out a photograph. She brought it over to Galean. It was a faded photo of a young man standing, a woman seated, both staring into the camera, and a small girl standing with her hand resting on her mother's knee. The man stood over them, stiff detachable collar holding his head erect. His expression said nothing.

"That's my mom and dad," she told Galean. Back on the couch now, Casey leaned her head back against the cushion, her energy depleted. She turned to Galean. "The rest of the story is predictable: a small angry child, a series of foster homes, me running away—many times." Casey was no longer telling her story to Galean, she was there, running along a dark road, *in* her story.

A vacuum cleaner's hum moved past Casey's office door.

"Oh my God, Galean, the cleaners are here. That means it has to be close to seven o'clock, Helena is not going to be happy. You need to go. Will you tell her it's all my fault?"

"But Casey, you haven't told me all of it. How did you rescue yourself?"

"Anger can be energy. If I wasn't supposed to die and if I was going to be alone, I had to depend on me. So I stopped running and made a plan. I was twelve years old by this point and I knew what I wanted to do and I knew how I had to do it: I had to be perfect. I had to be smart, and I knew how the world worked. I became good friends with a care worker, and she was the one who told me about my trust fund—no one else had ever said a word to me about it.

But I knew there had to be something. My parents … like Helena's … were wealthy. Wouldn't there be a will? Wouldn't there be money?"

"What?!" interjected Galean. "How could that happen? How could that be kept from you?"

"There are greedy, disreputable people in the world, and some of those people are lawyers and even people who work for child care agencies. They were collaborating, and I got them! They have served prison terms and have been totally discredited." Casey smiled. "All because of one courageous social worker who blew the whistle, put her own job at jeopardy and maybe even her life … and mine."

Galean sat, shaking his head from side to side. "Why didn't you ever tell me any of this?"

"Didn't think you needed to know. It's old news."

Galean made a split-second decision. "I'm going to call Helena right now, tell her what's happening and that I'll be home later."

"Not a good idea, Galean."

"No, Casey. I'm about to tell you my story, and then you'll see why the universe brought us together."

Casey laughed. "Galean Laihy, you are not the kind of man who believes in the universe."

"After hearing your story, Case, I think I might be." He got up from the couch then and walked to the desk, where he picked up the phone receiver and dialed his number.

Casey shook her head mouthing, "Bad idea."

But no one answered.

WHEN GALEAN LEFT, CASEY HAD AN UNCOMFORTABLE SENSE that something was brewing. Helena was angry, and that usually meant trouble. Casey knew things were becoming complicated, yet somehow she couldn't bring herself to feel regret. She had not heard Galean's story yet but knew sometime soon she must. He needed to clear a path forward.

Casey stood and walked to her jacket, took it off the hook and, as she threw it across her shoulders, a woolen orange-and-yellow scarf fell to the floor. When she knelt to pick it up, she noticed a paper on the floor by her desk. It was the page Galean had been so intent upon showing her. Putting one arm into a sleeve of her jacket, she began to read.

> *How do we discover true loving relationships in our short lifetime? Are we born searching? How do we know how it feels to love, to truly love? How do we avoid the prosaic? Is there room in our bodies, our hearts, our souls, for the longings, the exquisite and, ultimately, the losses As children, a young boy, a small girl how could we know what it felt to be loveable when what we knew was chaos? We did not know love.*

"Oh, Galean," Casey said aloud. "What are we all doing to one another?" In that moment she knew deep in her soul how ruthlessly deceitful everyone—all three of them—had been to one another, but even worse to themselves.

CASEY FOLDED HER SCARF AROUND HER NECK PULLED UP her jacket collar. Her boots were by the door. She picked them up and walked back to the couch. Sitting with one boot hanging from her hand, she looked down at Galean's page. To her it was his supplication to life. Oh, if she'd only read this earlier ... *I have to do something.*

Chapter Eighteen

And the sun set, and all the journeying ways were darkened.

—HOMER, *The Odyssey*

A ccidents happen, so it is said. A driver looks the wrong way down a cross street before proceeding, and her life changes in an instant; a driver in a pick-up truck swerves when a deer dashes across the road, and his life changes in an instant. Neither would have arose that morning expecting life to change. For Galean, he had known life to be unpredictable sometimes, but he certainly didn't expect someone to try to kill him, nor that that someone might be Helena.

SHE CLUTCHED THE STEERING WHEEL WITH FIERCE FURY AND pushed her foot against the gas pedal as the car's tires kicked up clumps of snow and ice pellets sprayed the road behind. Gaining on Galean's car, Helena experienced a rush—a cocktail mixture of anger, power and ruthlessness. She wanted to destroy him, expunge the possibilities he'd brought into her life. Helena's madness exalted in retribution. Her car swayed and shimmied as she got within a few car lengths of Galean. His car was swerving to the right, heading directly for a streetlight pole. With one last push on the gas, Helena rammed into the trunk of his car, driving him into the pole. The force threw her against the steering wheel. There was a brutal, grinding bang, then silence. Helena was slumped over the steering wheel, gasping for a breath, each one more painful than the last, at least one rib broken.

People jumped from their cars along the street. There was no movement from Galean's car.

A man ran to Helena's car and peered in. "Ma'am. Ma'am, can you hear me?" he yelled, opening her door slowly. "Stay still, please stay still," he urged her.

Three people ran from a nearby house over to Galean, who was unconscious, his head back against the seat, blood streaming down the side of his face.

"Roger, get back into the house and call 911," one of the older men shouted at a young boy.

In a few minutes the wail of sirens penetrated the chaos.

Two police cars and an ambulance, lights flashing, pulled up in a shower of snow and ice. Wasting no time, the paramedics gently lifted Galean from his wrecked car and placed him on a stretcher then raised him into the ambulance, all the while checking his vital signs. "Still unconscious but breathing," one medic commented.

Suddenly the man over by Helena's car shouted, "Hey, we need help over here!"

Helena was trying to push open her car door enough so she could get out, kicking wildly at the man who was preventing the door from opening fully. She held her arm across her chest as though holding the pain. Two policemen ran over to her. She was raving epithets, eyes bulging, her face scratched and bleeding. Both officers held her arms down, talking to her, leading her to the ambulance where, seeing Galean lying motionless, Helena screamed: "I want him to be dead! Why isn't he dead!?"

"We need to calm her," said one of the officers. "Take her over to the squad car."

One medic crawled into the back of the car to help Helena sit, speaking to her in quiet, gentle tones. She fell limp in his arms and slumped against the seat. Her eyes were listless, her face gray. The medic inched back slowly, almost out the door, letting go of her shoulders and letting her slip onto the seat. No protest, no sounds. A police-woman leaned in through the opposite door and lay a blanket across Helena.

Standing outside the squad car, the medic told the officer, "Follow us to the hospital. When you take her in, ask for a psychiatric nurse right away. This lady needs help. Major help." The medic then ran over to the ambulance and jumped into the passenger seat. After a quick glance at his colleague in the back who was attending to Galean, he instructed the driver, "Go! Now!"

The world had changed in an instant for both Galean and Helena; nothing would ever be the same.

MONDAY MORNING

A first day of promise in a long winter, a sun seemingly renewed. The sky sang out a joyful clear blue. Casey slipped her sunglasses out of the glove compartment, put them on and started her car. *I'm late, Alice is going to be wondering where I am,* she thought to herself as she backed down her driveway. Waiting for a passing car on her street to go by,

Casey turned on the radio and tuned to the local news.

"The police are saying little about the people involved in the accident on University Avenue last night; however, according to witnesses, the woman involved tried to run into the other car. Both have been taken to hospital."

"Hmm," Casey muttered to herself. "University Avenue. I wonder if Galean saw that on his way home last night." And backing onto the street, she headed for the university.

As she drove to her parking spot, Casey was surprised to see a police car in the parking lot. She opened her car door and stood for a moment, looking over at the street. All seemed quiet. Faculty and students were driving into the lot, some already running late for early classes. Just as she turned to lift her briefcase from the back seat, a car pulled up beside her. It was Dean Atwater.

Without shutting off the engine, he rolled down the window. "Casey, I'm so glad I caught you before your class. Can you come into my office for a moment?"

Some place in Casey sounded an alarm. "What's this about, James?" She slipped from her car and walked over to him, leaving the door ajar.

He locked his car and put his hand on Casey's shoulder. "You're a good friend of Galean's, yes?"

Casey stepped back, away from the news she'd been expecting for some time. "Has Helena done something?" Her words were almost a grated whisper.

The dean looked mystified. "I don't know about that. All I know is I received a call this morning from the hospital, telling me that Galean was in an accident and is unconscious."

"Oh God!" Casey's hand flew to her mouth.

He took Casey's arm and started walking. "Can we go inside? I'm freezing out here."

Casey moved away from his grasp and faced him. "What's happened, James?"

"Casey, please walk with me into the building and let me tell you what I know." He hurried off toward the steps, walking at a clip that meant *now*.

Finally she relented, closed her car door and sprinted after him.

James Atwater was familiar with academic issues, research and tenure, but he was not at ease with the news he needed to share with Casey. In his office, not bothering to take off his coat, he motioned toward two large wingback leather chairs, sitting in the alcove of a bay window. "Could we sit here for a moment?" he asked Casey. Without waiting for an answer, he sat down and let out a deep breath. He looked up at her, folded his hands, the tips of his fingers to his lips. A man seemingly about to pray.

Casey suddenly felt regret that she had shared as much as she had about her past with him. Was he too protective of her, whatever the situation might be? She sat on the edge of the other chair, facing him.

"Casey, Galean was in a car accident last night and Helena is in the hospital also, except she's in the psych ward." The words tumbled from his mouth, spilling into the air like rapid code.

Silence is like the spaces between the dots and the dashes in Morse code, which gives emphasis to each sound, one at a time. For Casey, her silence gave space for the bad news to penetrate, one word at a time. Her hands were folded in her lap; her fingers intertwined so tightly that the knuckles were white.

Dean Atwater paused. "I thought you'd want to know this as soon as possible. The nurse who called could only give me sketchy information about his condition. But it sounds bad, Casey. Galean has a brain injury."

She inhaled and whispered a question on the breath of the exhale: "When did it happen?"

"I think sometime around seven o'clock in the evening, from what I understand." He watched Casey's face become pale, watched her press the heel of her hand into her eye seemingly rubbing away some horrific image. He went on, telling her, "Casey, somebody across the street walking his dog said he saw two cars coming out of the university parking lot, one following the other. That must have been Helena, because this witness watched the whole thing."

"I have to go. I have a class." Casey sprung from her chair. "Thank you, James, for passing on this news to me. I'll be sure to let the other faculty members know."

"I've really upset you," he said, alarmed by her reaction. "I am so sorry."

"No, no, don't be. They're both friends of mine, so this news has come as a shock, but I'm fine, just fine. I'll get back to you if I find out anything else."

And she was out of his office, out the door down the hall before the dean could move from his chair. He sat there for several moments, perplexed. Why that sudden reaction? Were Casey and Galean or Helena all closer friends than he'd realized?

Casey ran down the hall into the faculty washroom, which was empty. *Thank God*, she thought. She leaned against a sink with her hands wrapped around its cold edge, and stared at her image in the mirror: she was wide-eyed, like a deer caught in the headlights. Her mind raced. *It must have happened after he left me. Helena must have driven to the campus and waited for him. My God, she tried to kill him. She's sicker than I imagined.*

Casey suddenly realized she was hitting her forehead against the mirror—an attempt to drive the unthinkable from her brain. Everything that had happened between her and Galean last night rushed back to her; their argument and the warmth of descending into one another. But now she felt a sense of horror. What were Galean and Helena thinking? How could they have gone ahead and married! If only Casey had been able to warn Galean about Helena sooner, he might have been more willing to hear her. She looked up at herself now in the mirror, her face tight and pale, "Oh, Galean," she whispered. "I'm so sorry."

Running the cold water tap, she splashed water over her face, grabbed some paper towel and brushed it across her forehead and chin. She took a deep breath then turned and walked from the washroom, down the hall toward her office. Casey now had precisely ten minutes to get to her Monday morning seminar with her doctoral advisees. Before opening the door into the outer office, she took another deep breath, preparing herself to see Alice, who always came in early. But before she could say good morning or pretend all was well, Alice rose from behind her desk and hurried over to Casey.

"Oh, Dr. MacMillan, have you heard about Dr. Laihy?"

How in the hell did the news travel so fast? Casey felt a stab of irritation. Walking directly to her office door, briefcase swinging from her hand, she turned to Alice, who had stopped, knowing that something was amiss with her boss.

"Police have been questioning people most of the morning," Alice told her. "Didn't someone stop you?" By now Alice was retracing her steps and moving to stand by her desk.

A pile of large brown envelopes on Alice's desk caught Casey's eye, giving her an idea. *Time to distract and divert.* "Are those my students' papers for this morning's class?" She asked Alice as she walked over to pick them up. Putting her hands on the pile, an overwhelming sadness caught her in mid-breath, almost a sob. "Alice, I'm so sorry. I'm being awful, aren't I?"

Without hesitating, Alice went to Casey and put her arms around her.

Casey buried her face into a welcome shoulder. For the first time on this tragic morning, she let herself feel bone-tired sorrow, but only for a few seconds. She moved away from Alice and let a long, slow breath escape her lips. "Time to straighten shoulders and go to class," she said, with her old and familiar determination.

THE COLD, BRISK WALK ACROSS THE QUADRANGLE TO SANC-tuary Hall gave Casey some time to make a decision. With her head down, collar and hood pulled up, briefcase tucked under her arm, she crunched through the icy snow, each step strengthening her resolve. *I'll go see him. Make sure he's going to be all right. And after that, it'll be done.*

Climbing the steps to the main door of lecture hall, Casey reached for the brass handle and stopped, pressed her forehead against the cold wood and quietly wept, ever so briefly. She had learned to allow sadness for only fractions of time. Pulling open the door, she tossed her hood back, dropped her briefcase down to her hand and strode down the corridor to greet her students and begin another day.

Chapter Nineteen

You seemed so brave and lonely.
I wanted to comfort you like a child.
I couldn't of course.
You wanted to ask me too far in.

—**KATHLEEN NORRIS**, "Answered Prayer"

Windows in Seminar Room 240, on the second floor of Sanctuary Hall, surveyed campus walkways twisting and turning through clusters of trees, branches black and naked against a dull metal sky. Students and faculty moved like silent specters along the paths, collars pulled around their faces and heads, scarves wrapping their expressions. The scene resembled a black-and-white still photo captured from an old movie.

Anya, Rob and Stephen waited in the quiet of the seminar room, thankful that nobody was compelled to talk. Each one was there holding thoughts about their theses and the places where Casey had encouraged them to go. She was their mentor and advisor, the one who rallied them forth to be brave and write about their own truths.

Today, though, would be different. Today it was Casey's story that needed air and light.

A voice greeted someone outside the door. Casey's voice. The door swung open. She strode in to her students' anticipation, greeting them, "Good morning, all. I'm impressed, everyone's here on time." She whisked her scarf from her neck, dropped her briefcase onto the oaken table. A brisk entrance—an attempt to mask her distress.

But not one of her three advisees in the room were fooled. Professor MacMillan was moving too fast, walking too briskly, eyes shining too brightly.

"Good morning, Dr. MacMillan." Rob was first to venture a hesitant greeting.

Anya sat silent, always alert to someone else's distress. She felt her heart quickening, her breath shallow.

Stephen stood and walked to the table by the window, where a coffeepot sat on a warmer next to cups, spoons, creamers and sugar, all there in tidy array. Stephen "the elder" as he called himself, often brought a morning coffeepot from his small grad student office, filled with the hot tempting brew, a wake-up call. He said nothing as he poured the dark liquid into a sunflower-yellow mug and walked it over to Casey, who was rummaging through her briefcase, head down and silent.

Stephen set the coffee mug beside her on the table, pulled the chair out and beckoned her to sit. "Seems you might need a couple of minutes, Professor."

Taking the mug, Casey wrapped her hands around it, feeling the warmth, giving herself a moment to breathe. She took a sip and placed it almost languidly on the table. "Thanks, Stephen. I could use that caffeine." A weak smile played at the corners of her mouth and she lowered herself into the wooden chair, which was cushioned with a yellow pillow that was given to her by other students to replace the frayed cushion she used to bring to class. A yellow pillow had become Casey's signature for comfort and well-being. Today she needed it.

"Dr. MacMillan?"

Casey looked across the table and waited for Anya to finish her thought.

"Do you want to take off your coat?"

"Thanks, Anya," Casey replied, "but I think I need the extra warmth this morning." And with that, she wrapped her coat more tightly and folded her arms across her body. Silence descended again.

"What's the cloak of silence about?" Rob smiled gently. He was feeding one of Casey's phrases that she often used, back to her.

Stephen nodded in agreement, encouraging her to share, "Dr. MacMillan?"

Casey watched and listened as her students prodded her to practice what she often preached to them: speak your truth. She smiled, grateful for their concern. Yes, she was struggling to hold the truth of her fears about Galean. Camouflaging her worry wasn't working.

One by one Anya, Rob and Stephen put down their pens and closed their notebooks.

Casey wasn't sure what might be happening back at the hospital. She sat with her arms still folded, her gaze fixed on drops of condensation creating tears on the window.

"Is there something we could do to help?" Anya's small voice hovered in the quiet.

Casey shifted and looked over to Anya. A recognition that passed between the two women: shared acknowledgment of past pain. Casey lifted her arms, shook off her coat and placed her hands behind her head. Leaning back into her chair, she looked beyond her students and began to recite lines from an Emily Dickinson poem, remembering from a time long ago, a distant place:

There is a pain—so utter—
It swallows substance up—
Then cover the Abyss with Trance—
So Memory can step
Around—across—upon—it—

When she paused, she noticed Rob was grinning, his elbow resting on the table, his head propped on his hand.

"That's part of my introductory chapter—that quote from Emily Dickinson," he explained. "I stole it from her, now you're stealing it from me." For the first time that morning, the air in Room 240 lightened.

"And a beautiful chapter it is, Rob," Casey said, moving her chair closer to the table. "You are all writing so beautifully. I feel as though we have become colleagues, no longer professor and students. And for that I am grateful. Yet this morning, I am feeling very sad, and I wanted to tell each of you that my work with you has been ..." she stumbled, words lost in a swallowed breath.

"No need to explain, Dr. MacMillan." Anya, gentle Anya, rose to the moment. "We've all heard about Dr. Laihy. We are so sorry."

Rob and Stephen nodded, but Casey resisted their good will. "No, please, this is neither the place nor the time." Somewhere within Casey pushed against her sadness. "What's happened to Dr. Laihy bears no discussion here. He's in good hands at the hospital." She waved her hand in the air as though swatting away any feelings of despair.

A chair scraping against the hardwood floor broke the silence, startling everyone. It was Stephen, now standing: "I think we need to leave and let Dr. MacMillan do what she wants and needs to do—go to the hospital. Hell, if a good friend of mine were lying unconscious in a hospital, I certainly wouldn't be sitting here." Giving legs and permission to Casey's true desire, he took his coat from the back of his chair, picked up his books and notebook and walked around the table to Casey. "Take our good wishes to Dr. Laihy."

Anya and Rob stood up and started sliding arms into the sleeves of their jackets. Stephen was already walking toward the exit, his coat over his arm, his boots flapping open on his feet. Soon all three stood at the door ready to decamp.

"Go. Please, now." Rob tossed the plea over his shoulder as he exited.

Anya walked back, over to Casey and put her hand on her shoulder: "Remember what you once said to me? 'Don't live with regret.'"

And they were gone, the door left open behind them. Casey sat for a moment astounded and relieved. Within minutes she was running down the hall.

CASEY HARBORED OLD FEELINGS OF DREAD WHEN IT CAME to hospitals, and they rose to the surface anytime she entered one. Flashes of childhood memories radiated: sitting on a gurney in a bright room, white shadows moving in and out; one standing by her, with a hand on her shoulder. Someone calling "Mommy." Today her dread translated into fear and concern for her friend.

When she asked about Galean's room at the desk in the front lobby, her fear became panic for a few moments. The volunteer receptionist did not cushion her anxiety.

"Oh, Dr. Laihy is not in a room. He's still in ICU."

"I didn't know he was in ICU." Casey clutched one hand

inside the other, holding so tightly that the veins protruded.

"Are you family?" asked the receptionist.

"No, no, but I'm a good friend, a colleague." Casey felt as though she needed this woman's approval. "He'd want me there."

"Well, you'll have to talk to the nurses at the desk outside ICU. They don't usually let anyone but family in to see patients in ICU."

Irritation flared, Casey felt her face warming. She inhaled. "Please, just direct me to ICU." Casey's best professorial voice sang across the counter.

The receptionist dutifully rhymed off the directions: "Take the elevator to the third floor and go to the desk on your right, there will be a nurse there to help you. She'll be the one to let you in."

For a moment Casey felt her aloneness, and the volunteer saw a woman in distress standing before her. She reached out her hand to Casey and said, "Take a few breaths before you go."

"Thank you," Casey replied. "Good idea."

She was grateful for the empty elevator as she rode up to the third floor, listening only to the whirring of the motor. One breath, one exhale; a long inhale, another exhale. When the elevator doors opened, Casey emerged, looking right and left, hoping to see someone who might help her find her way to Galean. Nurses moved quickly along the corridor of the surgical floor, their cushioned soles almost silent against the tiled floor.

To the right, she spotted a set of double doors, a counter and a desk. A nurse in blue cotton scrubs stood at the counter, a stethoscope draped around her neck. Behind the counter, a woman leaned against the desk, half sitting, half standing, her white coat signaling medical doctor. She held a clipboard and was flipping through sheets of paper, all the time talking to a nurse who was sitting, a phone receiver at her ear, presumably on hold.

No one looked up, no one seemed to notice as Casey walked toward them. She felt invisible, cloaked in a formless mass. When she spoke her voice sounded far away, someone she didn't know. "I wonder if there is someone who could help me?" her voice asked.

The doctor held a page on the clipboard still for a moment and looked up at Casey, her face possibly softening, Casey wasn't sure, but she felt her body returning and spoke with a little more volume. "Dr. Laihy. I'm here to see if I might ..."

"You know Dr. Laihy?" the doctor asked. She walked toward Casey and leaned into the counter. "Are you family?"

"Ah, no," replied Casey. "But I am as close to family as he might have." An unexpected feeling of protectiveness for Galean, for his aloneness, for his losses, for his determination, surged through her body. Whatever insane decisions he had made, whatever roads he had chosen, none of it mattered. He was her friend, and she wanted him to be safe and well. She wanted him to know how she loved him, even though she would leave him to the rest of his life with Helena, and she wanted him to know that he mattered.

"Ma'am, are you all right?" The doctor reached for Casey's arm.

"Oh, yes ..." said Casey, coming back to the moment. "Sorry, I guess I felt a bit faint."

What is going on here? I'm a mess. Casey feeling real emotions, was experiencing the depths of care, and sadness with the kind of intensity she'd learned to push away.

The doctor, reaching out for Casey, came around the counter's edge. "How do you know Dr. Laihy?" she asked, taking Casey's hand.

"He's probably the best friend I've ever had," she told her, then laughed. "I sound like a stricken teenager, don't I, Doctor?"

"Come with me." The doctor linked her arm through Casey's, leading her through the double-glass doors into the ICU.

Chapter Twenty

For I am full of spirit and resolve to meet all perils very constantly.

—SHAKESPEARE, *Julius Caesar*

For Casey, the next few days and nights of waiting, blended with hours of hoping, were not typical days for her. They became a space in time, as though nothing would resume until she knew Galean was all right.

The nurses greeted her gently each time she arrived "only to check on him," as she claimed. Tuesday morning, Wednesday later in the afternoon, Thursday at lunch.

"He's still in coma, Casey."

And she would leave, putting one red rose on his bedside table each time.

On Friday morning, in her office, at her desk, she read the newest chapter from Rob, while he sat clasping and unclasping his hands.

"Rob, could you not do that?" She smiled. "You don't need to worry, the committee is delighted with your thesis thus far. I'm making sure of that."

Knowing that there was a possibility she might not be here when Rob had his final meeting with his committee, Casey worked expressly hard to keep the three other professors informed. One woman and two men, who would ultimately decide Rob's doctoral fate. Her intensity, the way she shepherded her students, was legendary among the faculty. Now concerned about Galean, she had become like a mother bear, transferring her fierce caring onto her students.

A gentle knock sounded at her door. Alice appeared, her hand to her ear mimicking a phone call. "The hospital, Casey."

Scattering papers across her desk, Casey grabbed for her phone. "Yes?"

"Dr. MacMillan, it's Nurse Andrews in ICU. I have news about Dr. Laihy."

Casey's shoulders tensed, her breathing shallowed. Fear numbed her fingers clutching the phone. "I'm here."

"Dr. Wilson just came out to the desk, she asked me to call you. Good news."

Casey thought she might drop the phone, the words "good news" left her limp.

"Dr. MacMillan?"

"Oh, I'm still here. Please, what's happening?"

"Dr. Laihy is starting to wake up …"

"I'll be right there." Casey pushed back her chair started to stand.

Rob began to gather his manuscript, stuffing it into his leather case.

Waving him to sit down, Casey listened, the nurse still talking.

"Don't rush over, wait till this afternoon. Give him time to come back into the world, to absorb everything that's happened since Sunday. And the doctor needs to spend time with him. I'll see you later." And she was gone.

"Casey, is Dr. Laihy okay?" Rob sat, briefcase on his lap,

one foot in front as though ready to bolt from the room.

"I don't know, Rob. Apparently he's starting to come around, but," pulling her chair up, she told him, "you and I have work to do here this morning."

For the first time that week, Casey dropped into her daily familiar life. Professor MacMillan was emerging from her own self-induced daze. Like an animal crawling out of its protective lair, she straightened her shoulders and organized the scattered papers on her desk. Taking one page, she stood, walked around to Rob and sat in her favorite chair, the one graced with her yellow cushion.

"Your quote, Rob." She began to read from his chapter: "'One does not become enlightened by imagining figures of light, but by making the darkness conscious.' You and Jung, quite a combination. So then, how do we bear grief and despair when our world tries to shut those emotions away? I have to say, I admire your courage and your fierce determination to stay with the truth of your experience. It's a tough road you've chosen."

Quiet spread through the room. Rob settled back into his chair and watched his professor's face soften. A few minutes ago, it was a face tight with fear. Transformation. He felt it viscerally.

"I am so grateful we are working together, Rob," Casey told him. "We might even be transforming our lives in company with one another." She smiled. "However, there is much work to be done on both our parts, so let's begin. Now, this sentence here on your next page…"

Casey the professor moved into the life she knew well.

FIVE DAYS LATER, GALEAN LAY IN A PRIVATE HOSPITAL ROOM. Sunlight patterns rippled across the white bedsheet, five red roses graced the sterile chrome and pale wood of his bedside table. A tranquil sky welcomed his gaze out the window, allowing him the first glimmer of how lucky he was to be here, watching the sky. Here, alive. Dr. Wilson, his neurosurgeon, had been very clear about how close Galean had come to dying. The force of being projected through the car windshield had left him with a serious brain hemorrhage. The skill of many people, whose job it was to save lives, was the reason Galean could lie in this bed and marvel at a clear winter's sky.

When he turned his head very slowly, he caught a glimpse of the roses. *Casey.* The nurse had told him how she'd been in almost every day. *Casey, what now, my friend? What do I do now?* Without lingering on that thought, he knew. He knew "what now," and he felt an overwhelming sense of certainty. *I will not abandon her. I will not abandon Helena. I will not be another goodbye in her life.* His was a passionate promise coming from the depths of his past.

A gentle knock at his door. Nurse Andrews from the ICU appeared, who had taken a special interest in him, had come over to see him. She was not alone.

"There is someone here to see you Dr. Laihy, I'll leave you and come back later."

She smiled, "It's good to see you looking better."

A doctor whom Galean did not recognize appeared beside her, and Nurse Andrews backed out into the corridor.

"Dr. Laihy," said the unfamiliar doctor. "I hope what I have to ask will not upset you. I'm Dr. Mandel, your wife's psychiatrist. I was wondering if we might bring her down to see you." He paused, hesitating just inside the door, "Do you think you are up to that?" Again he paused. "I have talked to your neurologist and she's given the okay." More hesitation.

Galean, his head on the pillow, turned and looked back out the window at the sky. *What an extraordinary moment,* he marveled. *Should I believe in mystical happenings? I make a promise to Helena, and she appears.* He turned back to the doctor and tried to raise himself on one elbow.

"No, no. Stay where you are. If you're all right with this, I will bring her in a wheelchair and wheel her to your bedside."

Galean nodded.

The doctor took a step toward him, placed his hand on Galean's arm. "You need to know, she's quiet because of the sedation we've given her. But I think it would be good for her and for you, to see one another."

That was the moment Galean felt the wetness on his cheeks. Two people both traumatized, possibly beyond repair.

While the doctor went to get Helena, the nurses helped Galean pull himself to sit up. A white head bandage gave him the look of a man wearing a protective helmet. Leaning back against the pillows and the raised bed, he sat silently, watching as Helena was wheeled next to his bed, strapped into a wheelchair. Someone, he didn't know who, maybe one of the operating nurses, had dressed her in her blue-and-white cotton caftan. With her hair pulled back, some tendrils escaping around her ears, she looked like a young girl. Her vacant look, her face pale, scratch marks across one cheek gave Galean a moment of tenderness.

Then, he remembered. *She tried to kill me.*

Dr. Mandel leaned back against the wall, his arms and ankles crossed. "I'm not sure if she remembers anything about the accident. Do you, Dr. Laihy?"

Galean chose not to answer right away. His thoughts were chaotic, his feelings jumbled. One thought drove itself into his wounded brain, maybe into his soul: *I cannot abandon her.*

"I'm sorry, what did you mean, you can't abandon her?" asked the psychiatrist.

Galean realized he'd been speaking his thoughts aloud. "I'm ..." He stopped, looked away. "I remember leaving the parking lot. I remember a car following, from there all I can bring back is terror." He turned back to the doctor. "But now ... now I'm feeling, a kind of numbness." Struggling to sit up, to put his legs over the edge of the bed, he reached for Helena's hand.

Dr. Mandel moved quietly, swiftly to his side. "You don't need to do this right now."

All this time Helena sat staring at something visible only to her. When Galean put his hand over hers, she turned to look at him, a slow dream-like gaze. She spoke to him, almost in a whisper: "I'm sorry."

What can I say? Where do we go from here? Thoughts ran in spirals in Galean's mind. Fatigue and an aching residue of pain created a mist-like curtain.

Dr. Mandel, still beside him, bent over and put his hand gently on Galean's shoulder. "You need to lie back down. You don't want to undo the progress you've made over the past few days."

As Galean let go of Helena's hand, she breathed a sound, a sob almost like a child being awakened from a dream. She lifted her arm toward him, reaching again for his hand. Clear white recognition can crack open a heart. Helena's was broken, maybe beyond repair. The wild dark-eyed beauty, who had grasped Galean in her magic, seemed to have flown.

"Is it the drugs?" Galean looked to Dr. Mandel, beseeching him to say 'When the drugs wear off, she'll be back.'

"I wish I could say yes, she'll return to her normal self. But I'm worried that she's been headed for a total breakdown for a long time. Thanks to you Dr. Laihy, and your files, we were able to track down her history."

Galean put his hand over his eyes and closed them.

"I think with therapy, some medication, we can help her, but I'm really concerned for her long term." Dr. Mandel spoke gently, his eyes sad. "I'll ask the nurse to take her back to her room; you need rest and healing. It's not only that you've experienced a serious head trauma," he said, looking off out to the sky. "Your soul has been shattered; you have a deep soul wound."

Galean let a small smile quiver at the corners of his mouth. Being Irish, being who he was, he knew about soul wounds. He and Casey wrote about the ultimate deep wound; however, he did not expect a psychiatrist standing in his crisp white coat and shiny black loafers to know about soul wounds. Surprisingly, that insight lifted his spirits. "Doc, I think I'll be fine. I know what I need to do—I need to take care of my wife."

"She's one lucky woman," said Dr. Mandel quietly, so Helena couldn't hear. "I'm not sure if my wife tried to run me into a pole, I'd be so quick to forgive."

By now Galean, fatigued and achy, didn't feel as though he cared to explain what horror being abandoned could be. He just knew that he couldn't ever leave Helena, even when … Putting his head back on the pillow, he closed his eyes for a moment. When he opened them, he lifted his hand in a weak wave to Helena, whom he wanted to imagine gave him one of her brilliant smiles. But, in reality, she only settled back into her sedated world.

Dr. Mandel tightened the blanket around Helena's knees and began wheeling her to the door.

Ever so slightly, almost imperceptibly, her hand raised up from the arm of the chair. A wave?

"Helena," Galean called to her, sitting up on one elbow, his voice now faint from fatigue. "I'll be there. I'll be home."

Her fingers flickered on the arm of the wheelchair.

The door swung shut.

Chapter Twenty-One

You endure what is unbearable, and you bear it. That is all.

—CASSANDRA CLARE, *Clockwork Princess*

One month later, to the day, of Helena's episode (that's how Galean chose to refer to everything that happened that night, as "Helena's episode"), he wheeled her through the hospital lobby, Dr. Mandel at his side.

As they reached the outer sliding door, the doctor put his hand on Galean's arm and said, "I'm not convinced this is the best choice, taking her home by yourself."

Galean kept pushing forward, through the open sliding door, not pausing or looking over at the doctor. "I've hired a housekeeper with nursing experience who's going to come in every day," he told him. "She has agreed to take care of meals and to look after Helena's recovery." Galean spoke nothing of himself or his own injuries.

A nurse who had been following behind the three of them walked to the curb where a taxi was waiting. Just as they reached the curb, a car, moving faster than was allowed in the hospital turnaround, slid to a halt, barely missing the taxi. Casey jumped from the driver's seat and ran toward them, almost tripping on the curb. With a breathless exhale, she stopped and stood in front of Helena who showed no recognition of Casey. Only a bewildered stare.

"Galean," said Casey. "You and Helena are not going home in a taxi."

Surprise hung in the air. No one moved or spoke except Casey, who looked directly at Galean. "I want to drive the two of you home."

Galean looked away from Casey's gaze and put his hand on Helena's shoulder as though expecting her to lunge. "That's really kind, but," he started to refuse before being interrupted by Dr. Mandel.

"I think this is a very good idea, Galean," he said. "Dr. MacMillan has your best interests at heart. I know because she came to talk to me once when she went to see Helena."

Galean took his hand from Helena's shoulder and pointed at Casey. "You visited Helena? Why didn't I know this?" He turned back to the doctor.

A wavering voice floated up like the fade-out of a song. "Galean, I'm very cold." Helena lifted the blanket that was tucked under her knees and tried to wrap it around herself. Her movements were clumsy and awkward, drugged.

"Okay, Lena, we'll go. We'll go." With a gentle gesture, Galean bent over and tucked Helena's wool scarf into her coat collar, pulling it up around her ears.

Each person—Dr. Mandel, the nurse, the taxi driver and Casey—stood watching. What would be Galean's decision about going home? He seemed to be holding time at bay.

Finally he stood away from Helena's wheelchair and faced Casey directly. "I'm not sure what's going on right now, Case, but I'm going to take your offer." He reached into his coat pocket, pulled out his wallet and handed the taxi driver a five-dollar bill. "Here, sir. Thanks for hanging around."

WHEN THEY REACHED THE HOUSE, CASEY PULLED INTO THE driveway and parked. She turned to Galean, who was sitting in the front passenger seat, and said, "I'll help the two of you into the house, then I'll go."

"I've hired someone to help, actually," said Galean. "She should be here now." He grasped the car door handle and twisted around to look over at Casey. "Thank you for this. But … you've said nothing about why." He sat for a moment, awaiting her response. When none came, he opened the door, and she heard him say quietly, "Then again, life is confusing as hell right now."

Casey started to reach for Galean's arm, then pulled back before he noticed.

As he lifted one foot to step out of the car, Helena reached forward from the back seat and gripped his arm. "Where are you going, Galean?" They were the first words she'd spoken since getting into the car. "Don't leave me here." Her hand shook, her voice was tremulous. Helena was living in a tormented world that could descend upon her without warning. This was one of those moments. The simple act of Galean getting out of the car triggered a panic in her. It was an old panic, one that sometimes translated into fury; but today, only fear showed up.

Galean reached in and put his hand on her cheek, "Hey, Lena. We're home." He became the soother, the comforter. He became the promise he had made to her.

"Oh, Galean." Casey opened her door, jumped into the snow that had collected by the side of the driveway and, balancing herself on the cold steel of the car, walked her way around to get to Helena.

Galean called out to her to wait. "She'll be okay in a minute. We just need some time." He gestured with a nod of his head for Casey to move away.

Throughout Helena's stay in the hospital, Dr. Mandel and Galean talked in-depth about Helena's recovery. The doctor had hesitated to let her go home, he worried about suicide. Yet in some magical-thinking way, Galean hoped that home—their home—might be a healing place. The doctor believed that Galean was extraordinary, that his passion about caring for Helena was mystifying.

Now, standing in front of the house, an expression of recognition crossed Helena's face. Smiling, she stood and put her hand in Galean's. "We're home," she said quietly.

Casey watched it all with bewildered wonder. *Who is this man? The woman tried to kill him! Do I even know him? And Helena … where is she? Who is this meek woman?*

Helping Helena up the steps, Galean reached over and rang the doorbell. A tall, plumpish, gray-haired woman opened the door and greeted them. Mrs. Ferrante. Her smile was music.

"Dr. Laihy, Mrs. Laihy you're home." The housekeeper reached for Helena's arm and led her into the mirrored front hall.

Galean, feeling Helena's tension growing, was careful not to let her hand drop as he followed behind her. They were a strange parade, the three of them, following one behind the other, walking into the house.

Casey stood watching at the end of the drive, stamping her feet to keep warm and slapping her hands against her folded arms. She waited. The front door closed. "I don't believe this," she said to herself. The child in her, the one who felt abandoned and lost, picked up a handful of icy, frozen snow and threw it at the door. Casey knew she was experiencing the pain of old losses, but she knew too that wisdom, feeling, and reason often part company. Her frustration with herself, and how she'd helped create a mess, propelled her toss, just as the door opened and Galean emerged and stepped back outside. The snowball, the pieces of icy snow, landed with a spray against his shoulder. It stunned both of them—for a second. But in the next moment they laughed, great gulping seismic laughter. The first time in weeks.

"Did you really think I was just going to walk away?" Galean asked, walking down the steps at a fast clip and toward Casey.

As he approached her, Casey glimpsed their friendship reappearing and rising up. She remembered this man striding toward her.

"Thank you, Case," he said when he reached her. "I know why you did this. You are the kindest, most loving person. I know you care about Helena, and I know you care about me. Well, most days." He brushed the remaining snow and ice off his jacket. "Please take care of yourself, in Ireland." He paused. "Are you leaving in April, end of term? Can we get together before you go?"

"I've made arrangements with Dean Atwater," she said. "I'm leaving this weekend. This coming Sunday."

For a moment they became quiet, a barren space where words, any words, were like yesterday's snow. Head down, Casey kicked the packed snow away from the wheel well of the car.

Galean stood frozen, stunned, as her words sunk in. "I … well. I guess I thought …" he trailed off. He was a man lost.

"I am going," said Casey. "And it's time." Pausing, she walked around to open her car door. "You have work before you, Galean. Helena needs you. She needs the care you'll give her. God only knows, she may find her way back with you there." Now in her car, Casey turned the key in the ignition and looked up at him. "And you, my friend, take care of you."

Galean felt the shadows of the day descending. His head throbbed a bit; his sadness, for so many things, settled heavily on his shoulders. He leaned his forehead against the roof of the car and held the door open, afraid maybe that Casey might just drive away, before he could say ... say, what? And there it lay, the nothingness of a sad goodbye.

"Travel safely, Case." And he closed the door with a gentle click.

Casey backed out from the driveway, turned onto the street and drove into a fading afternoon.

When Galean turned to walk back to the house, he saw the rustle of a curtain at the upstairs window.

Helena turned away.

WHEN CASEY WALKED INTO HER HOUSE, SHE HEARD THE phone ringing. Tempted at first to ignore it, she listened to the echo of the third ring and then decided. She sprinted to the kitchen and picked the receiver up from the wall phone by the small white desk.

"Hello?"

"Casey. So glad I finally got you. I was talking to Jim, Dean Atwater, earlier today and he told me you're coming sooner than planned, that you're coming this Sunday. That's terrific!" Andy Kingwood's lyrical low voice warmed and encouraged her.

"It's all happened really fast, Andy. I didn't call because

I wasn't completely sure till the last few days."

Like someone coming to the edge of a cliff and jumping, Casey had decided to leave before the end of term. So much had materialized recently, it seemed the gods might be urging her on. She'd had her meeting with the dean, during which he talked about reasons she should go.

"You already have your sabbatical—it can begin tomorrow if you want. Everything is arranged, and you tell me that the place you intend to rent in your Irish village has come open sooner. Maybe it's all a sign, Casey. Time to lift your doubts, don your wings and fly."

Casey had never heard James Atwater, the pragmatist, speak in metaphors. And though it was tough and emotional, the meeting she'd had with her three advisees, Anya, Stephen and Rob, gave even more lift to her wings.

"If you are hanging around because of us, don't do that," Rob had said, speaking for the group. "We're going to finish and defend our theses. You have prepared us well."

And now today Andy Kingwood, her old advisor, was glorying in the prospect that she'd be in Ireland very soon.

"Are you still there, Casey?"

"Oh sorry, Andy. I just drifted for a moment," she said, coming back to the present. "Everything is a bit of a whirlwind right now. I'm trying to pack, I have a professor and his family who arrived out of nowhere and want to rent my house, and I'm turning all my university responsibilities over to Anne Morgan. You remember her, yes?" Casey felt as though she'd put her life into fast-forward, hurtling through the universe like a bursting star.

"Casey, you do what you need to do. I will be at Shannon Airport when you arrive. Just let me know when."

"Just a minute. I can do that now." She'd pinned her flight schedule on her notice board just above the phone. "Andy?"

"I'm listening."

"I'll be landing at Shannon at 7 a.m. on Monday, March the fifteenth."

"I'll be there," said Andy. "You know, the one grinning and waving like a fool."

As she heard him laugh, Casey felt the small cramp in her neck dissolve.

"Great timing, Casey. We can celebrate St. Patrick's Day together."

Another twinge in her shoulder. Gone.

"Andy, how far is Clonakilty from Shannon? That's where the cottage is that I'm renting. It's not too far for you to drive me there, is it'?"

"Dr. MacMillan, visiting professor, noted for her insights on love, loss and the human condition," Andy began.

Casey could hear the lilt of a chuckle in his voice.

"I would drive across this whole country to bring you here," he told her. "No, it's not a lot to ask, at all. If you will stop with me and have lunch in Cork, I can drive you past the university. Then it's only about forty kilometers to Clonakilty."

"Andy, you can't know what a blessing you are to me, right now, right this moment." Casey put her forehead against the rough cork of the board above the phone and squeezed her eyes shut to force back the tears. She swallowed. Barely a whisper emerged, "Thank you."

For a second they sat in the mutual silence.

"I think I do know, Casey."

"I'll see you soon." And with a gentle lift of her hand, she placed the phone back on its cradle.

Casey went over to the refrigerator and opened the door. Reaching in, she took out the bottle of champagne. It was time to signal the beginning of this the next chapter of her journey. A crystal champagne flute sat on the counter where she'd placed it that morning. Pouring the sparkling amber wine, she lifted the glass toward the window and sent her wish out into the afternoon shadows: "To you, Galean. May you be well and happy."

Chapter Twenty-Two

For that is happiness: to wander alone
Surrounded by the same moon, whose tides remind us of
ourselves,
our distances, and what we leave behind.

—HUGO WILLIAMS, *Collected Works*

A noisy, excited crowd collected behind the barriers at the Shannon Airport arrivals area. Some held up signs searching out the unknown arriving passengers, others ran around and through the crowd laughing in delight at spotting a friend, a brother, a long-lost aunt. Others stood anticipating, hoping that special person would come into view momentarily.

Casey, still numb from her eleven-hour flight from Toronto, fatigued from lack of sleep, searched the assemblage of faces looking for the familiar Andy Kingwood grin. Then she saw it, a sign larger than the others attached to some kind of stick high above the conglomeration of heads. It was being waved like a banner: WELCOME TO IRELAND, DR. MACMILLAN.

Casey laughed. This exuberant welcome was Andy Kingwood's style. Anticipation and adventurous excitement propelled her down the walkway and into a gratifying hug.

"You're here!" Andy dropped the sign behind Casey,

barely missing another passenger's shoulder. "You did it! You took the leap."

Casey allowed herself to rest upon Andy's bear-like chest for a moment, letting stillness seep through her body. Unfolding herself, she stood back and looked at his face. "You look wonderful, Andy. Ireland obviously agrees with you."

"I think you're going to love it here. It's been a long time since I've felt this contented. And now you are here."

Casey felt an uncomfortable twinge. *What does he mean, "And now you are here?"*

Reaching down and picking up the sign, Andy cracked the stick over his knee, crumpled the paper, walked to a trash can and threw them into it. Wiping his hands like a man satisfied with his work, he walked back to Casey and picked up her suitcase and her carry-on, as easily as though they weighed nothing. They held parts of Casey's life wrapped carefully, treasures she couldn't bring herself to leave behind. A poetry book that Anya, Rob and Stephen had given to her, a picture of her old cat who had been her constant companion for many years and had died only a year ago and another picture, Galean head back laughing, tossing his gold-tasseled Doctoral cap into the air. Slung across her shoulder was a bag holding the manuscript of the book she and Galean had begun together. She had not let it out of her sight.

"Follow me," Andy said over his shoulder as he moved toward the exit, wheeling one suitcase behind him, carrying another.

Casey, too tired to speed up, stopped and called to him. "Andy, I have to stop just for a moment." She rebalanced the leather bag hanging from her shoulder and stood still, taking a breath. The thrust of the last few days, the preparations to leave and her abrupt farewell to Galean, all created an impassioned state of movement. Now her body announced, "No more!"

Andy turned back to her and waited until she stood facing him. He dropped one suitcase to the floor, let the other sit beside it, handle still extended. Without words or warning, he stretched his arms out and, oblivious to the blur of people and movement around them, he bundled Casey into his arms. Resisting was useless. And for a short, sweet moment, Casey felt what a child feels arriving home. Something she'd lost many years ago.

"Thank you, Andy." She spoke into the rough wool of his jacket. And pulling back, she placed her hands on his shoulders, stretching her arms, looking into his face. "You are a dear man to do this, to be here and to be, I guess I could even say, rescuing a lost soul." Some passersby smiled as they witnessed what appeared to them to be a tender moment between two lovers.

Andy stepped back from Casey and spoke as he bent down to pick up her one suitcase and grasp the handle of the other, but his words drifted downward and were indistinguishable.

"What was that?" Casey asked. "I missed what you just said."

When he straightened up he looked off beyond Casey's right shoulder as though hesitant to speak what he was feeling. "Maybe we're a story of mutual rescue." He turned now to look into her gaze. "And maybe the story has more chapters."

Letting a quiver of misgiving fade, Casey took a breath and smiled up at him.

"All right, let's go now, give me the roller suitcase. Let's see what's out there in this land of saints and scholars for you and I. But first, can we have some breakfast? I'm starving."

LATER THAT AFTERNOON, CASEY STOOD ON THE STONE steps of her new home, just outside of Clonakilty, Ireland. Andy lifted his arm and waved from the car as he drove along the road, around the bend and out of sight. She rested against the stuccoed wall of the porch and leaned back, her arm still raised in farewell. *In an instant*, she thought, *everything changes.*

Beyond where she stood, sky and water hovered on the horizon. Light drifted across the bay, lending glimmers of shining softness; a gentle breeze lifted the grasses that seemingly floated to the edge of nowhere to a drop-off into the water below.

Casey's aching desire for quiet and solitude that had penetrated her soul over the last while now gave way to an unfamiliar sense of well-being, which was soon followed by a surge of guilt. *I've abandoned everybody. Galean, Helena, Rob, Anya, Stephen—all of my responsibilities …* Standing erect, she watched three gannets swooping and sailing in the air, wings spread aloft. And something shifted within her. *But I'm like those birds, sailing into new spaces.*

Turning toward the door—a bright yellow door—Casey lifted the latch, turned the knob and stepped into her new home. *This is how contentment must feel.*

ANDY, DRIVING OUT FROM CLONAKILTY TOWARD CORK,
pulled over to the side of the road and cut the motor.
Thoughts of turning around and going back to Casey penetrated his good intentions. The fact that she was actually
here, in Ireland, spoke to him of possibilities; their conversation in the car on the drive to Clonakilty rekindled a
hope. Casey was willing to drive over to Cork, "When I rent
a car," she'd said. She wanted to see the university, wanted
him to show her the work he was doing there, maybe meet
some of the exchange students from Canada and America.
Already she'd talked about the possibility of staying longer.

His thoughts whirring, Andy imagined driving back to
the little rented house and banging on the door. He envi-
sioned Casey running toward it and flinging open the door,
throwing her arms around his neck, pulling him into the
house. But then, rousing himself from a fruitless dream, and
with the image still dancing across the windshield, Andy
started the engine, turned onto the road and continued on
to Cork and into the day.

THE NEXT MORNING, CASEY AWOKE TO THE UNFAMILIAR
sounds of the ocean greeting her. The open window above
her head granted tranquility mixed with a sweet sadness.
Waves lapping onto the shore, gulls calling to one another.
A soft breeze brushing against her face. Lying there, she
offered up a small prayer of gratitude, something she realized she hadn't expressed for a very long time, if ever. Her
independent, determined nature had long ago jettisoned
the idea that there might be any kind of spirit or force who
cared about her. Yet this morning, thinking about the life

leap she had made, she wondered if there might be some essence moving her along.

Lifting her arms to catch the sea breeze, Casey thought about how Galean would love this moment. And right there in that second, she realized the substance of her sadness. She was missing Galean. Reaching across the bed to a small table, she took her red journal, picked up her favorite pen and put her thoughts onto the white page.

A sad note sits somewhere within, it sings of fare-
wells, of lives lived now far away. I am aware from
my skin to my heart how fragile and precious we
all are.
I need to experience the kind voice of another.
I want to be in the world, visible and real.

It was here that Casey stopped writing. She realized there was no going back, no re-creation of things that might have been. Her life as it had always been was separate from her yearnings. With that, she put her journal away in the drawer of the bedside table, swung her legs over the side of the bed, landed her feet on the floor and said to the walls, the open window, the sky beyond: "I begin again."

By ten that morning she'd unpacked and rearranged the desk and chair in the small living room, placing them under a wide window, where she could write and gaze out at the ocean below. Now she sat in a coffee shop, sipping strong coffee and munching on Irish soda bread. Sitting there amid the other patrons, Casey's attention was drawn to a woman wearing a beautiful cream-colored sweater and sitting at a table just beside her. It was the sweater that first drew Casey's eye, but beyond that, something else. The woman, maybe in her forties, rebellious hair swinging across her face, was writing. She held her forehead in the cup of one hand and in the other she held a pen, which furiously moved across the white-lined page. She was lost to her surroundings, her intensity palpable. Crumpled papers littered the floor around her.

The whole image was too much for Casey's curiosity. She spoke quietly: "You are an author?"

The woman hesitated and looked up, as though suddenly realizing the world had just reappeared and she was in it, there in a coffee shop with crumpled papers around her. To Casey's relief, she smiled and laughed and, in a lilt that Casey would soon come to love, said, "Are you a crazy writer too? I mean, look at me." She dropped her arms and pointed to the mess at her feet.

Casey smiled. "I am, I am. Or at least, I'm hoping to do what you are doing, write furiously. That's why I'm here in this town, in this country." Her words felt like a benediction. And then a thought occurred. Turning full-face to the woman, she asked: "Might you know anyone here in town who I could hire as a reader? I truly am here to finish a book and I'm going to need someone to read my chapters as I go."

"Tell me what you're writing. Fiction? Memoir?" A tilt of her head, a pen in mid-air. One writer to another.

Something within, a warmth, a connection, moved Casey to stand, pick up her chair and carry it closer to an unfolding friendship. "I'm Casey, Casey MacMillan. Can I get you a coffee?" She offered her hand.

"I'm Claire, lovely to meet you." Her handshake was firm and confident, her smile gentle. "A coffee would be lovely."

An hour later, the two were deep in conversation, heads nodding, hands waving through the air, occasionally stopping for a sip of coffee or a bite of bread slathered with butter and marmalade. Their shared joy of writing, their fierce passion for story, for ideas, gave energy to possibilities and friendship.

"A university professor, a writer, a thinker … who are the gods who sent you to this town?" Claire said, laughing. "And what's more, sent you into this café on this mornin'?"

The words Casey had written in her journal a few hours ago came dancing back to her: *I need to experience the kind voice of another. I want to be in the world, visible and real.*

"I think the gods are colluding or our muses are partying," Casey said, smiling. She inhaled and took another leap. "What do you do here in this town? I know you write, but you mentioned a pub?"

"Ah, when I leave you, in the next few minutes, I'm going over to Jimmy's, the pub where I work afternoons and some evenings. Would you like to come over and meet a friend of mine—Rori? She's a great girl, another writer. There's a bunch of wannabe writers gettin' together this afternoon. In fact, we've created a bit of a guild of writers. Well, more like a motley bunch looking for a muse." Claire grinned. "Have you got time to come over?"

Casey remembered Galean, who many times said, "We just need to sprout wings and see where the spirit takes us." She felt as though he were right there, lifting her from the chair.

"I'd like that," she said to Claire. "Yes, I'd truly like that."

Chapter Twenty-Three

*The constancy of the wise is only the talent of concealing
the agitation of their hearts.*

—FRANCOIS DE LA ROCHEFOUCAULD

Galean took a sip of his favorite single-malt scotch and stared into the glass. A man seeking the meaning of it all. The light that was hanging above cast a yellow gleam across his bent head and lit Dean Atwater's face, giving it a trace of beatific glow.

"Have you heard anything at all from Casey?" Galean asked the dean. He continued gazing into his scotch, as though more interested in the amber liquid than Casey's welfare.

"Only a telephone message left on my machine telling me she's 'ensconced' in her Irish cottage and loving it." Dean Atwater lifted his beer to his lips and watched for Galean's reaction. He had asked Galean to meet him here at Bottom of the Hill Inn, a favorite haunt fashioned in leather and wood. It was a place where faculty members and grad students collected, where conversation flourished and ideas hung in the air waiting for the next 'aha' revelation.

"I think she's doing fine, Galean," the dean added. "And I'm sure she'll connect with people at the university there, very soon."

Silence wafted between them for a moment.

Galean lifted his head, took a long swallow of scotch and put the glass between them on the table. He leaned back and threw his arm across the back of the wooden booth, attempting nonchalance. "When's she coming back?"

"You know, I'd rather talk about you right now, Galean. Not Casey. Although I do realize she's on your mind." Dean Atwater folded his arms on the table and moved toward Galean. He seemed to be huddling in as if to hear an important secret.

"Well, she did decamp kind of suddenly, so I guess I wondered if you knew why," Galean said, fixing his gaze on Jim Atwater. A look that might be called accusatory.

The dean chose to let the inference fall away, responding, "A lot of factors fell into place. Renting her house out, the house being available there, Anne Morgan at the ready to take over her responsibilities. And I think she wanted to go, *now*."

Galean shut his eyes for a moment, taking in the possible meaning of the emphatic *now*. "Are you thinking that possibly some of her need to leave had to do with me?" Galean, his face heating, balanced his elbow on the edge of the table, chin on his fist, and stared at the dean. "She's never been one to measure her decisions according to what I thought." His tone was tight, his words crisp.

"Whoa. There's an agenda here that's a little beyond me. Maybe I need to tell you why I wanted to get together this afternoon and … it really wasn't to talk about Casey." The dean leaned away from the table and lifted his beer to take a drink. Changing his mind, he put the glass down on the table and, before Galean could respond, forged ahead. "But I will say that, personally, I think it's a good idea for Casey to get on with her life and her career, away from here. Going to Ireland to write and teach is a grand opportunity for her."

He paused, considering whether to say what else he was thinking. But telling Galean that he thought he and Casey had been heading down a messy path was outside his jurisdiction as Dean, and maybe even as a friend. So he changed the topic.

"Galean, this is your friend speaking, you have a lot to deal with right now. I understand that Helena is home and you are caring for her?"

"We have a housekeeper who is a retired nurse," Galean said matter-of-factly.

Still pressing forward, the dean leaned into the space between them: "I want to suggest something to you, for the rest of the term. Your course will be ending in a week or so. Your students will be giving you their papers to read, and you'll be submitting their final grades by the end of the month. And I know, because you told me, as did Casey, that you've been working on a book together. I understand she'll be carrying on with her chapters in Ireland?"

Galean frowned and shifted back on the leather bench of the booth. Patience was not one of his attributes, and the dean was known to ramble. Galean right now felt impatient. "What are you suggesting, Jim? I need to get home soon, the housekeeper can't leave until I get there. So … what are you saying?"

"I want you to take a leave for this next term. Go back working at the hospital only and give yourself time with Helena and some breathing time for you. The last few weeks have been a bit of a nightmare."

With scarcely an inhale, Galean responded, "Yes. It has been a nightmare and yes, I do need time so, thank you for the offer."

Dean Atwater watched as Galean sat up, took a last swallow of his scotch and moved to ease out of the booth.

"Jim, I don't mean to seem ungracious by leaving right at this moment. I am truly grateful to you, especially as I'm sure all of this has brought you your own brand of grief." Galean offered his hand to the dean and told him, "You are a good man, and I think you are being more than kind. I'll go over to my office now and start clearing up." He spoke as though he'd already decided what to do before the dean had offered the leave.

Surprising both of them, the dean slid out from the booth, stood up and put his hands on Galean's shoulders. "I believe we can all learn from your constancy, Galean." He smiled, "I wonder, is it the Irish in you?"

Walking along the campus pathway back to his office, Galean had a sense of being carried along by a conviction of single-minded devotion to Helena. *I will not abandon her.*

Guilt and pain had drawn him into Helena's vortex of madness.

UNLOCKING HIS OFFICE DOOR, GALEAN COULD HEAR HIS phone ringing, reminding him that the world out there beckoned. Who might call his office this late in the afternoon? With measured pace, he walked to his desk, put his hand on the receiver and waited, possibly hoping for silence. But still it rang. He picked up the receiver.

"Yes? Dr. Laihy here."

"Dr. Laihy, it's Anna, the housekeeper. I'm ready to leave for the day, but I can wait till you get home if you'd like. Helena was quite agitated this morning, but since then she seems calmer and is wanting to make supper. Are you all right with that?"

"I think that's a good idea. She mentioned it this morning. I have a couple of things to do here, Anna, and then I'll be along. She had a bad spell this morning, which could be the agitation that you're seeing. Do you mind waiting just for another hour?"

"Well, if you think … well, all right. I can do that."

Galean put the phone down and sat at his desk, folded his hands under his chin. Just recently, he'd felt that Helena seemed to be having happier times, she even talked about going back to work part time. One evening, a few nights ago, she'd become the seductress he knew, with her abandoned sensuality and her fierceness igniting feelings that stunned him. But in the last few days, she had reverted to being the frightened child.

He thought of the scene in the bathroom that morning, when she had stood looking up at him as he shaved, her hair hanging in unkempt loose curls, her eyes deep in dark circles, her hands gripping the edge of the sink.

"You're leaving me, aren't you?" She had asked him, weeping. "Where are you going? Why are you leaving?"

The suddenness of her mood changes jolted him, even though he knew the unpredictable was predictable. He turned to her, shaving cream dripping from his razor, and placed his hand on her cheek, the way a father might do to reassure his child. "Lena," he told her calmly, "I'm going to the hospital, I have to see my patients. I'll be home this afternoon, later, the way I always am. We can cook supper together."

Helena, still weeping, sank to the floor like a child feeling rebuked.

Galean placed his razor in the sink, took a towel from

the rack and wiped his face, all the while bridling a sim-
mering distaste in the back of his throat—an irritation that
horrified him. He turned to Helena, who was on her knees,
arms folded around her body, her eyes closed, some grim
image tethering her to the past. She was rocking. Tears
dripped from her chin.

"Ah, Lena," he reached down, intending to help her stand
but then changed his mind and sank down beside her. They
sat there on the white bathroom tiles, he holding her, hush-
ing her; she becoming quiet.

Then, with a long inhale, she lowered her head to Galean's shoulder. "We'll have a lovely supper together, won't
we?" she said.

———————

SITTING IN HIS OFFICE, GALEAN LOOKED AROUND AT WHAT
had been his sanctuary but, as of today, was no longer.
Images came to mind of Casey sitting at his desk opposite
him, her eyes lit with the excitement of an idea for their
book, her no-nonsense determination when he would
suggest they go for a glass of wine and take a break from
heady thoughts.

He felt the spaces of her absence. He sat immobile, a
sense flowing over him of being pinned to his chair. Numbness crept over him and he wondered if he might be having
a stroke. But no, this was uncurbed sadness; regret for possibilities suspended maybe forever.

A photo within a silver frame sitting on his bookcase
stared over at him. It was taken outside the judge's office on
the day he and Helena had married. Her head was thrown
back in what he now recognized as her manic laughter, and

he was smiling at her. They stood apart. In that moment he realized the truth. *Oh, Galean Laihy, you believed you could save her.*

Walking to the door, he turned and looked from window, to desk, to bookcases crammed with years of collections. The clearing and moving from his office would have to wait. It was going to take more time than Galean had right now, and truthfully he couldn't face what needed to be done to prepare for his leaving. He spotted his copy of the unfinished manuscript, his and Casey's, just where he had left it, untouched for weeks. Looking at his watch, he decided to take just a few more minutes and read through the last parts they had written together when the world was simple, or so it seemed to him now.

Taking the manuscript, he crossed the room and sat down in an overstuffed brown corduroy chair, one he'd had throughout medical school and had kept for a time in his office at the hospital. Not only did it represent comfort to Galean, it said: "Come, leave the world for a while. Retreat." It was his "walled garden," as Casey would call it. As he sat back in the old chair, a hand-scrawled note fell from the pages.

Galean,
I've been thinking about what you said once about living inside the experience of our losses. Can we talk about that soon again? I don't want to lose what happened that afternoon. It was intense, wasn't it?
You said that you carry your story with you every day and that some moment, some happening, can bring the old demons rushing back. You've told me about your father dying in the streets of Belfast when you were just a baby. And then you were left—actually left (!)—on the

steps of an adoption home. Later brought to Canada to
work on a farm. You are extraordinary.
Are you living those experiences? Is that what you mean?
Or are you taking them and reconstructing your life out
of the pieces? (Forgive me, maybe the word "pieces" isn't
a good one, but I'm writing this quickly before class.)
In any case, I think you might be the bravest man I've
ever known.

The words began to blur on the page as Galean imagined Casey—intense, fierce Casey—hand holding her head, grasping strands of her hair while she wrote, pressing the pen into the paper. The blurred words? Caused by his own tears. But only for a moment did he allow himself this luxury. A new resolve settled in his body, one built on years of determination to keep going forward, leaving in his wake whatever must be jettisoned. Sadness and vulnerability were at the top of his list.

Galean put the manuscript with the note tucked inside in the drawer of his desk. Walking across the room, he quickened his step. Switching off the light, he opened the door, closing it with a quiet click. *I'm on my way, Helena.*

"ARE YOU SURE, MRS. LAIHY? I KNOW THAT DR. LAIHY IS ON his way home. I can wait till he gets here." Anna stood in the front hallway, her hand on the brass doorknob, her coat unbuttoned, scarf trailing on the floor. A woman uncomfortable with leaving.

Helena smiled. "Anna, I know I was a bit upset this morning, but I'm feeling so much better." In her best moments, Helena could convince the sun to shine. "You have your family waiting for you. I can sit for a while till Galean comes home. I may even have a glass of Chardonnay, it's been a while." She flashed her invented warm smile that could be so convincing.

"Please, I insist. Go on home, and I'll see you in the morning. Thank you for everything." Walking to Anna, Helena reached out and took her hand. "You are a blessing. I'm better than I've been for a long time."

As soon as Helena saw Anna drive around the street corner, she went to the kitchen and picked up the phone. "Hello, I'd like a taxi for 2255 Oak Street, and I need it in the next ten minutes."

Chapter Twenty-Four

All sorrows can be borne
if you put them in a story or tell a story about them.

—ISAK DINESEN

C asey and her new friend Claire spent quiet moments
together with unspoken sanction. Their friendship gave
space and time to each, to be in still silence in company
with one another. Walking along the shore, waves licking
their feet, cliffs rising into the green hills beyond them,
Claire and Casey wrapped themselves in mutual silence.

"Waves are like heartbeats, aren't they?" Casey mused,
while she watched her bare foot sink into the wet sand.

Neither woman felt the need to respond to Casey's
thoughts. Silence flowed over the two of them like the ocean
covering the imprints of their feet. The beach stretched
beyond them, curving into the distance; ocean and sky
blending into a harmony of soft grays and gentle sands.

After they walked a bit more, Claire stopped and pointed
at two large rocks just near the edge of the water. "Want to
sit for a minute?"

Casey nodded and followed her friend toward the rocks.
She sat on the edge of the one left vacant and lifted her face
to the morning sun, remarking, "I didn't expect Ireland
to be this warm in April." She closed her eyes and let the

unexpected warmth waft over her. "And really," she went on, "I didn't expect to feel this contented. I wonder, is this how it feels to be peaceful?"

Claire smiled, leaned down into the water, dragged her hand along and flipped drops up at Casey. "You are probably the most inveterate questioner of life I've ever met."

Casey in turn helped an oncoming wave splash in Claire's direction. "What are you talking about?" she asked, laughing.

"You're questioning your own contentment. Have you ever thought of just leaving yourself alone?"

"I'm not sure I could," Casey answered. "Seems to be who I am. It could be the writer in me." She let the thought hang.

"Well, I think we're all grateful that you are!" Claire stood and stretched her arms to the sky. "On that note, I have a proposition for you, oh wise one."

Claire's words caused Casey to feel a twinge of yearning. Lately she had been absorbing her own luxurious hours of writing, which created the quilt of her days. And the new friendships she was forging, particularly with Claire, had brought a lilt to her life. She had joined a group of four women who met in a small room over Claire's pub. (Casey thought of Jimmy's aka The Wordsmith's Pub as Claire's place.) They gathered there once a week. A room walled with bookshelves stuffed with W.B. Yeats, Elizabeth Shane, Oscar Wilde, Kate O'Brien, Elizabeth Bowen, Iris Murdoch, Margaret Atwood, women authors outnumbering the men. A true intent according to Claire and Rori both custodians of the collection. The moment that Claire and Rori had taken her upstairs to see the writing room, Casey had an eerie sense that she had been summoned. She had.

Claire's proposal was about to latch onto Casey's yearning, her idea hanging in the air like the gulls circling above them.

"Sorry," Claire said after looking at her watch and realizing the time. "I need to get to work, so while we walk back I'll try out my proposition on you." Standing up, she turned and extended her hand to help Casey to her feet.

They walked side by side for a few minutes. Casey intrigued; Claire forming the words.

As they approached the path that would take them up the hill and to where they'd left Claire's car, Casey's curiosity overtook her. "Okay, what do you want to ask me?"

"Will you be our writer-in-residence? We feel we have received someone golden within our group. Someone who might teach us and help to make our stories deep and fierce." Claire smiled and kept going, as though fearful of the answer. "I know you are here working on your book, and you said your friend Dr. Kingwood wanted you to work with him, but you have landed here in our town, like some kind of luminary. Just what we're all needing."

Casey's laugh emerged from some deep place within. "I'm no luminary, and where or on what planet did you find that word? Let me consider what you're asking."

They were now standing at Claire's car, door handles at the ready.

"Claire," said Casey. "I'm going to walk back to my house, it's only about three kilometers, and I need some sorting time."

"You sure about that? I can easily—"

"No," Casey insisted. "I need to walk and think. But thank you." She began to walk toward the road but then turned back for a moment. "One thing," she said. "If we decide to do this, I want us to tell our stories on the page to one another."

Casey realized no one here knew her story. And what was more, the one person who did know her story, she had abandoned. Galean. Sadness caught up to her and began walking with her along the road. Contentment evaporated like spray from the waves.

AS CASEY WALKED THE THREE KILOMETERS BACK TO HER rented house, the adventures of moving to a new country, a new continent, filled Casey's mind and inspired her to pause. The luxury of writing every day, whether it be in her journal or continuing the chapters in the book she and Galean had begun together all those months ago, energized her on some days, and then ... in moments like this, she felt overwhelming loss. A restlessness like pins and needles attacked her soul. Four weeks ago, she had left everything familiar and only an hour ago she'd felt a contented acceptance.

Reaching the front door of the house, Casey unlocked it and placed her hand flat against the sturdy yellow door, feeling the breath in her chest, the fresh air moving through her nostrils. She allowed herself to really feel her aloneness and, in that time and space, she gave herself a gift. She stayed with her body and felt her losses. Her knees weakened. She sank to the rough stone of the doorstep and wept—the noted professor, Dr. Casey MacMillan, on Love, Loss and Human Condition wept alone on her Irish porch, feeling sorrows too long in the shadows.

When the tears finally stopped, Casey folded her body

and hugged her knees with her arms. Words, always her mainstay, floated kind recollections across her memory. *I am alive. I begin again. The day calls. How will I answer?* A day, months ago now, when she had greeted her class at the beginning of term, asking them to speak their own truth, those were the words she had quoted to them.

I am alive ... her own words echoed back to her. She wondered why that particular phrase felt so urgent. *I am alive.* Gradually, gently she realized those were her words—a young Casey's words. And with a slow realization she remembered why aloneness in the world was her familiar place. She had been alone for a very long time. *I begin again.*

Unfolding her legs and pushing against the stoop, she stood and let the cool morning air brush against her body. When she opened the front door, she headed inside directly to her desk, sat down and picked up her pen. The words, a gathering of memories, fell from her hand onto the page in her journal: The accident. Losing everyone she loved and who loved her. Shattered pieces of remembering were sounds and images no longer willing to lie dormant.

Casey wrote as though pursued.

I remember.

The grating, jangling sound of steel on steel awoke me. My mother screaming my father's name, the car flying. My aunt Josh flinging herself across me. For a few seconds the world became a cacophony of sounds, shrieks and rending metal.

I remember ... smells, gasoline, seared tires.

I remember ... calling out Mommy, Daddy, and

hearing nothing, only silence.
I remember Aunt Josh, who wouldn't move. I tried
to push her. She couldn't move.

A jarring sound brought Casey hurtling into the present moment. Her phone was ringing. As she reached across her desk, her arms felt leaden, the way they might have on that day, when she fought to crawl from under her aunt. Her breathing was shallow as she lifted the phone receiver. She closed her eyes and let her shoulders drop. "Hello?"

"Casey, it's Andy. Are you okay? You sound a little strange."

Letting old memories onto the page had taken her to the horror of that day, but now Andy's gentle, deep voice and his concern brought her back, into the room. "No, I'm okay," she told him. "Just started to write, and I guess I'm still in the middle of it."

The images of twisted steel faded. Sounds of the ocean drifted though the half-door. Pages of Casey's journal fluttered in a gentle breeze as though some spirit of the past had just left the room, letting the present moment return.

She swung around in her chair, holding the phone to her ear. "Where are you, Andy? Aren't you working this morning?"

"Actually, Casey, that's why I'm calling. I just came from a conversation with the Dean."

"Before you go any further, Andy, I'm stopping you there. I know what this could be about, and I don't want to teach right now. I want to write my book." Her words hovered for a moment, leaving her emphatic tone hanging in the air.

"Whoa, can I finish?" Something in the edginess of Casey's voice sent out alarms to Andy. "There *is* something going on, isn't there? You do sound … well, tense."

A nagging thought played behind her eyes, like the beginning of an annoying headache. Guilt. It was guilt. Andy was the reason Casey had been able to come to Ireland in the first place, and she had not seen him or contacted him for weeks. She told herself that getting settled, finding her feet and meeting a new group of people were all real reasons for her "disappearance." Yet her intuition, which usually guided her well, told her Andy was on the move again. He still loved her.

"Casey? Are you still there?"

"I'm here, Andy." And taking a long breath, she said, "Tell me about your conversation with the Dean."

"Tell you what." Andy's voice was subdued. "Why don't I call you on the weekend? Maybe we can see about me driving over there. And we can talk then?"

"That'd be lovely, Andy. Let's meet at the pub, I'd like you to meet Claire. Now, truly, I really have to get to work."

"Casey," Andy started to reply. "You and I—"

She stopped him. "Andy, I really can't talk any longer, I need to get back to work. I'll call you on the weekend and we'll go from there. Okay?"

"Well, okay. You sound busy, so…"

"Thanks Andy. I'll call you. Take care. Bye."

Before Andy had a moment to say goodbye, Casey hung the phone on the cradle.

What is this fear? she asked herself. *Why am I running like a frightened child? Maybe because I* am *a frightened child?*

Casey left her writing desk to go make herself a cup of tea. Returning with the warm mug in her hand, she drew herself over to the bookshelf where the manuscript she and Galean were working on sat covered in a box. Lifting the lid, she pulled out a sheet lying on top. It contained a paragraph that Galean had written almost a year ago. As Casey read over the words now, she saw herself more deeply than she ever had. Her flight from Andy, her fear of being lost in someone else's need, her anguish about loss—it all flowed through her veins. Sitting cross-legged in an old stuffed yellow chair in a house in Ireland, just as she would were Galean there, she absorbed the sound and feel of his words:

> *Loss is in our skin; it flows in our blood streams and is imprinted on our souls. Despair is old, but love is older.*
>
> *Our human stories blend loss and love in a harmony that feels discordant yet is beautiful, like Stravinsky superimposing scales one on another, blending major and minor. The theme of life plays out, where music and rhythm clash and resolve; when Romeo and Juliet risk it all; Orpheus and Eurydice soften the hearts of Hades and Persephone in the underworld and Héloïse and Abélard become nun and monk in order to stay faithful to one another.*
>
> *If we stayed true to the narratives of our lives, might we move deeper into ourselves and the life of another? Might the truth of love permeate old fears and release us to feel what's possible?*
>
> *That is what my friend and colleague Dr. Casey MacMillan and I want to explore in this, our shared writing journey: what is it that draws us to the fantasy life and away from the beauty of pain, of loss, of love?*

The poet Wislawa Szymborska wrote:
Funny little thing ...
that even despair can work for you
if you're lucky enough
to outlive it.
—*from "Laughter"*

Casey uncrossed her legs, leaned forward, put the paper on the floor and stood. Her phone sat on the desk on the other side of the room. An overwhelming realization moved through her body; a dry riverbed suddenly flowing with clear water. Some untamed, unbroken part of her stirred. *Not today, Casey. Don't call him today.*

But she knew, someday, she'd make that call.

Chapter Twenty-Five

You must wake up with sorrow.
You must speak to it till your voice
Catches the thread of all sorrows
and you see the size of the cloth.

—**NAOMI SHIHAB NYE**, "Kindness"

He saw it right away: a note propped against a pot of daisies sitting on the windowsill in the kitchen. Helena's favorite flowers. Galean stalled in mid-step, a foreboding sensation chilling him. A glacial silence hung in the air.

He called out, "Helena, I'm home."

No response.

"Anna? Are you still here?"

Silence.

Galean, heart racing, reached across the table that sat under the window, grabbed the envelope and sank back into a kitchen chair. As he stared down at the envelope, his palms sweating, he ran his finger across Helena's distinctive oversized handwriting: her extra-large *G*, encompassing the *a*, an *L* falling into the *ea* and the *n*. His name bold and black. He opened the envelope slowly, methodically, pulling out a creamy note paper. Clenching it, his hands trembled.

Dear Galean,
It's all becoming too hard. I know you want to rescue me,
but, my darling, I can't be rescued. I thought I could find
peace here with you, and now I know there is nowhere
I can rest. All I seem to do is bring you pain. At this
moment death welcomes me. Forgive me, but I must go.
Sometime soon, remember the beauty.
Helena

Letting the note drift to the floor, Galean stood up and strode out of the kitchen down the hall, calling out Helena's name. Only silence answered back. Just as he reached the bottom of the stairs, the front doorbell rang.

Galean opened the door and found two policemen standing there. One female, one male. Both with hat in hand.

"Dr. Laihy?" asked the male officer.

"Yes," Galean barely whispered, not wanting to know why they were at his door, yet knowing.

"May we come in, sir?"

Moments became bits of icy fog. Words froze in Galean's throat, so he motioned for them to follow him into the kitchen. The note still lay on the floor where it had fallen. As Galean bent down to pick it up, he stumbled and grasped the edge of the table.

"Sir, let us get that for you," said the female officer, moving toward Galean. She took his arm and guided him to a chair.

The three—Officer Sandra Gail, Officer Andrew Wilson and Galean—sat at the table, letting the moments dissolve one into another. Galean wondered at their silence, it seemed endless. The note lay on the table. It was Galean who finally reached for it.

"You will need to see this," he told the officers.

"Dr. Laihy," Officer Gail said as she took the note from Galean's hand. "We are so sorry we have bad news. Your—"

Galean interrupted. "My wife has taken her life, hasn't she?"

A glance flitted between the officers.

"Yes, she has," confirmed Officer Wilson. "We have just come from the viaduct downtown."

"Oh God, no! She jumped off … Oh God, oh God." Putting his hand across his eyes, Galean shook his head and rocked.

Officer Gail, new to the force, reached for Galean's hand instinctively but then drew her hand back, correcting him, "No, no, sir. No, she did not jump." The officer paused, took a long breath. She hated these calls. "Dr. Laihy, your wife walked directly into the traffic that was crossing over the bridge. According to witnesses and the truck driver who hit her, she stepped from the curb and walked right into his path. He hadn't time to swerve, and if he had he'd have hit cars coming the other way. The driver has been taken to the hospital to be treated for shock."

Galean sat transfixed with his hands flat against the surface of the table, fingers spread. Neither officer spoke. His anguish hung in the air.

Suddenly a two-way radio crackled, breaking the silence. Officer Wilson stood up and, quietly pushing back his chair, took his radio from his belt and walked into the hallway. When he returned, he seemed to move with a renewed efficiency. He asked Galean, "Is there anyone we can call who might have seen your wife in the last few hours?"

Galean, amazed that he hadn't thought to call Anna, sprung up to go to the phone. "Yes, yes, our housekeeper—

Helena's caregiver. I'll call her. I'll call her right now." At this point, hope began its false story, and Galean heard a small voice in his head. *Maybe Helena is still all right, maybe she'd only tried ...*

Picking up on Galean's agitation, Officer Gail put her hand on his arm. "Dr. Laihy, just take a breath, take a moment before you call anyone. You can call whoever you like in a few minutes, but right now we want to let you know that a taxi driver called 911 after feeling apprehensive about dropping off a woman at the viaduct. We're trying to reach him now."

Galean's last sliver of hope was fading away. Piecing Helena's last hours together, it seemed clear now to everyone that she had decided to take her life and that she knew what she was about to do when she left the house. It was time to bring in Anna and others who had been the last to see her.

From the phone call to Anna and her tearful arrival, events began to speed up for Galean.

"Oh, Dr. Laihy," Anna said to him through her tears. "Mrs. Laihy seemed almost contented when I left her this afternoon. She told me what she was cooking for you for supper." Sobs muffled her words. "I'm so sorry, I should have stayed."

"Anna, it's not your fault," Galean told the distraught woman as he held her hands in his, almost in supplication to the numb grief that was seeping through his body. His heart felt as though it were hemorrhaging.

Officer Wilson, who had left the kitchen to take a phone call, returned. "Dr. Laihy," he began, "I just spoke with the taxi driver who called 911 this afternoon. His description of the woman he dropped off at the viaduct matches that of your wife." The officer paused before continuing. "He said that he'd called 911 because he had a bad feeling, but when he saw the woman walk across to the other side, he felt he had misread the situation and that she would be okay. After hanging up with the dispatcher, he started to drive away. That's when your wife turned and walked directly into the double lane of traffic coming toward her."

"Oh my God!" Anna threw her arms in the air and fell into the chair behind her.

Galean remained immobile. Staring. Hearing words that made no sense. "So then, that's it?" he asked the two police officers.

They looked at him, not knowing what to say. Galean's calm felt cold and eerie.

Head down, Galean went on to speak in a blurred murmur. "So it was Helena. She's taken her life, and involved all those other poor people." His next words stunned everyone in the room. "We were cursed from the beginning—everybody I love is cursed." Turning away, Galean walked through the kitchen, down the hall and into the living room.

Anna motioned to the police that she wanted to go to him. Following him into the living room, she called after him, "Dr. Laihy, is there someone I can call? Someone at the university or the hospital?" she asked.

Without answering her, he turned and crumpled into a chair. Hands to his face, elbows on his knees, he moaned and mourned for Helena's lost soul. He leaned forward, falling into the pain, letting his old cloak of self-protection fall away. Grief spread through his body like a merciless overflow. He invited the sorrow in.

DEAN ATWATER SAT OUTSIDE THE DOORS TO THE MORGUE at the hospital where Helena's body rested. Stillness defined him. Hands folded, eyes closed, he waited.

A head pathologist had taken Galean into an outer room, where he offered to provide a photo of Helena's corpse, intending to prevent the trauma of seeing it in person. Up to this point Galean seemed quiet, subdued, but now something broke.

"No!" he waved his hand, brushing away the idea, toppling the pathologist's good intention. "No, I have to go and be sure it's her. I need to see her, to look at her."

"Okay, I just wasn't sure, Doctor Laihy, if you wanted to see your wife after she ..." The pathologist paused, wondering how to say it gently—after your wife committed suicide in such a brutal way.

"Dr. Zabinsky, with all due respect, I know how she must look. She walked into a truck, for God's sake."

The pathologist stepped back and put his hand on the doorknob, possibly looking to escape this disheveled pale man. Just then the door opened, setting Dr. Zabinsky even more off-balance. A young woman ducked into the room, her hair pulled back in a tight chignon, tortoiseshell-rimmed glasses riding atop her head. A white cotton doctor's coat made clear her right to be there, but her approach toward Galean announced it was for more than a professional reason.

"Oh, Dr. Laihy. I am so, so sorry." She reached for his hand.

"Andrea?" Galean appearing dismayed to see her, put out his hand.

Without hesitation, she reached for him to put her arms around his shoulders.

Galean had been in this hospital morgue before, most memorably when he had been called to testify about a patient's death. Other times he'd been there with students who were studying forensics and forensic ethics. Andrea had been one of his students.

"As soon as I saw Helena's name in the logbook, I had to come," she explained. "I'm not on duty right now, please let me stay with you."

Andrea's compassion for her former teacher rattled Galean. He was so close to broken, yet not ready to surrender. When she reached for him he moved away, putting one arm up, ready to stop her. "No, no, this is not the time, Andrea. This is not what I need. More than your sympathy, I need your professional coolness. I taught you all about that, now please take me to Helena." Galean had indeed taught his students to distance themselves from their emotions and the pain of loss. "Just show me my wife's body, please."

Hearing his depth of anguish, Andrea moved toward the double doors that were the entrance to the morgue. She turned to Galean and beckoned him to go through. "I'm right here, with you, Dr. Laihy," she said. The student guided her teacher.

Cold steel and cold air greeted them. Lines of tables, banks of white doors—all belied the comfort of death that had been so sought after by Helena.

Andrea led Galean to a bank of shining white drawers, where she switched on a hanging overhead lamp and opened a drawer, pulling out the tray marked sixteen.

Helena lay covered with a white sheet.

Galean felt his knees weakening, his sight blurring, and he realized Andrea's arm was around his waist.

"You can just leave if you want, Dr. Laihy," she told him.

"We know it's Helena. Are you still sure you want to look at her?"

A voice spoke. "Yes," he whispered.

Gently, Andrea pulled back the sheet, still holding on to Galean.

Back curls came into view, and a pale visage marred with bruises and scratches, but it was undeniably Helena. No longer could Galean, nor did he want to, pretend. Unrelenting sadness permeated his body. Death had been part of his life since birth, and still it clutched him. He reached to pull the sheet back further, but Andrea stopped him.

"No, Dr. Laihy. You know it's Helena. You don't need to see anything more." As she said this, she moved him away from the tray and gently pushed it back into the slot. A sliding noise, a clank, and Helena was gone.

Galean knew why Andrea had decided that was enough. Helena had fallen beneath the wheels of the truck, which had allowed the tires to rumble across her body. He didn't need to see. Rote took over and he said, "Thank you, Andrea. I appreciate your being here. I guess I did teach you something in spite of myself." He turned away, then turned back as he approached the door. "Take good care of her." And he left.

LATER, AFTER A SILENT RIDE BACK TO GALEAN'S HOUSE, JIM Atwater pulled into the driveway and cut the engine. Putting his arm across the back of the passenger seat, he hesitated and then asked, "What can I do for you, Galean? Tonight, tomorrow, whenever."

Silence. Sluggish silence.

Galean looked down at his hands. Everything looked

peculiar to him, even his hands, as though he'd been channeled into someone else's body.

"There's to be a private service for Helena the day after tomorrow," he said. "I have to talk with the police again." He grasped the handle and opened the car door. "After everything is done …" And he paused as though pronouncing this chapter of his life closed. "Then, maybe I can tell you what I need, but right now …" he trailed off. Sitting on the edge of the seat, not rising, not moving, he seemed locked in some dark place. He turned back to the dean. "Actually, there is one thing you can do now. Let Casey know."

Not waiting for a yes or a no or a why, Galean swung himself out of the car and walked away, into the dark house.

CLONAKILTY, IRELAND. MAY 1982

Dark clouds hovered over the town as Casey parked her rental car across the street from Jimmy's Pub. As she stood outside her car waiting for a break in the traffic so she could cross, murmurs of winds quickening prompted her to pull on her rain slicker and hood. She ran from her car to the shelter of the overhang outside the pub. Just as she reached protection, the clouds delivered. Casey stood enthralled, watching the rain driven by wind gusts become sheets of water.

"What, for heaven's sake, are you doing, Casey?" Claire, running along the street, yelled out to her. "Get yourself inside!"

Gathering herself together, Casey pushed on the pub's heavy wooden door and stood aside to let Claire run in.

Shaking her very wet hair, Claire laughed, took off her rain jacket and gave her soaked umbrella a good shake. She beckoned to the stairs leading past the bar. "Quite a day to begin writing our stories, right, Casey?"

"I'm pretty sure I've never seen rain come on like that," remarked Casey, balancing her briefcase as she took hold of the railing and started up the stairs.

"You've been seduced a bit over the past weeks, the days have been lovely. I was beginning to think it was your charm, that you brought good weather and sun with you."

The two women bantered back and forth as they climbed the stairs. There at the top, they stood in a small room graced by a wide window that looked out upon the street below. It was a place that welcomed. Claire moved around, turning on the lamps that sat on the table where they'd be writing. Flipping a switch, she lit a fire in the gas fireplace.

Casey took a breath and exhaled a quiet, "Thank you."

A very furry gray-and-white cat lay dozing on a worn well-stuffed lounge chair. Not disturbed by the intrusion of humans, he stirred just enough to turn so he was now facing the back of the chair, where he continued his nap.

"Oh my," Casey commented upon seeing him, "there's even a resident cat. The scene is complete." She put her briefcase down, and dropped into one of four wooden armchairs placed around the table. "How did you do this, Claire? How did you make this perfect place to write?"

Claire shrugged and smiled.

Footsteps on the stairs and Rori strode into the room. Rori was a strider.

She reminded Casey a bit of Helena, without the edginess. She had the same unruly black hair, the same dark-eyed gaze that, if directed your way, sometimes seemed to penetrate your soul. But there the similarities stopped. Rori had been a social worker taking care of abandoned children who lived in foster homes. Rori, in her unhesitatingly calm way, had watched over these children. Now she told their stories. Retired, she transferred her passionate care to her friends, Claire especially. And soon Casey would become one other folded into Rori's kindness.

"Let the writing begin." Rori declared, dropping a crazy quilted green-and-pink bag onto the table.

With that pronouncement, Casey, Claire and Rori began the steadfast, steady task that women for thousands of years have embraced: listening to one another's stories and shedding light on old dark places. And as they did, the shadows of sorrows danced across the room.

Chapter Twenty-Six

Whoever you are, no matter how lonely,
the world offers itself to your imagination,
calls to you like the wild geese, harsh and exciting –
over and over announcing your place
in the family of things.

—MARY OLIVER, "Wild Geese"

Listening to the rain pelting, shutters rattling, wind howling, Casey imagined the gods grieving. She sat huddled in her wide bed with her legs drawn up to her chest and her arms wrapped around her knees. She had the white cotton comforter tucked under her chin, a yellow woolen blanket across her shoulders: her trustworthy cocoon. Cold dampness penetrated her bedroom. She thought of getting out of bed to walk across the room and stoke the glowing coals in the fireplace, but that bore a slim chance of happening. Casey looked over at the brightly lit face of her travel clock and sighed. 2:15 a.m.

Two hours ago, she had sat on the floor before the fire, wrapped in her flannel gown and a woolen blanket, watching tiny flames snagging the edges of the peat briquettes. Thoughts had swirled and spun around in her mind, each catching the tail of another.

I didn't call Andy back. Am I dragging my feet not

answering him?

Today, writing with Claire and Rori … maybe that's what I want to do.

I haven't looked at my chapters.

Galean … I wonder, how is he?

Does he wonder about me?

Am I lonely? Am I running?

When the fire had died down and the wind quickened, Casey had added more briquettes, before taking her thoughts, and climbing into bed. It was a mistake to have held on to her thoughts—particularly the one chiding her. *Galean, what is it that will not let me rest?* Tossing and turning, she navigated the doubts and the guilt.

Now, two hours later, sleep finally began to muffle the rattle of Casey's thoughts and she drifted. A jangling sounded beyond her. Somewhere a phone was ringing. There in the house.

Casey sat up. The ringing persisted—a chilling portent in the middle of the night. Throwing the comforter aside, she ran into the living room and grabbed the phone from its cradle. One hand over her ear to shut out the wind's roar, she shouted into the receiver, "Hello!"

"Casey?" A woman's voice. Her friend Anne, back in Toronto. Back at the university.

"Anne? Anne, what's wrong?"

"Casey, I'm so sorry, I know it's the middle of the night there, but I had to let you know. I couldn't put it off another day."

Closing her eyes, Casey rubbed her fingers across her forehead, wondering what her friend might be talking about.

"Casey?"

"I'm here," she responded. "What's happened?" Her

voice was low and hoarse and something chilled the back of her neck.

"Helena. It's Helena." Anne's voice dropped away.

"Anne, oh no … has she hurt Galean?" Casey's first thought arose like the wind and rain rattling against the house.

"No, Casey," said Anne, her voice almost a whisper. "She's taken her own life."

In the seconds it took to absorb Anne's words, Casey heard only the wailing of the wind outside. She closed her eyes, hoping maybe she was back in her bed, dreaming. But then realization penetrated and bleak sadness flooded her body. "Helena … oh, Helena." Dropping onto the chair by the phone, Casey held the receiver to her ear, propping her elbow on her knee and bowing her head. "Oh, Galean." A whisper.

"Casey, what can I do for you?" Anne broke into Casey's lament.

"I don't know. Have you talked to Galean?"

"No, he's not talking to anyone except the dean and some friends at the hospital. I heard through the dean's office that there's already been a private service."

Casey knew exactly what Galean was doing—shutting himself away from the world.

"Anne, I'm grateful you called. It must have been a hard decision for you, not to mention this is a very long distance call. By the way, how did you know where to find me?"

If Casey were to see Anne at that moment, her friend, familiar with Casey's lapses, was holding the phone away from her ear and rolling her eyes. "Uh, Dr. MacMillan, absent-minded professor? You wrote a lovely letter to me when you arrived there, remember? And in that letter gave

me your address and your number, with a fervent promise
I was not to give it to anyone, except maybe Dean Atwater."

Barely able to hear Anne over the noise of the shutters
banging against the house, Casey clutched her flannel gown
at her neck, pressed the receiver closer to her ear. Gusts of
wind intensified, railing against the house. Were the gods
angry, or was it Helena wailing from some lost depths?
Casey inhaled and held her breath for a beat before asking,
"Anne, do you know how she took her life?"

Only silent air responded.

"Anne?"

"Casey, it was awful," Anne said reluctantly. "She walked
across the Bloor Viaduct—you know, the one downtown
over the subway tracks—and when she got to the other
end …" Anne's voice quavered, covering a sob. "She turned
around and walked right out into two lanes of traffic, directly
into a truck."

"Oh my God," Casey whispered.

Inexplicably, the exasperation she'd felt when Galean
had first told her about Helena now rose in Casey's mouth
like ulcerated decay. And just as quickly, she quashed it.
Helena was so angry, all her life, she thought to herself. *And
now the anger's destroyed her and it has its grip on Galean.
Maybe that's what she intended. To destroy him.* Even as she
conjured the possibility, Casey extinguished the thought. *No,
Helena was confused and tormented, she wasn't evil.*

She stood holding the receiver to her ear. Breaking her
long silence she spoke. "Anne, I'm going to hang up. I need
to call Galean. He can't think he's been abandoned, not now."

"Casey? Are you going to be all right there by yourself?"
Anne imagined her friend, distant, alone, absorbing the
brutality of it all.

"I'll be all right. I just need to talk to Galean." Casey placed the receiver back on its cradle, hearing Anne's farewell only faintly.

Calm for Casey was a mug of tea, a pillowed couch, a yellow woolen blanket. The wind's ferocity was spent, like her anguish, which was now just a gentle sadness. Regret coursed through her body, a lament for Helena.

Casey sat lengthwise on the couch with her legs stretched before her and her ankles crossed. She wrapped her fingers around the warm mug of tea sitting on her lap. Closing her eyes, she tried to conjure images of Helena, the young spirited woman who pushed against her demons and anyone who tried to love her.

In the beginning, Casey—the young, idealistic social worker—embraced Helena's spirit yet dreaded and feared her wild recklessness. *How many times,* Casey thought now as she sipped her tea. *How many times did I wrap blankets around her while I held her shivering with terror? How many times did I sing to her, like a mother to a small child?*

Putting her mug of tea on the side table, Casey rose from the couch and walked down the narrow hallway to her bedroom. There the comforter lay rumpled on the floor where she'd tossed it when she ran to the phone. The room felt different. The walls encircled her, reminding her of other walls, other rooms, where she had sat beside a young Helena weeping into her pillow. Casey hadn't thought of that Home at all since arriving in Ireland. Now those memories intruded.

Dropping to her knees, she peered under the bed and pulled out a red duffel bag. Sitting down on the floor, she pulled the comforter over her knees, kicking the thick cotton down over her feet. She leaned against the bed and the softness of the mattress. A glow from the bedside lamp cast a light across the contents of the bag. Casey pulled out a photo of her younger self smiling, her arm across Helena's shoulder. Helena was leaning toward Casey, yet her head turned away a bit. They sat on the steps of a porch, and behind them at an open door, a tall, gray-haired woman stared out at the camera, possibly one of the nurses, watching the two of them. All those years ago, and Casey remembered that moment as though it were yesterday.

It took a while for the tears to come, but come they did. All the pain, all the bits and pieces of tragedy and hopelessness that Casey had pushed into the farthest corners of her life, rose slowly into her chest, into her throat, and grief became a presence, pleading to be acknowledged. Images of Helena filled the room. As the night became dawn, Casey wept, giving light and air to old anguish and to all she had abandoned throughout her life. She held Helena's photo against her chest. *I could have given her more, I could have helped, I should have known.*

Summoned mental pictures of Casey's own life stories tangled themselves around one another. She saw herself, that little girl pulled from a mangled wreckage. Suitcases and foster homes with blank, forlorn windows. A parade of young girls, looking to Casey for solace and the ones she'd left behind. Helena.

Casey realized she'd created her own losses. She'd broken her own heart. Looking at the clock now, seeing it was almost seven o'clock, she made a decision to gather up the pieces of herself. She picked up the phone and dialed.

"Hello?" answered a quiet voice with a gentle lilt.

"Hi Claire, it's Casey. I know it's really early, but I wondered if you'd like to have breakfast together?" And with that, for one of the first times in her life, Casey MacMillan reached out across the abyss between one human being and another. She made herself vulnerable.

When she arrived an hour later at the café, Claire was there, sitting at a booth. She waved, pointing to the coffee she'd already ordered for Casey.

Sliding onto the bench of the booth, Casey sat for a moment, still, before speaking. "Claire, something horrific has happened."

Her friend placed her coffee mug gently on the table, reached over to Casey and covered her hand. "Ah, Casey. You look stricken, like you've seen a ghost. Whatever is the matter?"

"Helena," began Casey. "It's Helena. She ..." Stopping, Casey swallowed and reached for the words in her throat. Grateful now that she had told Claire the story of Galean and how she had felt such humiliation about Helena. Thankful, too, that Claire had never sat in judgement, only expressing compassion for all of them. "She took her own life," finished Casey. Somehow the words "committed suicide" seemed too brutal and cold.

A moment. Claire gave them the gift of a moment before saying, "Oh, my love, what do ya need? What can I do?"

"I need you to help me decide," said Casey. "I'm spinning and I can't find my feet. I think the last time I felt this out of control, out of my body, was when they wouldn't let me get back to my mom and dad in that wrecked car. God ... I was four years old." A sob, deep and wrenching, escaped Casey. Her past swept into the café.

Claire stood, moved around the booth, slid in beside Casey, and enwrapped her in her arms. No words. No murmurings. Only a gentle space.

Wiping her eyes with fierce fists, Casey sat back, still clutching Claire's arm. "What I want to do is call Galean right this minute and tell him I'm sorry about everything … all of it, from the beginning. I left him, just like everyone else has. I abandoned my best friend." Before Claire could respond, Casey brought her hand down flat on the table as though declaring herself in the company of all. "I need to carry on the best of Helena's spirit. I need Galean to know he's loved."

"And, what might I do to help you?" Claire had one arm across Casey's shoulder, holding her, emboldening her.

Turning to face Claire, Casey smiled. "You have a spirit that reminds me of Helena in her best moments; you kindle something in me. And truthfully, I need a cheering section right now 'cause I have work to do." For the first time in many hours, she sighed a full breath.

"And?" Claire urged her on.

"And," Casey continued, "I want him to come back home—to Ireland—to finish his story here, and then move on." She paused. "I want to be here when he comes. I want him to know that nobody's leaving him on the steps anymore. That story is done. I want him to come home."

Very gently, in almost a whisper, Claire asked, "Home to you or home to him?"

Casey leaned back against the board of the booth. Claire released her arm. They sat with their shoulders touching.

"Both, Claire. Both."

Chapter Twenty-Seven

Living is a kind of wound;
a wound is a kind of opening;
and even love that disappeared
mysteriously comes back
like water bubbling up from underground,
cleansed from its long journey in the dark.

—TONY HOAGLAND,
"Message To A Former Friend"

September 1982

As he made his way down the hallway toward his office, Andy Kingwood spotted an envelope taped to the door, which was an unusual sight. Notes seldom were taped to a professor's door here at UCC. Andy thought perhaps it was from an advisee who needed more time before handing in his chapters and was too embarrassed to speak to him directly. But when he approached the door, recognition set in. The matchless perfection of Casey's handwriting stood out in black relief on the front of the envelope.

Dr. Kingwood:
I am at the library working. If you have a moment,
could we please talk?
Sincerely,
Casey

Pausing only to take down the envelope, Andy turned, retraced his footsteps and headed for the library.

The main area of the UCC library was a cloister-like space watched over by a stained-glass window. Each time he walked toward the building, Andy felt a shiver of gratitude for the time he'd been given abroad, the time to relish in research and feel the energy of learning. Today his anticipation centered on Casey and her sudden appearance on campus. He still hoped for a deeper friendship with her, but he felt cautious about why she'd asked to talk with him.

He spotted her sitting on a bench by the front door of the library, head lowered, pen in hand moving across a page. He moved toward her.

"Casey?"

She looked up and smiled. "Shall we go get a coffee, Dr. Kingwood? Um … Andy?"

"No, actually, Casey, it's very pleasant right here. Do you have something to show me? I see you still carry your lucky briefcase." He motioned toward her book bag leaning against her leg.

"Only when I have something important to share with my advisor." Letting a small grin play at the edges of her mouth, Casey reached down and pulled out a single paper— Galean's paper, the one she had found in the draft of the manuscript. "First, though, I need to apologize for my disappearing act. You're the one who smoothed the way for me to be here having this extraordinary experience, and I seem to have abandoned you."

"No apologies, please," said Andy. "You needed time to settle in. The point is, here we are now."

Casey felt the uneasiness she always used to feel when Andy intimated there might be something more. "Here we are now" sounded like hopeful anticipation to her. She scurried to quash any expectation of a deeper friendship.

"I brought something that Galean wrote a while ago when we started our book together. I wanted to show it to you, and let you know what I'm thinking." Her words tumbled.

"Shall we just sit here?" Andy pointed to the empty space on the bench beside her.

Nodding her head she said. "Yes, this is a good place to talk."

He sat down and turned to Casey, reaching for the sheet of paper. "Let's see what you have."

Instead of handing the paper to him, Casey placed it in her lap and turned to face him. "Andy, before you read it I want to let you know what I'm intending to do. I'm going to call Galean." Her definitive tone clearly broadcasting "not for discussion."

Andy paused for a moment, waiting for Casey's next words. When she seemed to be struggling, he filled in the hesitant space. "What's happened?"

"Galean's wife, Helena, has taken her life. Did you know that?"

"What!"

A student walking by, startled by Andy's reaction, stopped in mid-step and looked over at the two of them: a man and woman frozen in a strangled moment. Silence wrapped around the two of them for a few seconds; Casey staring down at the paper, Andy shaking his head back and forth absorbing the news.

"She walked in front of a truck on the Bloor Viaduct," Casey said.

"How did you find out?" asked Andy. He lifted his face to the sky, still shaking his head.

"Anne Morgan called me," she told him. "And when I leave you today, I'm going to try to call Galean. But I needed to talk with you first."

Now the penny dropped for Andy Kingwood. Casey wasn't here to express new feelings for him; whatever her intentions were, Galean was on her mind.

Andy turned away and looked out over the paths and lawns of the campus. He watched the students moving along. Some were intense, purposeful, their heads down, while others were laughing. As Andy had learned to do once before, he shed his hopeful fantasies about possibilities for the two of them and slipped into his familiar role, the person Casey needed. Her advisor. Her friend. He straightened his back and turned to her. "What do you need from me, Casey?"

"I need your wise counsel, and I need you to read this." She handed Galean's paragraph to Andy and watched as he leaned forward, elbows balanced on his knees, and began to scan the words.

Two sentences seized his attention right away: *Loss is in our skin, it flows in our bloodstream and is imprinted on our souls. Despair is old, but love is older.* He slanted his head to the side, looked over at Casey. "Do you want me to critique?" he asked her. "What exactly am I doing?" An edginess crept into his tone, like sandpaper rough against wood. "I feel like an interloper, like I'm meddling where I have no business being." He waited, not moving.

Casey rested her back against the ironwork of the bench. As though considering what to say, she took a moment to fold her arms. A gray squirrel scampered across the pathway leading into the library. Staring after the squirrel, Casey took a breath and decided. She turned, arms still folded and faced him. "Andy, I have not been fair to you. You were a brilliant advisor when we worked together, before I fled from you and from my own fear of being cared for. Were it not for you, well, I'm not sure where I'd be right now. It's time for me to leave the cocoon of your care, even though I walked away from you all those years ago, I guess I still depend on you. What you think of me matters, but … damn it, I'm falling all over the words." She leaned forward, face in her hands, elbows on her knees.

Andy set the paper on the bench between them, put his hand on her shoulder. A soft connection. And he chuckled. Casey looked over at him between her fingers.

"Casey, I'm no match for the kind of friendship that you and Galean have. I just honestly don't know why the two of you haven't seen what everybody else sees and has seen. God, I remember the two of you when you met. Watching you in conversation at a seminar was like watching a great tango. So quit apologizing for how you feel. You did it once already, but this time when you walk away from me, do it because you bloody well know what you want. Not because you're afraid." Andy sat back, and then forward, rocking the bench. "I'm not the one who should be sitting here with you. I want to … by God I want to. But, well, are you listening to what Galean is trying to say?" Andy picked up the paper. "Listen: 'If we stayed true to the narratives of our lives, might we move deeper into ourselves and the life of another? Might the truth of love permeate old fears and release us to what is possible?' What a testament to being alive those words are. What a testament to you!" Andy waved his hands upward as though invoking the heavens to agree.

"Start listening to yourself, Casey," Andy continued. "Listen to Galean. Whatever it is you're afraid of, walk straight into it and—pardon me, but—screw the fallout. I thought it might be me you were running from, even now. But it's not, Casey." He stood up, turned back to her and pointed, one finger extended, almost berating her. "Hell, you came all the way to Ireland because I paved the way for you to come. So, it's not me you're running from, is it?"

Casey felt a surge of something new—irritation. She was letting herself feel anger. "I didn't come here just because you invited me, Andy." Her voice was low and taut.

"Okay then, why *did* you drop everything and come?" he asked her.

Feeling pushed, a bit invaded, Casey's face flushed. She stood up said, "Because it was too hard to stay back there."

Sometimes truth makes its way to the light in spite of all the ways we've learned to push back, this was one of those moments for Casey. The two of them stood now, facing one another, hands at their sides, waiting for the next moment.

Andy reached out a hand toward Casey and she took it, folding her fingers into his palm. He told her, "You wrote the most brilliant thesis—no, it wasn't a thesis; it was a wonderful piece of work. A story about yearnings that was full of courage and longing." He entwined his fingers around hers, as though reluctant to let go, then dropped his hand. "It was one of the best pieces of soul work I think I've read in my career." He smiled. "The day you left; the day you fired me—"

Casey started to protest, but Andy held up his hand gesturing for her silence.

"The day you fired me, you ran. Not from me—you ran from what you were uncovering in yourself."

Three young women ran down the steps of the library, chattering, laughing. When they sighted Andy and Casey, they dropped their voices to low-pitched sounds as they walked by. Something in the manner of the two standing facing one another, their stillness, projected intimacy, a need for privacy.

Andy waited for the girls to pass. "It really wasn't me who uncovered your story—you did that. And yes, I loved who you were becoming, but you ... you saw me through fearful eyes. "

Turning away from him, from his penetrating gaze, Casey picked up the paper lying on the bench. Her face no longer flushed, her eyes now soft, she began to read. "'If we stayed true to the narratives of our lives, might we see and love ourselves anew?'" Smiling, she said, "Well, Dr. Kingwood, as always, you've taught me well. What was it you just said a few minutes ago? You're not the one who should be sitting here, it's Galean's words I need to hear?" With that, she gathered up her book bag and her satchel, threw her sweater across her shoulders. Taking Andy's hand again, she gave him a professorial shake and, laughing, kissed him on the cheek. "Do you remember the last paragraph of my thesis?" she asked. "I know you have a copy because I sent it to you."

Andy laughed. "I'm good, Casey, but I'm not that good. I remember a memorable thesis, just not word for word. So, please remind me, what was the last paragraph?"

Dropping her bag onto the path, Casey folded her hands, put the tips of her fingers to her lips. She paused. "I even remember where I was when the words came to me, in full sentences. I was walking early in the morning by Lake Ontario, and I'd called Galean to meet me for breakfast. He was just coming off a rough night at the hospital. One of his patients had died." She paused again.

Andy sat down on the bench, leaned back and spread his arms across the wooden slats. Knowing Casey as he did, he thought to himself, *She needs to tell me the whole story, and it gives me just a few more minutes with her.* He beckoned to her to sit beside him.

Casey sat down and went on with her story. "Galean came down to the lake. I remember he cried. The patient he had lost was a newborn, hardly even in life before she left again, that's what he said to me."

Andy wasn't sure if Casey remembered he was still there. Her eyes reflected a far-off gaze; her hands were folded loosely in her lap.

She went on. "And when I told him my last paragraph and how it had just come to me, he said he thought the words were miraculous."

"So, what were they?" Andy's voice now was gentle.

"I remember them," said Casey, "word for word: 'There will be a time when you take back the moments that were pure, those childlike moments. And you will know. You will know everything is a mystery and everything is connected—every event, every loss, every hope, every yearning and every joy. Nothing is superfluous. All of it is life. Bless it all.'"

It took a small breath before Andy could trust himself to say anything. He felt as though he'd been given some kind of benediction. When he put his hand over Casey's hand, still folded in her lap, he had a sense of endings. This would be their last intimate moment. He knew that. "You need to go and write that book," he told her. "Go change the world, Casey MacMillan. Or, or at the very least, go out and create some chaos—please, no more caution. Go live." He stood up, patted his hand over his heart, turned and walked away.

THAT NIGHT IN THE QUIET OF HER STONE COTTAGE, DRESSED in her frayed flowered kaftan, Casey sat before the turf fire she'd built in the fireplace in the living room. She had purposefully left the lamps off. Only the flickering flames reflecting across the walls gave light to the room. The storms of the past few days had abated, leaving only the soothing sound of waves lapping the shore below. Staring into the fire, Casey began to let herself feel the truth of her life—the torment as a little girl when her family was wiped out; being shunted from foster home to foster home, always leaving somebody behind. She allowed a lifetime of pain to sweep though her body and she greeted it with a strange sad exhilaration, like a shell finally loosening from the sand of the ocean floor. She stayed with the feelings and pushed against the walls that survival had erected. Being the queen of pretense was no longer an option. She decided aloud, "It's time."

Getting up from her place in front of the fire, she walked across the room to her desk, turned on the lamp and sat down upon the weathered chair. Letting the lengths of her hair fall, she leaned forward. She thought for a few minutes about all that had happened throughout the past months; all that had brought her to this moment, this place. Taking her pen from its holder, smoothing the paper with the palm of her hand, she paused, and began to write.

Dear Galean, she wrote.

Chapter Twenty-Eight

Keep some room in your heart for the unimaginable

—**MARY OLIVER**, "Evidence"

Galean watched the truck back out from his driveway. The large print across the side spelled out words that belied his feelings: Goodwill. There was nowhere in his body, his spirit, or his mind that he felt any goodwill. As they turned to drive away, the two young volunteers from the organization waved and smiled. Wendy and Brian, good people, driving around the city picking up used clothing. *Used clothing. Helena would be horrified.*

Galean stared down at the itemized records of Helena's belongings that the Goodwill people had left with him. A list of her belongings now gone, dispatched. Nothing of Helena remained in the house, no piece of clothing, no hairbrush, not even a favorite pen. Nothing except a wedding picture, the one taken outside the city hall on their wedding day. Why he'd kept it sitting there on the dresser in his bedroom was a mystery. His desolation and anger were so tangled, he couldn't feel where one feeling ended and the other began. Giving away all of Helena's possessions was a way of clearing, of finding a way forward through brambles of bewilderment.

In the kitchen now, Galean reached into the liquor

cupboard just above the fridge but then took a step back, closed the cupboard door. It was Monday morning. He was due at the hospital by nine o'clock. He had students from the university medical school waiting.

Lately his world felt like a string of freight cars on a hill, each coming uncoupled from the one in front. Moments following moments, each one detached from the other. He stood in the middle of the kitchen wondering what to do next, which direction to take. His medical, rational self knew what was happening. Grief and shock. His world was in freefall.

Shaking his head, flexing his shoulders, he walked from the kitchen to the front hall. Opening the closet door, he took down a gray wool jacket and grabbed his blue scrubs that were wrapped in a plastic garment bag. Every movement was rote. Arm in one sleeve, his jacket hung off his shoulder. Keys on the hall table under a pile of mail. Letters, ads, a package, all left where he'd tossed them each day. This time, as he dug for his keys, a letter fell from the pile and landed by his foot. It was a personal letter. Postmarked Ireland, the return address, Clonakilty. When Galean leaned down to pick it up, his hand shook for a moment. He exhaled, blowing breath between his lips, his cheeks puffed. His legs felt like jelly. Ripping open the envelope, he walked to the living room and threw his garment bag on a chair. *Time—I don't have time.* But he knew he had to read Casey's letter. Everything else, everyone else, had to wait. He sat on the edge of his couch and pulled the letter from the envelope.

September 9, 1982
Dear Galean,
I am so, so sorry about Helena. She was beautiful. She was magical. She loved you. And when she loved, as

*you know probably more than anyone, she loved with
a warrior-like fierceness. And she knew all too well how
painful it was to love someone; how frightening.
How must it be for you, trying to understand. Wonder-
ing what were those moments like when she decided …
How many unanswered questions are you sitting with?
I'm so sorry that I'm not there to be across the table
from you, and listen. I'm sorry that you are there, alone.
So, my dear friend, might you consider something?
Might you consider coming over here to Ireland? To
stay with me, walk by the ocean, sit and weep. Bring the
broken parts and we'll try to put them back, you and I.
Come. Come home. Come find where you began.
We've talked a lot about feeling as though we've left
pieces of ourselves behind, and we need to go back and
find them. Maybe that's what we could do. Help one
another find those we left behind. Maybe we might even
finish that book?
Bold of me to say all this? Now? Probably, yet this may
be exactly the right time.
Anne Morgan has my number.
Casey
P.S. Do you remember these words?
"If we stayed true to the narratives of our lives, might
we move deeper into ourselves and the life of another?
Might the truth of love permeate old fears and release
us to what is possible?"
You wrote that, Galean.
C.*

Galean placed the letter on the couch but let his hand
linger, his fingers still holding the edge. He could hear
Casey's voice, could imagine how she closed her eyes and
pressed her lips together when thoughts from somewhere

inside stirred. *Help one another find the pieces? Oh, Case, what a romantic you are.* His heart beat against his chest. Warning him? Or urging him on?

The phone jarred him. Reaching across the letter to the side table, he picked up the receiver. "Yes? Dr. Laihy here."

"Sorry to interrupt you, Doctor. You have some students waiting in your office."

Galean glimpsed at his watch and discovered he'd lost thirty minutes somehow since he last checked the time. He quickly gathered his things again to leave and, as he was locking the front door, he paused. Running back into the house, he picked up the letter and stuffed it into his book bag. He felt something that could have been called hope.

"ANNE MORGAN HERE." SHE SPOKE WITH THE ASSURANCE she'd gained during the past few months.

Dr. Morgan had assumed the role of Chair almost immediately after Casey had departed for Ireland. Last April, winding down the semester, had been busy enough that Anne now understood those times when Casey had called her at the end of a day, saying, "Anne, meet me at the Inn. I need wine or I may have to commit an illegal act." Of the challenges that she had inherited from Casey, the latest was a faculty member who showed no interest in teaching and made no secret that she only wanted to further her research. She held a tenure-track position, so firing was out of the question. Anne suspected that the student who was due in her office any moment for a scheduled meeting was coming to air another complaint, and it was only September.

Phone receiver balanced on her shoulder, awaiting a response, she nodded toward the new doctoral student who appeared just then at her door. She beckoned him in, pointing to the chair by the window where she liked to sit and talk with students. Motioning to the phone, she mouthed, "I'll only be a minute," and waved to the chair.

"It's Anne here," she said again into the phone.

"Dr. Morgan, it's Galean Laihy."

Anne knew right away this call was not going to be "only a minute."

"Galean," she said, "I have a student with me. Could you drop by my office later today?"

The pause was long enough for Anne to think he'd hung up.

"Galean?"

"Sorry," he stammered. "I—I just wanted to get Casey's number in Ireland."

"More reason for you to drop by." She was protecting Casey, Anne thought, from herself. She needed to know what Galean was thinking, why he wanted Casey's number. "Five o'clock?" she suggested.

Galean agreed. Five o'clock.

"THERE," ANNE SPOKE TO THE EMPTY OFFICE. SHE PUT THE coffeepot on the tray along with two mugs, cream, sugar and, just in case, a small bottle of Drambuie to charm the coffee. As she prepared for her guest, it occurred to Anne that Casey and Galean's once-ordinary lives were surprisingly tumultuous. From the moment of Casey's stunning announcement in January ("I think he's going to ask me to marry him!") to now, with Casey gone, and Galean and Helena's marriage ended after Helena's suicide. Anne worried that more tragedy might be hovering down the road. *So unlike Casey to get everything so wrong. So much tragedy.*

The buzzer for her office rang. Walking to the door, she opened to see Galean standing at the threshold, a phantom of himself. She remembered him being a tall, vigorous man with shining eyes and an easy smile. This afternoon, that man had disappeared. He'd lost weight, his jacket hung loose on his shoulders. He was a portrait in gray: gray skin, gray demeanor, gray smile—or the want of a smile. Right away Anne thought, *Drambuie it'll be.* Here was a man who needed a friend. Everything about him portrayed someone abandoned.

"Let me have your jacket. Here, come sit." Anne took his arm, guiding him. Still holding his arm, she looked into his face. "Oh, Galean. Such tragedy. I'm so sorry."

Seeing the concern in Anne's face, Galean grimaced and said, "Guess I'm looking pretty bad." He dropped into the chair by the window and immediately recognized it: it was the leather chair from Casey's office. If he believed in encouraging signs, this could be one.

"Coffee?" Anne held the pot and waited.

"Thanks, I will, and a little drop of that," he said, pointing to the Drambuie.

Anne prepared his coffee and handed it to him. Settling in, Galean leaned back in the leather chair, his fingers laced around the coffee mug. Anne sat opposite him, letting the moment hang in the air.

"I got a letter from Casey today," said Galean. "She's asked me to come to Ireland."

Anne waited. Watching his face, she wondered, *Has he*

come to ask what I think? When Galean didn't continue, she prompted him: "And?" She sipped her coffee, her eyes just above the rim, zooming in on Galean's face.

"Casey told me I could get her phone number from you."

Anne lowered her mug to her lap, splashing drops of coffee. The conversation was moving faster than expected. "So, you've decided? You're going?" she asked him.

"Yes," Galean responded, surprising himself, because up until that moment he hadn't been sure. But, sitting here in Anne Morgan's office, his intuition, his disappointments, his grief, his regrets, all accumulated like the final paragraph in one of his articles or the chord that resolves dissonance into harmony. All said, go, now.

"Yes," he said again. Gathering himself and dropping his mug onto the side table with a resounding clear intent. "So, what's her number?" And he smiled easily for the first time in months. Relief tracked through his body. Knowing that he'd go felt right, inexplicably right.

Anne stood up from the chair, placed her mug on the side table and walked to her desk. Pausing, she turned to Galean and smiled. "I think maybe you two are listening to one another, finally." *And why did it take tragedy to make it happen?* she wondered. Taking a pen, she opened a top drawer and pulled out a red scribbler, one that resembled a school composition book. As she leaned forward and opened the book, she heard Galean getting up from his chair. She looked up. "Are you leaving?"

"In a moment," he said. "As soon as I get that number. But I want to show you this." Galean took Casey's letter from the book bag he'd dropped to the floor. "This is the reason I need and want to go." He handed the letter to Anne and waited while she read it.

After what seemed a long time to Galean, Anne finished reading. When she looked up at him, she was smiling. "'Help one another find the pieces' ... that's our Casey, ever searching. And, how beautiful, that she is asking you to come home." she handed the letter back to him. "Here's her number in Ireland. Write it down—now."

After he'd written the number into his pocket notebook, Galean offered his hand to Anne.

"Oh, for heaven's sake," said Anne, refusing his hand and instead opening her arms to draw him into a warm embrace.

EVERYONE—HIS COLLEAGUES AT THE HOSPITAL, JAMES ATWAter at the university, his medical students—all sighed a collective relief when Galean announced he was taking a leave and going to Ireland. They'd always known his intensity, and lately they sensed a man who was bearing deep sadness. They noticed his weight loss, his sentences that drifted into the air and his eyes, dulled.

James had conferred with Galean's colleagues at the hospital who had wanted to convince Galean to talk to a professional, someone who would help him untangle his guilt from his grief. Thus the day he requested a leave to go to Ireland to study, to find his home and maybe his birth family and to write. He was given unquestioned consent by the hospital and university administrations.

Within two weeks of receiving his letter from Casey, Galean was ready to go.

SEPTEMBER 10

Casey had been marking off the days since mailing her letter to Galean. Once she wrote the words, once she began to hope, urgency set in. Andy's words spurred her on. *Whatever it is you're afraid of, walk straight into it and, pardon me, but screw the fallout.* That's exactly what she was doing.

Casey was in her favorite corner of the small living room. The desk, the typewriter, the lamp and the window looking out over the Atlantic Ocean, all giving her a sense of comfort. She sat looking out to the horizon. The latest chapter of the book was stalled. Preoccupation with the possible reactions Galean might have to her letter clouded her mind. In the last half hour she had typed only seven words:

Loving is possibly our most creative act ...

Leaning now into the typewriter, hands poised above the keys, she continued.

and losing love sends us reeling into directions that change us forever.

The phone rang. Casey jumped. Looking at the clock, she saw it was twelve noon. Maybe it was Claire calling, wanting her to come for lunch. Or maybe?

She picked up the phone from its stand. "Hello?" Damn, how she hated that hesitant, girlish tone. "Hello," she said again, this time firmer, more confident.

He laughed that deep, rolling chuckle. "Yeah, Casey, not good to be too tentative. Be assertive."

"Galean Laihy—well, well!" She rolled her eyes again. *What a ridiculous thing to say. Of course it would be him.* She knew. She knew he would call.

"Let's make this succinct," he said.

Some things never change. Galean getting on with it.
Casey grinned at her reflection in the window. "Okay, here's succinct: What's going on?"

"I'm making arrangements," he told her. "I'm coming to Ireland. You and I are going to finish that damn book and I'm going to figure out where I truly come from. Put that to rest for good. Got a place for me there?"

Casey heard both urgency and hesitation in his voice. She had to ask. "Galean?"

"Yes?"

"Are you sure about this?" She waited throughout his silence. "Galean?"

"I'm still here, Casey. And, yes, I'm very sure."

Eyes closed, her forehead furrowing into deep lines, Casey clamped her fingers around the receiver. She drew in a long, slow breath and let it slip through her lips before saying, "Nothing is the same, Galean. Do you know that?" Right away, Casey wanted to breathe those words back into her chest. *Of course he knows nothing is the same. His life is in pieces.* "Oh, Galean, I'm really sorry," she told him. "What a stupid thing to say."

"Case, no apologies. We're going to be tripping all over one another in the next while, let's just …"

Casey broke in, "Screw the fallout?"

Galean snorted. "Screw the fallout?"

"Just something I'm learning to do lately," she explained. "I've decided to stop tiptoeing through life. And that's why I wrote the letter." Something in her chest changed. Breath wove its natural path and the old pinched feelings loosened, like a steel brace unlocking.

"Good letter, Case. It'll be a fine prologue to our book."

"Come soon, Galean, before we lose our nerve again."

Chapter Twenty-Nine

Beginnings are such delicate times.

—FRANK HERBERT, *Dune*

"You know those times when you find that final jigsaw piece under the couch, days after you've given up on the puzzle?" Casey said to Claire, who was standing next to her with four pints of Guinness balanced on a tray. The pub was ringing with laughter, men standing at the bar leaning into the latest town stories. Cigarette smoke floated like fog across the room.

Casey had her own pint of Guinness in one hand, the other hand was shoved into the pocket of her jeans. "You know what I mean, Claire? That's how I'm feeling right now. Any minute Galean's going to walk through that door. And he'll be the missing piece."

"Could ya give me a minute, Casey?" said Claire. "You're flying meters above the rest of us right now." She laughed as she nodded across the room. "Let me take these over to that table, then we'll go upstairs and you can tell me everything."

The "room upstairs," as Claire liked to call it, had been transformed over the past months. The windows that overlooked the street below shone like the hopes of the women who arrived each week to write. A table that had been donated by Jimmy, who'd been part owner of the pub, took up the center of the room. It stood on sturdy, curved legs that spoke of another era when furniture made a historical statement. The chairs placed around the table were "odds and sods" as Casey called them, each one different like the stories ground out by (or, on a good day, flowed from) the women on Wednesday afternoons. Two floor-to-ceiling bookcases were home to favorite books brought in by the writers, many from Casey's collection. A portrait of Oscar Wilde over the fireplace stared down at the room as though daring those who came here to be dangerous and brave, to be bold and write.

Casey climbed the stairs, walked down the narrow hallway at the top and opened the door into the writing room. The air held anticipation and trepidation.

Yesterday afternoon eight women sat around the table listening to one another's unfolding stories. Some were poems, some imaginary narratives of lives wished for and some glaring descriptions of lives held up to the light. Many afternoons, Casey was stunned by the depth of story the women brought into the room. A grandmother wrote about—and through—the pain of being estranged from her daughter and her grandchildren, a family torn apart by The Troubles, her son-in-law killed in an IRA bombing. One young woman, a mother, found release in the whimsical, writing about an Irish faerie who helped single moms raise their children. No idea was ever quashed. Casey could not remember a time when she felt so called to her craft as a writer and a teacher. Breaking away from her old life back in Canada cleared a path, one where she tripped over the possibilities.

"Hello?" called Claire. "Are you in there?"

Casey looked up to see Claire standing in the doorway.

She hadn't heard her enter the room. "Oh sorry, guess I was drifting."

"So, my friend, what's going on?" Claire asked as she flopped onto an orange, nubby wool couch, a donation from John, who was now part-owner since Jimmy's death. The Troubles were not far from home, even this old pub.

"I've heard from Galean, and he's coming to Ireland." Casey's voice smiled.

Claire watched a red blush leak into Casey's cheeks— and were those tears? Yes, there were wet drops easing from the corners of her eyes. "What are the tears for?" Claire sat up, ready to comfort her friend, yet not sure if that's what Casey needed. She opened her hands; a bidding, an invitation to her friend. "What do you need, Case?"

With a startling thump, Casey dropped her forehead to the table. She spread her arms like wings from her body, assuming the posture of a novitiate nun prostrate before her altar. A faint and muffled sound rose. It sounded to Claire like a mixture of laughing and weeping.

Casey raised her head and caught Claire's curious glance. "I think I'm finally entering my body," she explained. "I think I found that piece of the puzzle under the couch, and it's not him at all. It's me."

"Okay, Casey. You're kind of scaring me, because I really don't know what you're talking about."

Sitting back into her chair, Casey rubbed the spot on her forehead that had hit the table. "Woo, that hurt. But maybe I needed to get my attention."

Claire moved from the couch and walked over to sit beside her friend. "So?"

"I've been living somebody else's life, thinking every-thing was fine." As Casey spoke, her hands flew into the air like two exclamation marks. "I've been tiptoeing around, being intellectual about everything, pushing back anything or anybody who tried to interfere with my pretend life story."

Claire sat forward and rested her chin on folded hands. She'd known Casey only a few months, from May into September, yet it had been long enough to know conversations with her required wait time—interludes during which she needed to air her thoughts before landing upon what she wanted to say. Thus, Claire waited. Bursts of laughter from the pub below traveled through the floorboards.

Casey, still rubbing her forehead, mused for a moment with closed eyes before she let the words spill into the air. "Remember yesterday when we all sat in this room and just talked before we started to write?"

Claire nodded, still waiting.

"Marissa, the youngest in the group, was sitting right where you are now. How old might she be, maybe thirty-two?

"'Bout that, I'd guess," answered Claire.

"Do you remember how she stunned all of us?" asked Casey.

"Okay, Casey, I know you are going someplace with your thoughts, but I really am getting older here."

Both woman laughed.

"I'm almost there, Claire, almost. Give me another minute." Casey reached across the table and slid a small pile of papers over to where her friend sat. "These are some of my notes from that session." After flipping through the pages, she stopped and exhaled a triumphant "Yes! Here it is. Forgive me for being dramatic, I think what Marissa said was life-changing." Without a pause or chance for Claire to comment, Casey started to read from the page.

Life hones us and chisels us into becoming more,
until we seemingly arrive quite distant from where
we began and yet at the same time we are aware of
having come full circle.

Casey placed the page on the table and put her hand over it, asking, "Is that not wisdom?"

Claire raised her eyebrows, cocked her head to one side and opened her mouth to respond.

Casey, though, was too quick. Grabbing another paper, she said, "And, here's Elizabeth, maybe the oldest in our group, our grandmother. She wrote lines from a Shakespearean sonnet when she wrote about her estranged daughter, remember?"

Claire, realizing there was little point agreeing or not, sat back biding the few seconds it took for Casey to read the lines.

When to the sessions of sweet silent thought,
I summon up remembrance of things past,
I sigh the lack of many a thing I sought
and with old woes new wail my dear time's waste.

This time Claire grabbed Casey's arm, and said, "You're right, Case, these women are good, but what's your point?"

Looking crestfallen for a moment, Casey took a breath, then recovered. "I'm supposed to be here, Claire. I'm supposed to be in this town working with these women, we've all landed here to teach one another." A tinge of excitement bordered her words. She paused. Then, curling her fingers into fists, the next words exploded: "I'm here because it's time for me to begin again. The days of waiting to see what might happen if, are over." Putting her hand over her mouth, Casey paused again, let her hand fall onto the table. "Claire, I feel as though I might have been party to Helena's death."

Claire took Casey's hand. "No!"

"Wait, let me finish," she told Claire. "Helena needed her friend—the friend I had been to her once, long ago—and I wasn't there. I was too busy feeling humiliated. Too busy thinking Galean was on the road to destruction, so I did all I could to sabotage their relationship. Not consciously. But I wasn't there for either of them, Galean or Helena."

The banter and joking in the pub below seemed quieter now. Casey took a sip of her Guinness. She dropped her head and Claire thought she might be weeping. But when Casey lifted her head, Claire could see her eyes were clear.

"You know, Claire, I've been running since the time those ambulance drivers pulled me from that wrecked car when I was little." Telling the story of her parents' deaths had been Casey's way of beginning to work with the women in the writing group. She ushered in her bravery and encouraged the others to follow her.

Claire knew more than anyone how the accident affected Casey, and she reached now for her hand. "What do you need to do?" she asked.

A remarkable moment occurred for Casey as she sat there. For the first time in her life, she knew what she needed, and she let the words go. "I need to forgive myself. I need to forgive myself for surviving that accident, for not being able to fix Helena's shattered life—which was beyond fixing, I see now." A long inhale, then: "I want to sit with the old sadness and let it drift away."

Claire, still holding Casey's hand, squeezed it. And they both smiled. Something had just happened in that room upstairs. Something left unsaid.

"EXCUSE ME, SIR. WE'RE GOING TO BEGIN OUR DESCENT TO Shannon Airport soon, so I need to ask you to put your papers and pens away and push your briefcase under the seat. Many thanks." The flight attendant stood, hand on the back of Galean's seat. She smiled. "Writing a book are you sir?"

Galean gathered up the manuscript he'd been reading and revising as he crossed the Atlantic from Toronto. "Well, actually I'm co-writing with a good colleague of mine. Her name's Casey MacMillan." He had no idea why he needed to tell an anonymous woman about Casey, but saying her name was like a reality check for Galean. He was truly about to see her again, within hours.

The pages now safely lodged in his briefcase and under the seat in front, he sat back, reached into the breast pocket of his suit jacket and pulled out a letter. He'd written it after the lights had dimmed on the plane, when he knew he'd not be disturbed by his sleeping seatmate or a flight attendant wanting to know if he needed anything. It was a letter to Helena.

Dear Helena,
Wherever you are, I want to believe you can hear me, or you can feel me. It doesn't seem strange at all to be writing to you. In fact, it helps the ache. We did have an unusual bond didn't we, you and I?
Before I get to Ireland ... yes, I'm on my way to Ireland ... I need to say some things that I didn't get to tell you. I need to clear the decks.
We were phenomenal, you and I. You were my phenomenon. You were like a comet, a celestial body flashing across the sky. Nothing and no one could hold you

*for long, you needed to move on. Maybe I caught you
just as you were heading for the sun. Maybe you were
already on your way home when we met, when I saw
you in that operating room, you moving with such grace
and deftness, you outshone even the surgeons.*

Galean felt the gentle downward movement of the plane,
the leveling, and the descent. He swallowed to clear his ears,
and only then realized the wet on his cheeks. His seatmate
hadn't stirred from his cross-Atlantic slumber, for which
Galean felt relieved. How does one explain writing to his
dead wife? Surreptitiously wiping his cheeks, he went back
to the note,

*And you captured me. Enchanted me. I remember feel-
ing crazed. When I discovered in those early days how
haunted you were, I wanted to swoop you up, rescue
you from your demons. I think I failed you, Helena. But
please know that, for whatever reason fate led me to you,
I am changed because I knew you. I am braver and I
am surer that what I'm about to do is true. Remember
how you used to say, when you got exasperated with
me, "For God's sake, Galean, just show up in your life,
just once"? Well, here I am. Showing up.
May you be at peace, my darling Helena.*

As the wheels of the plane touched the ground, the man
beside Galean unfolded his arms, opened his eyes, turned
to him, smiled and said, "Ah, we're home."

A KETTLE BOILING; A TOASTER POPPING; HAM SIZZLING;
music from a radio on the mantel above the fire: Casey was
taking care of her friend.

The crackle of flames in the fireplace, the one built into the white stone wall in the living room, reached into the depths of Galean's oldest memories. He fought the urge to close his eyes *only for a moment*, he thought. When he opened them, a soft woolen blanket covered him from his neck down to his stretched-out legs and feet. Casey sat opposite him in an old brown leather chair that bore a resemblance to every brown leather chair he'd ever known her to own.

Something soothing flowed through Galean as he peered through still half-shut eyes at Casey, who was sitting with her legs curled under her a hand folded against her cheek, her hair falling over her face, the proverbial book open in her lap. "What time is it and how long have I been asleep?" he asked her.

Casey looked over at him and smiled, "Oh, I think you fell asleep the moment you hit that chair after we arrived back from the airport."

"But weren't you cooking breakfast? Did we eat and I missed it?"

"No," she told him. "I had only just started when I came in and saw you sound asleep, so I put everything away for now."

Shaking his head, Galean sat up and folded his hands over the blanket. "Thanks for meeting me at the airport, Case. That was very kind. It must have been early for you."

"It was and that's fine, so be quiet." She grinned.

Galean felt as though he'd been transported through a time warp or a parallel universe and everything from his childhood on had shifted into a happier place.

"I put your things in the bedroom," Casey said. "When you feel like it you can make yourself comfortable in there, unpack, whatever you need to do."

"Um," began Galean. For the first time in many years, he experienced a shy hesitancy in the company of Casey's forthright manner. *Was there just one bedroom? One bed?*

Sensing his uncertainty Casey said, "We haven't talked about the details, have we? Don't panic: I'm going to sleep out here on that wonderful old couch over there by the window."

She pointed to the far end of the room to a daybed with great high-scrolled arms and pillows tumbling across it, a wool blanket draped over the back. The couch sat away from the wall, just below the long window that opened to the cliff and the sea beyond. Casey had no reservations or qualms at all about spending her nights out here among the rows of bookshelves and the sounds of the ocean. She felt an unfamiliar sense of contentment and ease. Her friend was home.

"So," she said as she unfolded herself, stood up and took the blanket from Galean's lap. "Let's go have breakfast and talk about what's next."

Chapter Thirty

She had no need to ask why he had come.
She knew as certainly as if he had told her that
he was here to be where she was.

——**LEO TOLSTOY**, *Anna Karenina*

Experts at dodging real feelings, Casey and Galean found themselves in unfamiliar territory. Life resumed as though they had escaped to a parallel universe. Casey drove to Clonakilty for her classes. Galean walked the beach, wrote and thought about what he needed to do next. Here in this new place, this new time, they were careening off the beaten path of safety and plunging ahead like two explorers on their way home.

A week passed, then two weeks.

Casey continued to drive into Clonakilty to work with her fellow writers each Wednesday afternoon. Word was moving throughout town that the professor from Canada who rented the old O'Neill cottage was giving writing courses—free! Casey, who still received her salary from City University while on sabbatical and whose trust fund from her parents sat accumulating in the bank, was not concerned about being paid for her passion, teaching.

Claire was largely responsible for word spreading about Casey's class, because a writing workshop upstairs in the pub, she felt, enhanced the place. And now, with growing numbers of hopeful writers, Casey decided to create a second group on Friday evenings, this one accompanied by rollicking music from the pub below.

She had discovered a renewed vigor stirring within herself. Letting her cloak of survival slip from her shoulders, she experienced a lightness in her body and she dared to consider that her soul might be healing. There were mornings when her feet touched the floor with a sense of anticipation Casey had never known or allowed herself to feel.

One afternoon after the last writer had left, Casey, feeling reflective and thoughtful, wondered aloud to Claire, "Maybe that little girl's spirit that I buried all those years ago when my family was whisked away, maybe she's come alive?"

Claire's response was less philosophical and more of the moment. "Any chance you might be feeling how it is to be admired and loved?" she asked Casey. "You know, right out there in the daylight? If that's true, then hang on 'cause it's a hell of a ride. No wonder you're finding all this new energy—that, and the Guinness, will do it." Claire grinned, her eyes, cheeks, and mouth all in playful harmony.

AT THE COTTAGE, GALEAN HAD LITTLE PROBLEM SUCCUMBing to Casey's care. She cooked for him, found audio tapes of his favorite Mahler symphonies, watched and waited when he found his way to the ocean for his morning solitary walk. She noted the first time he laughed his infectious chesty laugh. She kept their manuscript out of sight, biding her time and his, waiting for the moment when the words would come to him again.

Two weeks into his stay, Galean went to pick up Casey at the pub where she was meeting with her Wednesday afternoon writing group. It was his first venture beyond the cottage and the ocean; his first attempt at driving on the "wrong side" of the road.

When he arrived at the pub, he walked toward the bar, smiling, ready to greet Claire, but there was still a sadness in his dark blue eyes that belied his smile, as did his unkempt appearance. His khaki jacket was gently rumpled. He needed a haircut.

As soon as she spotted him approaching the bar, Claire realized right away who he was and understood why Casey wanted to care for him. *This is a man who could be wearing away*, she thought to herself. To him she said, "And you must be Galean?" She reached across the bar, offering her hand. "Are you here to pick up Casey? I think she may be almost finished up there. Go on up if you like, or you could make yourself comfortable here and I'll pour you a pint."

"I think I'd just like to stay here and wait," said Galean, pulling out a stool and taking a seat. "Casey's told me what a good friend you've been since she arrived."

"She's definitely invigorated the wannabe writers in our town," said Claire. "Who knew there'd be so many?" She handed him a Guinness and offered a basket of chips, which Galean accepted and ate with gusto. Watching him devour the chips, Claire smiled, "Is the woman not feeding you? And would you like something more substantial? I have meat pies, they're my specialty."

Galean shook his head no and, with a handful of chips, smiled a thank you. He felt himself settling into Claire's welcome.

UP ON THE SECOND FLOOR IN THE WRITING ROOM, SIX
women sat around the old round table, each one listening and leaning into the story being told by Nancy, who'd
arrived that afternoon excited about what she'd written in
her journal. She read with the lilt and confidence of someone who was finding her own voice.

Casey listened with her eyes closed and allowed the
words to wash over her. The moment felt familiar. Inner
lives unraveling in the company of trusted others. What was
noteworthy was the quality of attention the women offered
one another. This was Casey's gift to them. A safe place to
be seen, to be heard.

Nancy paused when she noticed Casey's eyes shut.
"Casey?"

Opening her eyes, Casey shifted in her chair and turned
toward Nancy, asking her, "Why did you stop? You write with
a flow and you have such care for your own story. It shows."

Nancy still hesitated. "I wondered what you might be
thinking. I may look as though I'm feeling confident …" she
said with a look to the others, "But some of that bravado
leans on your approval."

Around the table others nodded their heads.

Casey straightened in her chair, placed her hands on
the table and folded them, her fingers intertwined. "This is
probably some of the scariest work we do, reveal ourselves
to others, even in as safe a place as we have. It's also some
of the most beautiful. Think of your reflections on your life
as a gift to the rest of us. And to yourself."

Nancy smiled at Casey's words and, feeling encouraged,

picked up her journal and read the last few sentences.

Whenever I'm not sure about the road ahead or even the ground under my feet, I look for the details around me that speak of hope. And I remember the poet Emily Dickinson, who wrote:
Hope is the thing with feathers, that perches in the soul
and sings the tune without the words
and never stops at all.

Casey smiled over at Nancy and said, "You chose one of my favorite poets, and one of my favorite lines."

Nancy hesitated for a moment and then grinned, like a child receiving an unexpected award.

"Hand me your journal," Casey said to Nancy, taking the yellow notebook. Without pausing she wrote a note across the bottom of the page:

You are a seeker, so wonder at the details and particulars, hold them up to the light. Yours is a story of adventure, of hope, of courage kindled.

She handed the journal back to Nancy, who glanced at what Casey had written, and her grin broadened. "Thanks, Casey."

"Glad to share that with you. I'd like to say that quote is mine, but someone—my thesis advisor, actually—wrote it in a letter to me once. Many years ago." Casey paused, wondering at how that note from Andy remained clear and distinct in her memory.

For a few minutes there was only the crackling and hissing of the peat burning in the fireplace. There was a comfort in the silence. The world outside the room was troubled and rancorous, but for these women, for that afternoon, Casey was giving them "ground under their feet."

When the session came to a close and the women were making their exit, Casey listened to the buzz of their voices as they walked down the stairs and into the pub. They usually stopped for a drink before heading out, and today was no exception. Sitting there, soaking in the silence of the vacated room, Casey listened to the muted hum of voices below and one voice stood out: Galean's. Somewhere inside she smiled. Reaching across the table, she gathered up the pens and pencils, blank papers and some notes left by her writers. After she'd placed everything in her book bag, she made her way to the door and switched off the light. She paused at the top of the stairs and let a sense of pleasure stream through her body. He was just a few steps from her, down in the pub, chatting to the regulars, no doubt having a Guinness.

As she emerged from the hallway at the bottom of the stairs, Casey looked around the room and saw him sitting at the bar. He turned toward her as though he'd been waiting and anticipating, which indeed he had.

"Over here, Dr. MacMillan." Galean grinned and beckoned her to take a seat at a stool beside him at the bar.

"This man has been waitin' here for hours." Claire told Casey, looking pleased.

"Not so, Case," said Galean. "I arrived a while ago, but not hours."

They were all playing with one another like young teenagers who knew secrets about one another.

"Come, sit here, Casey." And again he beckoned to the seat beside him. "I want you to meet this man who's been telling me all about ways I might search out my family. He's suggesting I go to Northern Ireland, to Belfast. That's where

I was adopted as a boy, remember?"

His eyes were brighter than Casey had seen for a while; the darkness was beginning to lighten into the clear blue that she remembered from years ago. She took a seat on the stool and shook her head no to Claire, who was holding up an empty tulip-shaped pint glass. Offering her hand to the man beside Galean, she said, "Hello, I'm Casey. What's this about sending him to Northern Ireland?" She smiled, but part of her felt a twinge of hesitation.

Since arriving in Ireland in April, Casey had heard a lot about The Troubles, of the civilians being killed and maimed in bombings in Belfast and Derry. And, in July, Claire had arrived at her door one day distraught and worried because a friend had called from London to say she'd been in Hyde Park, the day the IRA detonated bombs in Regent's Park.

"Fortunately," Claire had reported in between gulps of air, "Ginny was on the fringes and came away relatively unscathed." That day Claire had suggested to Casey that she not travel into Northern Ireland for a while, "till things settle down a bit," she had said. So now, hearing Galean talk about going to Belfast unsettled Casey.

"Do you think that's wise, Galean?" she asked him, then signaled to Claire that indeed she would have that Guinness.

"I'm not thinking immediately, Case. We have work to do, you and I. That last chapter needs rewrites and we've hardly had time to regroup. So no, if I go at all, it'll be just before Christmas. Not to worry."

Claire set the pint in front of Casey and said, "And anyway, Casey, no one's going to do anything nasty like bombings or shootings in the Christmas season."

"Well, all right, I'm listening, Claire. However," she

swung around facing Galean her mouth set, her eyes flashing, and told him, "if you go, Galean Laihy, I'm going with you."

LATER THAT EVENING, GALEAN AND CASEY PULLED TWO OF the plump, cushioned chairs over to the fireplace. The fire blazing up with new peat cast golden reflections around the small room. The sounds of the fire were gentle, not the crackling or hissing of wood. There was almost no sound, only the glow of the flames.

"What do you think about starting to write tomorrow, Casey?" Galean stared into the flames. He spoke softly as though thinking aloud.

"Do you think you're there? Are you ready to write again?" Casey looked over at his face lit by the fire. She experienced a lump in her throat that threatened tears. She shifted to sit upright, placed her feet on the floor. She extended her hands to be warmed by the flames.

Galean rested his head back against the chair, closed his eyes. Without opening them, he started to talk, his voice still soft and reflective. This was Galean from the inside out, vulnerable, exposed and unshielded. "Do you think it's time, Casey, that we began to mend our heartbreaks? You and I have tried to circle around our aches for too long. Maybe we need to try something new." And he smiled over at her. "Maybe we just need to be in the middle of it all, together. As messy and uncertain as it is."

Casey let a breath go, the air warming her lips. Still gazing at the fire, she took an inward breath and asked the question, afraid in so many ways to hear the answer. "What are you saying, Galean?"

He sat up, opened his eyes and turned to her. "I'm saying, it's time we moved on ..." He paused, waiting for the next word.

Casey felt the old panic, the memory of humiliation when she had misinterpreted something he'd said to her. *Please God, not again.* But she waited for him to finish.

"Together," he completed the thought.

His meaning now clear, the lump in Casey's throat dissolved.

THAT NIGHT CASEY MOVED BACK INTO HER BEDROOM. SHE and Galean; one room, one bed. She cleared out drawers in the dresser, moved her clothes to one end in the closet, emptied a shelf in the bathroom cupboard. Like beginning the third act of a play, the intermission over, the two of them moved quietly around one another, Galean unpacking a suitcase still holding shirts and sweaters. Casey making room on shelves. Not much said except the practical questions, the businesslike work of the unspoken. They were about to become a couple, sharing one another's space, not yet certain what it might mean.

"Casey, where shall I put my typewriter?" He had not taken it out of its case since arriving. He stood in the middle of the room, holding the case at his side.

Casey stood at the threshold to the bedroom with her arms folded, leaning against the doorframe. "Galean, tomorrow is another day; a new day. Let's decide how all that will be, in the morning. You look tired." She walked to him, took the case from his hand and placed it on her desk by the window. Turning back toward him, she put her hand on his cheek, kissed him on his forehead. "Let's call it a day, my dear."

Chapter Thirty-One

We live and breathe in this touchable, sensual world, and through trauma, through grief, through recovery we heal in order to be touched again in the right way.

——**DAVID WHYTE**, *Consolations*

ife brings the unresolved to the top in unexpected ways. Casey's ever-present mantra was no longer a hoped-for ideal or a thought. It was reality for her and for Galean. The two of them lived unexpected moments over the next few days; moments when they saw one another with new eyes.

One morning, three days after they had decided to share a room and a bed, Galean came in from his walk along the road to the beach. He was breathless, his hair wind-blown, his face flushed. "Casey," he called from the doorway. Excitement propelled him through the threshold.

Thinking something had happened, Casey dropped the frying pan onto the stove, eggs sliding across it, almost slipping over the edge. "Are you all right?" she called out as she darted from the kitchen.

"Whoa, I'm fine," Galean assured her. "But I had an epiphany out there." He whirled his arm, reaching toward the ocean. "Remember we talked about clarity yesterday?" Before Casey could nod or answer, he barreled on through.

"What we have, you and I—right here, right now—is the kind of clarity you get when you wake up in the morning and you know the answer to the calculus problem you've been working on for days." He flopped onto the couch, reached his arms up, folded his hands together behind his head. "You and I are like that calculus conundrum. We've worked on it so long that now, suddenly, it's clear."

Casey cocked her head to one side, squinted at Galean, hand on one hip. "It's clear? Umm, I'm not sure ... what you mean."

"Okay. Tonight, we're going to the pub, Case, we're going to sing and dance. We're going to celebrate."

She walked over to the couch and sat down, facing him. "What's going on?"

"This morning I woke up and I watched you sleeping. You had your arm thrown over your forehead and I could swear you were smiling. It was the most beautiful thing I've seen for a long time. I felt like Rip Van Winkle waking up from a very long nap. And I knew I'm exactly where I need to be." He looked over at Casey, letting his arms fall beside him, "Casey, can we move on? You and I? Not today," he continued, smiling. "But someday, soon, can we ..." He paused, looked down at his hands, "I'm not even sure if I'm in a place to ask you ... but when I come back from Belfast can we talk about, maybe ..."

Casey exhaled a slow long breath. The details of life, the eggs on the stove, the toast popping, the smell of freshly brewed coffee, all were a backdrop for the leap Casey and Galean were about to make. Into the unknown.

She leaned forward, elbows on her knees, chin cupped in her hands. She inhaled, seemed to be holding her breath, then air escaped through her lips as though she were releasing months, maybe years, of wondering. "I've been waiting, wondering what's next, for such a long time," she said to Galean. Turning to him, she offered her hand. "Now I'm scared."

Galean furrowed his forehead, as though trying to absorb Casey's doubt. "This was not the reaction I was expecting," he said. "I thought we were moving past the 'being scared part.'" He reached over, took her hand.

They sat for a few seconds like two people introducing themselves to one another, their hands folded together. Casey started to draw away, but Galean held his grasp.

"You're scared, because?" he asked her.

"The other night, when we first slept in the same bed, I was terrified that you'd want to…that you possibly assumed that…" she stopped.

"We'd make love?" Galean guessed.

"That's partly it. Afraid we might, and afraid we might not. Try and figure that out." Casey shook her head. "I feel stuck, Galean. Stuck in my old story that tells me that loving only means losing someone, eventually, so why even go there? I took that leap with you once, and we both know how that one turned out." She smiled, an ironic smile.

"You know what, Case? We need to move this conversation to clear, fresh air. We need to begin again, let's leave the old memories, the old stories, here by the fire, and let's you and I go walking." Galean stood up and, grabbing Casey by the hand, told her, "Turn off the stove, get your coat. We're going out."

A COOL FALL WIND PLAYED GAMES WITH YELLOW BIRCH leaves scattered across the grasses by the cottage. Silver branches waved to Casey as she stepped from the house. A hesitant sun drifted from cloud to cloud. Wrapped in a new Irish knitted shawl and her wool scarf that tucked its warmth under her chin, Casey pulled on her waterproof hiking shoes, tied the laces, stood up and walked down the front steps, out to the road where Galean waited. His black leather jacket and a herringbone wool scarf tossed around his neck kept the cooling wind at bay. He stood looking out toward the water, the wind catching that lock of hair over his forehead, the one he kept trying unsuccessfully to smooth down. Pausing for a few seconds, Casey stood on the front path, watching him. Pure pleasure moved across her skin. A new feeling. No denials, no rebuffing.

"Want me to drive, Casey?" Galean asked when she neared him. "I'm getting good at driving on the scary side, haven't hit anybody yet." He grinned.

"No thanks, we don't have far to go and I feel like driving. Anyway, I'm supposed to be the only driver, according to the rental people." Standing at the open car door, Casey called over to Galean, who was about to open the passenger door. "Where are we going?"

"Drive along Inchydoney Road," he told her. "We can park there and walk to the beach."

Climbing into the car, they settled themselves into a comfortable silence.

Casey smiled to herself as they drove along N71 to Inchydoney Beach. Galean's take-control manner that morning was in some peculiar way, freeing. She felt an impetus, a momentum, something shifting.

FOR A WHILE, GALEAN AND CASEY WALKED ALONG THE beach, the sounds of waves and wind accompanying them. Rippled sand drifted over their boots. Occasionally a scoundrel wave tried to wash over their feet, causing them to dance a two-step that is a familiar part of the beach stroll. They walked, their shared silence enclosing them in a cocoon.

"Mind if we sit on that rock over there, or would you rather climb up to that bench?" Galean asked, pointing to a weathered wooden bench sitting just over a dune, partially hidden by waving long grasses.

"Let's go over to the bench." Casey said.

In a few moments they reached the bench, where they both sat, arms folded, Casey wrapping the wool shawl closer around herself, Galean zipping his jacket and tightening his scarf around his neck.

Staring out at the ocean, Casey spoke into the breeze. "So. About our stories. What did you call them—our 'old' stories?"

"I think we've let them get in the way of what's possible," Galean said while he, too, stared out at the ocean. "For you and I." Taking a moment to let his breath feel easier, he leaned into his story. "I am through being—can I use your favorite word, Casey? Being *cloaked* in my old story. I'm finished with living out of everything I think has been done to me, by people I don't even remember." Hard edges crept into his words. *People I don't even remember.*

Casey turned her head only slightly. "I think I know exactly what you mean," she told him.

And they began the historical human practice of clearing

the way forward, telling one another the truth of what had brought them to this place, this time. Galean took the lead.

"My father, so I'm told by my adopted mom in Canada, was a raucous Irishman, maybe almost a caricature of the fighting Irishman." Galean threw one arm across the back of the bench and continued. "Maybe I'm hoping for the impossible, but I need to know what happened. That's why I want to go to Belfast to search out anything I can find about him or about his family. I know his name, it was James McCann and he lived in County Antrim in the North. Mom finally told me stories before she died. But I need to know more. I mean, was he shot because he believed in something, or was he just a rowdy?"

"Galean, how will you ever find that out?" Casey asked him gently.

"I don't know the answer to that question, Case. Maybe I won't discover anything I don't already know, but I'm here, and I need to try."

"When did he die?" she asked.

"I think it was sometime in the late nineteen thirties. I should know when, shouldn't I?" His head dropped forward onto his chest for a moment; his hand still rested on Casey's shoulder.

She reached up and intertwined her fingers with his. "Not really, Galean. Life's taken you in a whole other direction." She took her hand from his, pulled her shawl across her body. "Why do you need to know?"

The question startled Galean. Wasn't it clear? "He was my father, Casey. His blood runs in my veins. What if he was a violent man? Maybe I might be too."

"Galean. Let that thought go, let it fly. You are one of the gentlest men I know."

He grinned. "How many men have you really known? Remember, we've been friends for a long time and I haven't seen crowds of men surrounding you."

"Stop it!" Casey punched Galean's shoulder, a light, playful smack. "You know what I mean. Look how you were with Helena, how gentle even at the worst of times." Casey was immediately sorry she'd mentioned her.

Galean bowed his head again, put his hand over his eyes.

"I'm so sorry," she told him. "That was stupid of me. I should know better." She put her hand on his sleeve.

While Casey was struggling to regain the moment, Galean stood up. "It's getting cold here and the wind is picking up. Why don't we go back to the house?" He started to walk back along the beach.

She watched him walking away. Remaining on the bench for a moment, Casey wondered if he noticed she wasn't trailing after him. Just then he turned.

"You coming?"

"Are you going to finish your story?" she asked him.

Galean let his shoulders drop, plunged his hands into the pockets of his jacket. "Okay, but can we do this back at the house where it's warm?"

Casey jumped from the bench and ran past him along the shore. She wanted to lighten the moment, bring the two of them back to where they'd been before the mention of Helena's name, before Galean's spirit darkened.

BACK AT THE HOUSE, CASEY HELD HER HANDS TO THE GENTLE flames in the fireplace while she waited for Galean to sit beside her and return to his story. Two steaming mugs of strong tea sat waiting on the coffee table.

Since arriving back at the cottage, he'd disappeared into the bedroom, door closed. When he emerged, clean-shaven, hair smoothed down, he walked to Casey and stood over her. He folded his arms. She wondered, was he cold? Uneasy? Upset?

The answer appeared.

"Casey?" said Galean. "Will you understand if I ask you not to talk about or mention Helena for a while?"

He seemed restless, walking away from her, then turning and walking back. Sitting down on the edge of the couch, he leaned forward with his elbows on his knees. A man wrestling with a demon? Trying to say what he was feeling?

"I'm trying very hard right now, to separate myself from everything that's happened in the last year," he explained to Casey. "It's the only way I can see going forward."

Moving back against the softness of a woolen cushion, Casey folded her legs and feet under herself, yoga-like. She sat for a moment, wondering how she might respond. And she decided. "No more interruptions, Galean. I promise." But Casey knew they'd have to return to this moment. Sooner than later. Or they'd be traveling down the same old path, avoiding the tough moments, glossing over real feelings.

As though there had been no interruption, no uncomfortable moments, no mention of Helena, Galean picked up his story from where he'd left it back on the beach.

"After my dad was shot, my mother, the woman who birthed me, was left with four children: me, a brother and two sisters. She was left with nothing, which tells us more about my father, doesn't it?"

Galean took a moment to sip on his tea. Casey waited.

He looked over at her, his eyes shining with tears he refused to shed.

"Can you believe?" he asked her. "It's like a B movie. I was the youngest, so she tried to keep me with her. My brother and my sisters were left at some kind of adoption home, and I never saw them again."

Casey looked away. How hard it was to sit silently, letting him go directly into the painful places. How hard it was for her not to say, "It's okay, you don't have to do this," because she knew eventually he'd have to go there, and … so would she. She had not ever heard Galean's whole story. She only knew, and only from him, that he'd been brought to Canada as a boy when he was seven years old. Brought to live with a farming family. And she had never quizzed him about where his life actually began. She had her story, he had his, and she'd been content to leave it that way; to leave their past lives back there with everyone they'd left behind. It seemed now that this might not be an option any longer. Something was shifting like tectonic plates in the earth, silently, surely.

Casey realized she'd drifted away for a moment. The whack of Galean's mug landing on the small table startled her, brought her back into the room, where the fire glowed and a misty rain began drizzling against the windows.

Galean went on. "She left me, a baby in a basket, sitting on the steps of a children's home. Left me. Left me …" His voice trailed into silence.

Casey reached for his hand and chose to be quiet while he pulled these old images from his past. Galean needed clear air to continue his story. Here in this cottage, he needed her to be his friend and hold this space. Their conversations over the years had sometimes been heartfelt, but never like this. All those years of buried emotions that, like weeds, can tangle and suffocate feelings, were mingling in this moment.

"How does a woman leave her child, her baby, like that and walk away?" He covered his face, ashamed that he could no longer hide the sorrow of being left, of feeling diminished.

Casey knew as much as another can, how much pain he held. She wanted to reach for him and draw him into her chest, yet knew this was the moment he needed only her presence, nothing more. She knew this, because it's what she wanted too, just his presence. And so she sat, bearing the years.

"Actually, I guess in some ways she rescued me," Galean mused. "When the people at the Home arranged for me to travel to Canada in later years with a group of young orphan boys, I was the lucky one, placed in a farmer's home, where I was taken care of. I went to school and lived a normal life with a new family. Now though, I need to find my birth family, or at least some answers, and maybe discover who I am." Galean stared into the fire, as though seeing himself, that young child.

"Do you think there will be answers in Belfast?' A cautious question. Casey treading softly.

"Casey." Galean picked up the now cold tea and held the mug in both hands. "Really? I don't know. But right now, here in this room, I can tell you that I have to at least try. And I need to go soon, before I shut down again."

And, just as suddenly as he had traveled to his darkest places, he seemed to arrive back in the room. His expression, the old Galean, anticipating. Ready to move on. Pushing against the softness of the couch, he moved to stand. Walking toward the kitchen, he whirled his hand in the air, the helicopter signal they'd had for years saying, work awaits. He called back to her.

"Casey, let's have something to eat, make a hot pot of tea. It's time for you and me to get to work. We promised one another we'd write, and I'm not going to Belfast—or anywhere—till we put some words on the page."

Casey recognized his cunning maneuver. Work was the antidote to pain.

"Come back here, Galean," she said. "I don't think you're done yet. Don't you think you need to do what you came here to do, before you go to Belfast? You know, purge your demons?" She could hear him filling the kettle. Then silence.

He appeared in the doorway, kettle in hand. "I'm done with purging for now," he said. But," Galean held the kettle in the air, pointing toward Casey. "Maybe it's your turn to tell your truth."

"I might not be ready," Casey replied and started to walk away, heading for the kitchen, edging around him.

Galean reached for her hand and instead grabbed her arm. "Okay. I'll give you this." Taking a long breath, still holding her, he ventured into their no-man's-land. "You and I have lived so long in our heads, dodging, weaving, running for cover from real life. We've fed our mutual demons. We've become emotional cripples. Maybe we need to write about that, or maybe we should just stop right now and see what honesty feels like."

Casey tried to pull away from his grasp. Galean held on.

"You're right, Casey. I'm not entirely done yet. But I want to clear up something that I think is the elephant in the room. Yeah, maybe one of my demons."

And he took his hand from her arm, walked to the

window and looked out over the yard, out to the road. When he turned back to Casey, he folded his hands prayer-like, put his fingers to his lips, waited a moment and spoke, words he was sure were going to penetrate, and possibly hurt, Casey.

"Okay, here goes. For all the anguish Helena experienced in her life, for all the pain she felt and for all the confusions we caused one another, I know without a doubt, she was out-loud alive. She was here in the world. She did not hide away in her head."

"Well," said Casey. "So much for not bringing up Helena's name. Really, Galean, deal with that demon. You really need to deal with all of that—the marriage, your guilt. So don't infer that I'm hiding away. Call me when Helena has left the room." She turned toward the door into the kitchen and stopped. Turning back, she folded her arms across her chest. Old shame took over. "I think I might have said this once before, Galean: you can be an idiot. And today, right now, you've just outdone yourself." Casey disappeared into the kitchen.

Oh the fragility, the delicacy of telling intimate truths.

Galean yelled after her, "Have we finished?"

A door banged.

Chapter Thirty-Two

Someone I loved once gave me a box of darkness.
It took me years to understand, that this too, was a gift.

—**MARY OLIVER,** "Thirst"

Confusion, bewilderment and embarrassment. Three rogue spirits accompanied Casey along the path behind her cottage. A misty rain coming in off the ocean cooled her frustrations, most of which were about herself. The muddy path she followed collected tiny eddies of water, squishing underfoot like protests. Her thoughts flogged the self-assurance she'd experienced not that long ago. Older voices, critical ones, chattered inside her head. She felt propelled into the wind, leaving the warmth and safety of the cottage and Galean behind.

Casey stopped when she realized she was charging ahead, not knowing why or to where. A small sign with an arrow pointed toward Clonakilty. She looked back at the cottage, a distance behind her, misted in the fog and rain. Standing in what was becoming a drencher, Casey thought about her conversation with Claire one day after writing class, and her own words bounced back to her: *I need to forgive myself. I need to forgive myself for surviving the accident that took away my family. And forgive myself for not being able to fix Helena's shattered life.* Disregarding her wet hair, sodden sweater and gradually soaking shoes, she experienced what Galean might have called an epiphany.

"Helena?" Casey called out. "You were one powerful lady." Her voice shouted into the wind and at that moment, she turned toward the road that partnered the path to town. Birches and small shrubs waved as though beckoning her to pay attention. A car, Casey's car, was creeping along the shoulder. The window on the driver's side lowered. She could see Galean peering out at the rain, squinting through the fog. Stumbling through the wet grasses, avoiding dripping tree branches, she floundered out to the road.

"Casey, what in the hell are you thinking?" Galean called. "Are you nuts? You're soaked through!"

For a second, Casey considered turning back into the woods, but instead she threw her hands into the air and shrugged her shoulders. Running around the car, she jumped into the passenger seat. Galean leaned across her to shut the door, saying no more.

Casey stared through the windshield, watching the rhythm of the wipers. The two of them hunkered there in silence, each waiting for the other to speak. Finally Casey twisted around to face Galean, her left hand balanced on the dashboard. He steeled himself for a Casey chiding, but instead she nodded her head and smiled, slow and apologetic.

"I'd like us to start this conversation all over again, Galean. Yes, I want to go where there's music tonight. And yes, we need to talk about how we dodge and weave around one another. And yes, Helena was 'out-loud' alive. And yes, I'm an idiot." She turned and looked out at the pouring rain, intertwined her fingers and dropped her hands into her lap. "So, here goes."

Thus on the drive back to the cottage, twisting her fingers in and around themselves, Casey began to yield up her buried truths to Galean. She talked, she squirmed from side to side, she paused, she rocked. Anything to release the tangled web of old survival stories.

Wise and cautious, Galean drove along without comment. He concentrated on watching the road through the sheets of rain, yet he heeded what was happening here beside him. Casey's voice beat a kind of cadence in the car. The energy of holding primitive experiences.

When they pulled into the drive and parked the car, Galean leaned across Casey (who was still talking) and opened her door. Afraid to break into the stamina of her story, he waited till she stood at the door of the cottage, before getting out of the car. He watched a new Casey, a clearer Casey, an enlivened Casey. Putting one foot on the ground, he eased from the car and stood up. For all the thought-out reasons he'd decided to come to Ireland—his father's death, resolving his own anger—he realized at this moment that the real purpose waited there at the door of the cottage.

"Are you coming in or are you going to stand there getting drenched?" She called back to him before disappearing into the warmth.

Once they were both inside, Casey walked on into the bedroom, saying she needed just an hour or so to get dried off and that she needed "some alone time."

After her door sighed shut, Galean listened for a moment, wondering, *Should I knock, make sure she's all right?* Never had she been so forthright with him. Never so vulnerable. He decided to honor what she needed. He walked over to his briefcase, took out his pens and notebook, sat on the couch and wrote everything she had spoken about in the car. Not wanting to lose any of the pieces she had given into his care, he sat in front of the fire putting her story onto the page.

I was one of the luckiest, most-loved little girls.
My dad would walk with me after he got home from
work in the evening. We'd go across the street to a
wild, grassy field, and we'd walk and talk. He'd
quote lines of poetry that he remembered, and I'd
ask him to tell me more. He never got impatient.
He'd just walk along in silence for a while and then
would offer another line, another poem. I guess I'd
be about four at the time, can you imagine? My
mom would wait supper for us and in the winter-
time, it might be dark by the time we arrived home.
I sometimes wonder if I just dreamed all this, but
I can hear him, I can smell the wool of his jacket.
I only remember one time when he got cross with
me—one time. I was playing over by our house, he
was raking leaves. I picked up a stick and started
whirling, not knowing that Tommy my neighbor was
whirling with me. Stupid boy! I whirled too close and
caught him on the edge of his eye. Probably could
have taken his eye out, but I kept whirling and he
crumbled to the ground, crying. My dad just let a
yell out, picked Tommy up and ran into the house,
shouting at me to get in the house. I was so startled
to hear him raise his voice, I froze right there. He
actually came back to me a few minutes after he'd
taken Tommy into my mom, who was a nurse. He
gathered me up, sat me on his knee, and he apolo-
gized. Apologized for yelling! Can you imagine?

But everything changed, everything disintegrated.
One Sunday afternoon drive. That's when it hap-
pened. The car racing through a stop sign, out there
in the country. Crashing into my dad broadside,
sending us spinning and rolling. My aunt with
me, in the back seat, falling across me. She saved
my life. My dad's chest was crushed, my mom was
thrown through the windshield.
That's when everything disintegrated. That's when
I lost my way.
But it was also when I knew there was only one
person I could depend on—me. That's how I made
my way through the maze of foster homes. The
people who pretended to love me. That's when I
discovered the mythology of love and the truth of
loss. And I survived.

Back in the warmth of the cottage, Galean imagined
Casey as she had been in the car, telling her story. He held
the pen hovered above the page of his notebook that was
balanced on his knee. He closed his eyes. When he opened
them, Casey was standing there watching him.

"You're writing," she said. "Are you working on the last
chapter?"

He put his pen down on the page and beckoned to her
to come closer. Leaning forward, elbows on his knees, he
rested his chin on folded hands and looked up at her.

"What deep thoughts, my friend?" Casey asked.

"I wonder," said Galean, "if you are able, can you tell me
the rest of your tale? Just the way you've summoned it? What
would you think of changing the beginning of our book? What
would you think of telling our own lost stories right up front?"

Casey said nothing, only stood still, watching him.

"I'm thinking about the kind of book we envisaged when we started, Case. Seems a long time ago."

"And?" she asked him.

"Your story, my story," he replied. "Real loss, not just what the scholars write about. Maybe that's where we need to start. Our own disappointments, our own illusions." Galean sat farther forward on the couch, as though urging himself, and her, on. Watching for the stubborn, tightening of Casey's jaw, he sat back against the cushions.

She folded her arms across her body, squinted a bit and cocked her head. "I'm not sure what you mean."

He patted the sofa cushion beside him. "Don't run and hide on me now. I mean we tell it all: your family, the foster homes, Helena. My dad."

"And what about everything we've written thus far?" Casey asked, lowering herself onto the couch.

"It would still be part of what we want to write," said Galean. "But we—you and I—need to show up on those pages, just like you did today. In the car."

"Okay," said Casey.

Galean hadn't expected agreement. He'd expected an argument; a polemic on the rules of scholarly writing. Startled, puzzled, he cocked his head, looked over at her apparent calm and waited.

Getting to her feet, Casey turned to him. "And when we're done? When we've finished unraveling ourselves and writing about it? What then?"

Galean shrugged his shoulders and opened his hands. "Let's see what happens."

Casey walked over to her desk, sat down, put her hands on the keys of her typewriter. "Okay."

HOURS LATER, AS THE AFTERNOON THREATENED TO WANE and the rain became a mist, Galean leaned away from the table in the kitchen where he'd set up his portable typewriter, his notebooks and his pens. He folded his hands and interlocked them across his chest. Casey, at her desk by the window, was typing steadily, her gaze intent upon the words that were emerging.

Both had promised to write until they reached the depths of what each had pushed away and down, until they found the place where love had been left in mothballs (Galean's word). She was struck by the length and breadth of his new-found compassion, not only for her but for himself; he marveled at the energy generated in the silence between them.

"Casey?"

"One minute," she responded. "I'm almost there." A minute later came a final click—a period. Casey lay both hands on the desk, one on either side of the typewriter. She exhaled a small prayer, something she hadn't done for years. *Thank you.*

Galean stood and walked over to Casey and, without hesitation, he put his hands on her shoulders, leaned down and kissed the top of her head. "Let's go have a Guinness."

Casey leaned back and looked up at him. "Aren't we going to read?

"Not right away. Let's let what has happened here this afternoon breathe." He brushed his hand across her neck. "Like a nice red wine needs air and time, so do we."

THEY COULD HEAR THE MUSIC AND THEY COULD FEEL IT TOO as they stepped from the car outside Claire's pub.

"Ah, listen to those fiddles, hear the bodhrans," Casey said as she skipped a few steps just ahead of Galean.

"Bodhrans? Come on, Case, you've been here longer than me." Galean grabbed her hand to pull her back beside him.

"Drums, Galean. They're drums. You have to know this if you want to live in Ireland."

For a moment everything around them faded. Only the words "if you want to live in Ireland" hung in the air.

"I mean … I mean …" Casey stammered.

Galean took her arm and put it through his. "I'd say you're making what I've been wanting to say really easy."

Calls of greeting welcomed them into the gaiety. Casey believed it was the first time in her life, she knew how being lighthearted might feel.

Claire approached through the crowd, her sweet-sounding voice welcoming the two of them. Linking her arm through Galean's she led him to the bar "Good talk, good conversation—that's why you're here, Galean Laihy."

Casey spotted two young women she knew from her writing classes, and she walked over to sit with them at their table. An older man far at the end of the room was singing a lament in company with the fiddle. Claire's son, Peter, just turned fifteen, tended a peat fire that was taking the chill out of the late autumn's chill. How far it all was from the dilemmas and the wounds of just a few months ago.

Up at the bar, Claire handed a Guinness to Galean and introduced him to the tall man standing to his left. "Galean Laihy, meet John MacAuliffe, the man who lets me run his pub."

John clasped Galean's hand in a firm handshake, which belied the sadness in his eyes.

Claire leaned over the bar and placed her hand on John's shoulder. "John and his brother were one-time co-owners." She let her hand linger on John's shoulder while he leaned into the bar, wrapping his hands around the pint. For a second and only that long did the man's face sadden, a memory echoing and fading. His broad shoulders sagged within his greatcoat. He bowed his head.

When Galean looked over at Claire with a quizzical expression, she shook her head, placed a finger to her lips.

In the next moment, John stood up, reared his shoulders and said, "Jimmy was me brother."

Claire picked up a cloth and began polishing the oak, not taking her eyes off John. Several patrons who were nearby, standing at the bar, quieted their voices. Galean saw the wet at the corner of John's eye.

"Mindin' his own business up in Londonderry a few years ago, was Jimmy. Was in the wrong place … got caught in crossfire. One of those times when it was hard to tell the bad guys from the protesters or the police. He shouldn't have even been there." John paused, looked at Claire. "And it's not over yet, 'specially in Belfast," he added.

Galean and Claire both glanced over at Casey, who'd been laughing and smiling with her writer friends but was now quiet, looking over and mouthing to them, "What's going on?"

The unusual quiet at the bar drifted to the tables and made more obvious the last resonant note of the fiddle.

John smacked his empty Guinness onto the scarred wooden bar. "Let's have a song for Jimmy."

The fiddle began a long, slow lament. The bodhran was silent, the pipes lay hushed, the flute quiet. No one spoke. Without warning, and with almost a joyous rush, Claire and John began double-clapping their hands in the air. Then John broke into a broad grin and Claire whirled out from behind the bar. The drum took up their rhythm, the fiddle the song, and the flute joined in along with the pipes. Galean, watching it all, felt something old, like a melody humming from a far, distant place.

Two women sitting at Casey's table stood and pushed back their chairs. They pulled her up beside them as they began to sing:

Whack for my daddy, oh
Whack for my daddy, oh
There's whiskey in the jar, oh

Soon they had Casey skip-dancing across the floor over to Galean, who without a hesitant breath, took her hand and danced her around the tables. Music sang out across the room. Casey sensed a vitality she was sure could be seen. Her hand in Galean's, she felt that not only was she dancing, she was the dance.

Over by the bar, John lifted his glass toward the ceiling, "Here's to you, Jimmy. I love ya." And his pint in one hand, the other arm reaching for Claire, they step danced around the room.

Love and loss, things invisible and beautiful, uncertain and hopeless—all led to Jimmy's pub that November evening in 1982. And life carried forward into the next day, where it announced hope.

Chapter Thirty-Three

May the wind always be at your back.

—IRISH PROVERB

"Do you think lives have a trajectory?"

Casey, warming the soles of her feet, perched her heels on the leather stool directly in front of the fire. Her mind wandered around the edges of thoughts, like small flames catching the contours of peat briquettes. They were home from the pub.

As she hunkered down into the cushions on the couch, Galean, who was sitting on the shaggy carpet, leaned against the pillowed edge, resting his head by her leg. Before he had a chance to say what he thought about trajectories, Casey mused on.

"I think our lives—yours, mine—have been headed to this place for a long time. Maybe we are exactly where we're meant to be, right this moment." She was aware of the warmth of his face on her leg.

In fact, Galean was smiling. He continued staring at the fire, looking into the flames, taking a moment to be sure about what he wanted to say. "Before I try to answer that deep, dark question," he began. He liked to tease Casey's introspections every so often. "I need to tell you something. Or, more to the point, I need to ask you something, which might answer your question about trajectories."

"Galean, you're making fun of me and you're being dim."
She patted the top of his head, a teacherly gesture. And she
laughed a shrugging, breathy laugh.

He hoisted himself up onto the couch beside her. "Casey,
when I go to Belfast I want you to stay here; that is, if you
are still thinking of coming. It would be time alone for you.
Time to write and time to consider what I'm about to ask
you."

"Wait a minute," she stopped him. "Don't I get a say?"

Putting his hand over hers, he shook his head. "Not
about this."

When she started to protest again, Galean placed his
finger lightly against her lips. "Too much is going on there
right now. Shootings, bombings. I talked to Claire and John
about it at the pub and they agree, you shouldn't go. But—"
and he pushed on through, before she could interrupt. "I
want us to do something, and maybe this is what our trajectories have in mind." He paused and inhaled a long deep
breath. "Before I leave in a couple of weeks, I want us to
write that book, maybe even finish it and be able to send it
back to the university to our editor."

Taking another long breath, Galean pressed on. "I want
us to walk by the ocean, dance again, sing again, and ..." He
closed his eyes for a second, like the diver on the top board.
"And ... would you think about marrying me?" Then, just
as quickly as he had uttered the words, he moved on, telling her, "But you don't have to do that today. I mean, think
about marriage. You know, we can ..." He sputtered.

A sound escaped from Casey. It was somewhere between
a burst and an intake of breath, close to a choke. "Are you
kidding me?" she asked him. Moments after the words were

out in the air, she wanted to stuff them back into her throat. The old Casey, who had learned to survive by resisting love, was terrified. The person she was becoming—the true Casey whom she'd hidden away all these years—turned to Galean, raised her legs onto the couch and curled them under herself. Sitting cross-legged, rather like a wise shaman, she rested her hands on her knees. She looked over at the man sitting before her. He smiled.

"Casey, maybe for the first time in our friendship … our long, long friendship—"

She cut him off. "Galean, quit loitering." She grinned. That word—it had to do with one of the first disagreements they'd had in the midst of coming to know one another. Galean had accused her of "loitering" around the point.

"I'm feeling like a grown-up, Case," he continued, more to the point. "I'm going to Belfast. Going to put the broken parts of me back together. Then I will return to you, stay for a while, go back to Canada." He paused then, waiting, watching her face.

"Whoa, whoa," she said. "Let's just start here, now. To answer your last question? Yes."

"Yes?"

"Yes. Life isn't going to wait around for the next time our trajectories crash into one another. So go fix your story. Make peace with your history. And, Galean," Casey said, then paused to take a long breath and let it whisper between her lips. "Make your own peace with Helena's spirit. And then, my love, soon you'll be back." Here she stopped, words backing up into her throat.

Galean waited, wise man that he was.

"Then, we'll go home," she said.

THAT NIGHT THEY SLEPT, CASEY'S HEAD ON GALEAN'S shoulder, her arm across his chest. Once every hour or so, Galean awoke and shifted a bit, but Casey, feeling like the protected child for the first time in many years, stayed right where she was.

"SUN, GALEAN! LOOK—SUN!"

Dazed and befuddled from the restless night and the Guinness, Galean struggled to open his eyes. When he could see beyond the fuzziness of early-morning waking, he found Casey at the window with her arms outstretched to the blue sky and the sun. She was childlike in her delight; innocent in her faith that all will be well. In fact, those were her very words—"All will be well"—as she had drifted into sleep the night before.

Galean watched her for a moment, his head still foggy. Then, lifting himself, he turned his body toward the sun, toward Casey. Propping his head on his hand, his elbow dug into the pillow. "Casey, you once said to me that you and I would never make love; that sharing our stories was intimacy enough." Sitting fully upright now, leaning against the brass rails of the bed and the pillows, he asked her, "Would you maybe ...?"

Looking over her shoulder, a gentle smile playing at the corners of her mouth, she waited a few seconds (a long few seconds in Galean's perception) before responding. "I did say that, didn't I? That part about 'sharing stories is intimacy enough.' Well ... let's just say I may have changed my mind."

Casey's stroll back to the bed, back to Galean, was like a walk along a very long, very high bridge, and finding certain ground on the other side.

LATER THAT DAY, THEY SAT SIDE-BY-SIDE AT CASEY'S DESK IN the living room: she in the old leather wing chair, he perched on the edge of a chair made of pinewood that he'd dragged from the kitchen. Casey's hand rested lightly on Galean's leg.

Earlier, as they had lain in the grace and tenderness of one another, Galean laughed at gentle murmurs emerging from the two of them. Casey swore they were like sounds coming from the universe. Later Galean would call it, with a smile and in his doctor voice, "post-coital euphoria." Both laughing, they'd risen from the bed, stepped into jeans, threw on thick sweaters and shuffled out to the living room.

Neither wanted to undo the depth of feelings. Each knew something mysterious had occurred, as though they had experienced one another fully—both body *and* soul. Two people who historically circled one another, not daring to land, were discovering the mystery they had only ever talked about: love.

Beyond, in the bedroom, music from Casey's cassette player drifted as background to what they needed to say, needed to write. Mahler's *Adagietto*, his Fifth Symphony; his tribute to his beloved wife. Delicate musical longing filled the silence.

"We have to find the right words," Galean mused. "We need words. This is what we write about, Case—this. Our journey."

On this late autumn afternoon, Casey and Galean were discovering the length and breadth of one another.

"We're learning how it feels to show up in our lives, Galean," said Casey. "Maybe that's what we've been missing. We've been so afraid of breaking hearts, one another's and our own, that we created our own mess while trying to avoid the messiness." Moving her hands toward the typewriter, she let her fingers search out the words.

"Quick!" Galean said as he grabbed a pen and a notebook. "Write what you just said!" Without waiting for her, he started scrawling her words.

And so they began. And over the next hour, they talked, they wrote, they exclaimed "Yes!", they shook their heads vehemently, they laughed, they sighed.

The daylight now dimming and the wind rising across the grasses out by the road, Galean sat back with his hands behind his head. "I think we have it. I think we know where to take the last chapter, and we know now, how to change the prologue. We've done it, Case. We've done it." Her non-response slowed his elation. "You don't look convinced. What's wrong?' he asked.

"Wait a minute," said Casey and then disappeared into the bedroom. After a few minutes she came back, accompanied by the drifting strains of Mahler's Fifth. "Listen, listen," she told Galean as she stood still with her eyes closed. "The music … it's all about being broken and finding the way back."

Taking a seat at her desk, Casey typed some words then pulled the paper out and read what she had written. She gripped the page, as though keeping the words from disappearing.

Burn your way through the fog of old stories. Walk straight ahead into your own truths. Be brave, be dauntless; love as though your life depends upon it. And it does.

And when the loss occurs, and it will, take it in as you might a homeless soul. Take care of it. Be generous, be gracious, be grateful that you chose the hard path and the broken heart. Now you can say, "I am alive."

Galean seemed to stop breathing. Exhaling one slow breath of air, he lifted his hand up toward Casey's face. "You are extraordinary," he whispered.

She shook her head. "No. *We* are extraordinary."

The moment passed and the writing moved forward. Every so often, one or the other would go into the kitchen to pour some tea, grab an apple. There were silences while Casey typed, her fingers flying across the keys as though her life and Galean's life were unfolding onto the page. They wrote about their hopes; they wrote about their anguish; they wrote scholarly opinions of love; they wrote about the experiences of love they'd collected from their students and colleagues, friends, ordinary people. Nothing of them, of their longings, their disappointments, or their forbearance had appeared on the page before this day. Till now.

At one point Galean said, "Wait, just one moment." He went over to his briefcase and pulled out a sheaf of papers, which he rummaged through until he miraculously found some journal entries he'd written. "Look at this, Casey. Its's a Rumi quote that I kept from when we were working together, years ago." He paused for a moment, remembering when he'd first come across the quote. Never had he allowed himself to think the words might be about the two of them. "I never showed it to you because I thought you'd think it was too emotional, not scholarly, maybe too close to the bone."

Casey stayed seated and silent while Galean stood there, holding the page. She looked up at him as he read the quote to her:

The minute I heard my first love story
I started looking for you, not knowing
How blind that was.

Galean stopped. Swallowed, then began again.

Lovers don't finally meet somewhere.
They're in each other all along.

Both took a long breath.

Casey turned back to the typewriter and rested her fingers on the keys. Staring at the darkness out beyond the window, she waited, let her shoulders drop. Speaking as though to the landscape, the road, the cliffs and the ocean, she said, "First we live chaos, misunderstandings, mistakes, then we discover truth. And then we do it all over again, and again and again …"

"Great quote, Case. Who said that?"

"I did. One day in class when Rob—remember my handsome student Rob? When he wanted to know if we humans ever get life right."

"And do we?"

"Depends what you think 'right' looks like."

Galean smiled. This was the Casey he knew and loved. The thoughtful, ever pensive, ever hopeful Casey.

"Okay," said Casey, "let's not get off track. We need to

keep going. If you're leaving sometime in November, we have work to do!"

Ah, yes, of course, he remembered, *Casey the director*.

The jangle of the phone jarred their return to the pages. Casey started to reach over to grab the receiver but Galean stopped her.

"I'll get it, Case. I know who that might be. John at the pub said he knows a good car rental agency." He smiled. "Actually it's his. Seems people in this town are multi-talented. They own pubs, or manage pubs, and they rent cars."

One more ring, and he picked up the receiver. "Hello? Oh my god! Anne? How good to hear your voice. No, not at all, we were just about to finish up for the day and Casey will be delighted to talk to you."

Taking the receiver Galean handed to her, Casey leaned forward and placed her elbows on the desk. She balanced her chin on one folded hand and held the phone to her ear. A broad smile lit her face when she heard the voice of her old friend from City University. "Anne!" Casey exclaimed. "How lovely!" And then, less than a beat later, "Okay, what's wrong?"

"Nothing changes," laughed Anne, who was sitting in her office remembering how Casey was quick to anticipate trouble. "You always go for the worst. Nothing's wrong—I just got into the office. Dean Atwater met me in the parking lot and was asking about you and Galean. So here I am, ready for news and ready to report back."

Casey had relaxed into her chair and was sitting back with her eyes closed, listening to the familiar low-throated cadence of her friend's voice. "All is well here," she told Anne. Actually, you called at a good time. We've been writing all day and we think we've got something worthy of all the time we've spent trying to say what we needed to say."

"So, taking a sabbatical was a worthy choice for both of you?" Anne asked.

Casey paused for a moment and looked over at Galean, who was intent, reading over their day's work. "Oh yes, it's been more than we hoped for." A bit of a flush began at her neck and rose to her cheeks. "And how are things there, Anne? You must be getting ready for second semester, going crazy trying to satisfy everybody's scheduling requests."

"Not to worry," said Anne. "That's all in motion. Really what I wanted to know is, how is Galean doing? He was not in a good place when he left here a few weeks ago."

Another glance over at Galean, who was still reading, whirling the pen intertwined in his fingers—his way of physically concentrating. "I'd say he's doing ..." and Casey paused for a second, lowering her voice, before saying, "very well. It was a good idea for both of us, coming here. For both of us and for many reasons. Galean is leaving soon for Belfast. He's going to search out his family's story, and maybe find some peace for himself."

"Are you going with him to Belfast?"

Anne's question was Casey's first opportunity to consider what Galean had said this morning—she answered, not hesitating. "No. I need to stay here and keep working on the book, and he needs to be on his own, not worrying about me while he does his family search."

Galean looked up from the papers. He smiled.

"When is he going?" asked Anne.

"Soon," Casey told her. "In fact ... I think he's intending to rent a car soon, near the end of November."

Not looking up, Galean nodded yes.

An evanescent moment passed between Casey and Galean. Sadness? Melancholy? It drifted into the dust particles that were dancing in the late afternoon sun.

"Well, I just wanted to check in with you," said Anne. "Make sure all is well ... and that you, Casey, are fine?" She seemed to be wanting to say more.

"Everything I hoped for, Anne, is landing on my doorstep. The book is well on its way—I'll be writing a new last chapter while Galean is in Belfast, we'll finish it up before he goes back after Christmas ... and ... Galean and I are talking about marriage, maybe as soon as end of December." Her smile took flight.

"Oh Casey, that's wondrous! For both of you."

Casey felt a flash of unease at the memory of the last time she and Anne had had a similar conversation. "Okay, Anne, I'd better get back to work. Galean seems to be beckoning. I'll call you again after he leaves for Belfast. Take care of yourself."

"Good. Yes, Casey, you take care of you, and be happy. Your life is unfolding."

Casey smiled as she put the phone down. *Life unfolding,* she mused. *Sounds so tranquil.*

THREE WEEKS LATER, MID-NOVEMBER NOW UPON THEM, Casey stood at the front door and waved Galean into the darkness of an early morning. She watched until the flicker of his taillights faded into the distance and then stooped down to pick up the paper from the step. She felt an early morning chill run through her body as her eyes registered the news on the front page: another incident of paramilitaries ambushing soldiers in Belfast; Margaret Thatcher's anger, part of a visceral editorial; tanks at the border to Northern Ireland; people being searched on the streets of Belfast. All of it intruded upon Casey's unfolding life.

She wished she'd gone with him.

Chapter Thirty-Four

If you suddenly and unexpectedly feel joy, don't hesitate.
Give in to it.

—MARY OLIVER,
"Don't Hesitate"

Sitting in the old dark-leather chair, Casey stared out the
window, watching the sky blend into ocean off on the
horizon. Her hands rested on the worn arms of the chair.

Feeling unsettled and restless, she had walked a mile
and a half that morning along the stretch of beach she and
Galean had frequently strolled. Bundled in her navy wool pea
coat, a red wool toque pulled down to her eyebrows, jeans
tucked into her all-weather boots, Casey was the image of
the proverbial seaman who left the harbor every morning for
the day's catch. She had chuckled at her appearance as she
passed the mirror in the tiny front hall on her way out the
door. But her brief lightness of heart soon faded. Keeping up
her brisk pace did nothing to dispel the unease that roiled in
her chest and caught in her throat. *I should not have listened
to the morning news,* she had scolded herself. Thoughts pum-
meled her as her footsteps pushed into the wet sand, one after
another. Radio commentators were predicting more violence
in Northern Ireland. All of it seemed surreal to Casey. Three
hundred miles from her that morning, Irish were killing Irish.

Back at the cottage, she had changed into a heavy sweater, dry woolen pants and thick socks. Warmth and comfort snipped the edges from her fears. Now, sitting at the window, she sighed as she watched the light fading.

So this is how it feels to love someone, she thought to herself. *Well, MacMillan, you'd best go and write, stay busy.*

As Casey rose from her chair, the jangle of the phone rang insistently. She ran, almost falling across the table, to get to the phone on her desk. "Hello?" she breathed, gasping into the receiver.

"What did you do, run up from the beach?" Galean laughed into her ear.

"Oh my God, where are you?" Worry and fear clipped her words, raised her voice.

"Hey, hey!" said Galean, now alarmed. "What's going on there? What's wrong?"

For a second, Casey thought she might weep. Taking a long inhaled breath, she closed her eyes and waited a moment to speak.

"Casey? Case? Talk to me," said Galean. "Are you okay?"

Slumping down onto the chair by her desk, she gave herself another moment. "It's me just being a bit spooked by all the news from the North. I feel, after listening to the news this morning, like I've sent you off into a war zone. And the truth is, I have."

Galean's silence on the other end felt foreboding.

"Galean?" Casey prompted.

"It's funny you should use that phrase," he responded. "I was just having a conversation with my B&B host and he used the same words when we got talking about the last fifteen years. There's a kind of stalemate going on between the Northern Unionists and the Irish Republicans that doesn't seem solvable. At least not right now."

Listening to Galean, Casey sensed his concern. She could hear it beneath his measured words, his quiet tone. "Are you sure you want to stay?" she asked him. "Maybe you need to just come back here. We'll go back to Canada, stay for a while, finish our book, and then when things settle down …" She felt as though she were pleading.

"Ah, I think I'm fine, Case. Really. I'm here now. I'm not stupid. I'll go to safe places, like libraries. I mean who wants to bomb a library?" He laughed.

"Just stay safe, please." Casey felt the next words coming before she could stop them: "Galean, I love you." Virtually a whisper. The first time in forever she'd said those words to anyone. She imagined Galean at the other end, his hair flopping over his forehead, more gray than black; his dark eyes closing as he was wont to do when emotions overtook him.

"I will be back safe and sound," he assured her. "We have life under our feet and a book to finish." He took a respite breath. "And Casey, I love you."

———

THE DAYS BLENDED INTO ONE ANOTHER OVER THE COURSE of the next week. Sun and clear skies encouraged Casey to take long walks on the beach in the mornings. During the afternoons she sat writing, inspired by the fresh new feelings that were overtaking old fears. Each evening, just at suppertime, Galean would call to tell about his pursuit of his father's story and his search for family.

One evening he called, elated. "Case! I think I'm on to something!"

"Wait just one moment, Galean." Putting the phone down, she ran into the kitchen, poured a glass of wine, then quickly returned to her desk and picked up the receiver, "Okay. I'm ready to make a toast." She smiled. "This sounds like news that's worthy of celebration."

Galean's words tumbled over themselves. "I discovered, with the help of a lovely young man in the library here, that my father had a brother. And, Casey, he's one Michael McCann and he's alive living in Ballykelly, which is an hour's drive and a bit from here. He's seventy. My library friend thinks he can help me find him there."

Casey could hear the excitement in Galean's voice, and her only regret at that moment was not being there with him sharing his exhilaration. She waited, knowing he wanted to say more.

"I'm not feeling so abandoned anymore, Case. There's a family out there I belong to, and—" his voice caught, nearly breaking. "You are back there," he finished, then paused before continuing. "Maybe we are family, you and I, Casey. The family we've been looking for. Think about that. I have to go. but I'll call you from Ballykelly. Then I'll be on my way back to you."

"Be safe, Galean."

When Casey put the receiver on its cradle, she stood for a few seconds listening to the quiet. The day, which had been clear and bright, was fading now into a gentle evening. Returning to her typewriter, she picked up the sheaf of papers she'd left on her desk. As she read what she'd written that afternoon, she revisited her thoughts. Wrapping herself protectively within her plaid woolen shawl, her writing shawl, Casey let the words penetrate.

We are suspended in time. The past tries to hold
on as though afraid we might disappear without
our memories to keep us there. But one day the old
stories lose their power and the way opens up. Be
ready for that moment. Be ready for a world of pos-
sibilities. Be ready to discover yourself.

Just as she turned on the typewriter and scrolled the page back onto the roller, headlights flashed across the window. A car door slammed. A moment later, a loud knock came at the door followed by a voice. "Casey? It's Claire."

Opening the front door, she found Claire standing, shivering; no coat or hat, just wearing her red sweater, blue jeans and checkered scarf.

Claire pointed to the car, engine still running out in the driveway. "John's out there in the car. We've come to get you," she told Casey. "Your self-imposed solitary confinement is over for now. Your women—your writers—are asking what's happened to you." She continued talking as she walked into the house. "We haven't seen hide nor hair of you in days. Get your jacket. We're going to the pub. We're missin' ya."

Casey realized in that moment, that she was missing them, too. She truly had been isolating herself to write, to fulfill her promise to Galean and have the last chapter finished when he returned. Tonight, though, a celebration was fitting.

THE CHATTER OF VOICES, THE RHYTHM OF THE MUSIC AND the occasional hoot of laughter welcomed them. One of her writing students noticed Casey as she walked into the pub. It was the grandmother who'd been writing about estrangement from her family. Breaking ranks at the bar, the woman turned, grinned, and beckoned to her.

"Casey! We've missed you," the older woman said with genuine affection. "You haven't given up on us, have you? I hope not. You have brought light and life to us, the struggling writers here in this town. It's a gift, you must know that." Without waiting for a response, she encircled a surprised Casey in a warm hug.

Others at the bar turned and invited her in among them; some, Casey had met before, some were strangers, yet all were welcoming. Claire handed her a glass of white wine and pointed to a table over in the corner. Making her way over there, Casey experienced a sense of friendship and camaraderie as she moved among the people. She let the feelings of warmth and harmony flow over her and into her body and, without resisting, she realized something: *I matter.*

The two women took a seat at the small table, which offered a quieter place to talk, being in the corner away from the boisterousness and the music. "Are you all right?" Claire asked, reaching out and resting her hand on Casey's arm. "I've been wondering how you've been since Galean left."

Casey took a moment. "I'm not sure how to answer your question. But, I think I'm really okay."

Claire shifted her head to one side, crinkled her brow. "Not sure you answered my question. Could you take another run at it?" She yawed a bit to the left, smiled, put her elbow on the table, chin on her hand, and waited.

Casey sighed. "Honestly, I'm okay."

"But?" Claire pushed further.

"Okay," Casey relented. "Yes. I'm worried about Galean wandering around out there with bombs going off and people shooting people. And," warming now to her fears,

Casey carried on. "He asked me in his usual unusual way to marry him."

Claire hooted and cried out, "Excellent!"

"Well, yeah," said Casey. "And then he left for Belfast."

Inexplicably, the two women began to laugh, leaving Casey feeling lighter than she had for a few days. An image of Galean proposing marriage and running out the door, prompted them both to dissolve.

Inhaling a staggered breath, Casey wrapped her arms around herself and sputtered, "Thank God for laughter."

Claire, still smiling, reached for her drink and raised it toward Casey. "Here's to laughter and here's to you, my friend. All will be well." Then she stopped and her smile faded. "But, oh. Does this mean we'll be losing you soon? Will you go back to Canada when Galean gets back?"

"Here's the thing: we haven't even got as far as deciding what'll happen when he returns. My sabbatical isn't up till the spring, and … I'm really not ready to leave—I'm happy here."

"Do you have to decide right away? Maybe when Galean gets back … I know!" Claire threw her arms in the air, bringing them down onto the table with a bang. It was loud enough to startle those sitting and standing at the bar nearby. "Why don't you think about being married here? One of our regular patrons is the local priest."

"Claire, neither one of us is Catholic." Casey spoke almost apologetically.

"Well then, John'll marry you. He was a captain in the Navy."

"Claire, you are probably one of the nicest friends I've ever had, and maybe one of the nuttiest," Casey said with affection. "Anyway, let's wait till Galean gets back. He's excited right now about what he's discovering about his family, in fact, he's on his way to Ballykelly to search out his uncle. He sounded almost joyous on the phone."

In just that moment, conversation ceased. Voices rose from across the room and the fiddle took up the tune. "Deck the Halls" rang out.

Claire grabbed Casey's hand. "Come on over to the bar. It's a tradition. John'll be singing his favorites soon, and he loves people to join in."

The Christmas season had arrived. An unfamiliar elation caught Casey by surprise. Something feeling like happiness? Whatever it was, it was a feeling that stayed with her for the rest of the joyful night.

LATER, AS SHE WAS ABOUT TO LEAVE THE PUB, CASEY RAN back to speak to John. Claire waited for her out in her car.

"Thank you, John," Casey told him. "Thank you for making me feel so welcome. And thank you for telling me the story of your brother Jimmy. You are a lovely man." And she kissed him on the cheek.

She could not remember when she had felt so enfolded into a company of friends. If she dared, she might have called them family.

THE NEXT MORNING, CASEY AWOKE VERY EARLY. SHE THREW her legs over the side of the bed, tossed on her warm wooly bathrobe and slipped her feet into sheepskin slippers. Heading directly to her typewriter, she flipped over the page on the daily calendar sitting on her desk: Monday, December 6. Galean had said he'd head home on Wednesday, and she wanted to have the draft of the last chapter ready for him.

She felt inspired. When she took the cover off her typewriter she found the page she'd left when Claire had arrived the night before. It now beckoned to where Casey had begun to write the last sentence, or what she hoped might be the last sentence of their book, if Galean approved and agreed.

> *Galean and I did not begin this book intending to reveal ourselves. We meant to continue upon our shared scholarly paths, entrusting our communal knowledge to you, our reader. Yet, the unexpected moments drew us in, and thus we were changed. We discovered the depths of being alive.*
> *Love and loss are the marrow of our human lives. They create the meaning we yearn for. They are the food of our personal history, the adventures we risk if we choose to be bold. Each day when we awake, we re-experience the grace of being alive. Be there, pay attention, if only for a moment. Invite the unexpected in, do not hesitate.*

Casey sat reading her words aloud, letting them float out into the room. Her historical fear of writing her own truth, without the protection of scholarly references and credited sources, caused her some discomfort. But then she began to smile. *I am alive. I begin again. The day calls me; how will I answer?*

Her quote, her thought, it was how she traditionally had begun her classes each new term. Now the words took on new substance. She leaned back and grinned. She realized she hadn't had breakfast or even made herself a coffee. As she stood, she saw the mail carrier on his postal bicycle stop at the end of her path to the road. Not used to getting much mail, she ran out the door, still in her robe and slippers.

"Good mornin', ma'am," the postman called as he held out a letter to her. "Looks pretty official, from a university."

Casey laughed as she took the envelope from him. She wondered happily if he would like to stay around and see what this woman was doing getting a letter from a university. "Thank you, sir, and the best of the season to you."

"And to you, ma'am," he said before cycling off down the road.

Walking back into the house, Casey looked at the return address: *Dr. Andrew Kingwood, Queen's College, Cork.* She set the letter on the kitchen table and went to make herself a mug of coffee before sitting down to read the letter. To her surprise, it was an unexpected invitation from her former advisor.

Chapter Thirty-Five

There will come a time when you believe everything is finished.
That will be the beginning.

—LOUIS L'AMOUR,
Lonely on the Mountain

Dr. Andrew Kirkwood
Department of Sociology and Philosophy
Queen's College Cork
Cork, Ireland
November 26, 1982
Dear Casey,
I am trusting that all is going well for you since last
we talked.

Casey smiled at the formal manner Andy was choosing.
She read on, intrigued.

We are busy here at the university with some reorgani-
zation and some hiring, which is the main reason for
my letter. I have been given a new role by the dean and
the provost, which is exciting; however, as universities
will do, it's added to my teaching load.
They are asking me to head up an exchange program
with City University back in Toronto, the intent being
to encourage and bring in more exchange students,
particularly at the master's and PhD level. One of my
responsibilities is to bring in a professor to assist me and

direct the program. There would be teaching responsi-
bilities as well. Because it will be a term position, I'm
free to appoint someone of my choosing. Of course, who
did I think of right away? Dr. Casey MacMillan.
The teaching responsibilities do not actually begin till
September 1983. However, the dean and provost would
like the person to come on Faculty sometime in the
spring term.
Of course, I understand all this is coming out of the
blue, and I'm not sure what your plans are when your
sabbatical ends. If you are interested at all, I would be
glad to work with City University in freeing you to take
on the position. It could always be seen as a plus for the
university there and for your department.
If you could, please get back to me with your initial
feelings right after the Christmas break.

Placing the letter on the table, Casey sat back, picked up
her coffee mug and folded her hands around it. She gazed
down at the letter and continued reading as she took a sip
of coffee.

You can call me here at my office, or you can write to
me. Let me know what your questions are and what
your doubts might be.
If you choose not to take the position, I'll understand.
However, do give it some thought. It's the kind of chal-
lenge and innovative position that I know might appeal
to you. A whole new world.
Take care.
As always,
Andy

Casey's first inclination: *Maybe a few months ago, but*
probably not now. Yet she could feel some pull, some intui-

tive call that said, *Sit with it; wait; talk to Galean. But how could I come back here, take on this role and marry Galean? No! I've spent all my life letting my fears of commitment and love call the shots. No more. I'll not say anything to Galean now. I'll wait till he comes back, talk it over with him. Then call Andy. There—that feels right.* She folded the letter back into the envelope, walked into the living room and put it by the lamp on her desk.

The afternoon began to fade into early evening. Casey, dressed in a comfortable white silk caftan, let her hair hang loosely onto her shoulders. She stood in the kitchen wondering whether to call Claire and John at the pub and invite them for supper on Thursday, the day after Galean would arrive back. Looking in the refrigerator, she realized that her self-imposed exile had not included keeping groceries on the shelves. Only a few eggs, some orange juice, cold ham that appeared it might qualify for an experiment, and a lot of cheese. That seemed to be it. *Grocery shopping tomorrow,* she mentally noted to herself.

Taking some bread and cheese and some tomato relish given from Claire's kitchen to hers, Casey took a frying pan from the drawer and began making her favorite meal, grilled cheese with tomatoes. The kettle on the counter announced tea. As she poured the boiling water over the leaves, she glanced up at the clock. It was almost six-thirty, about time for Galean to call.

When the clock struck seven, Casey wondered if he had decided not to call because he was coming home the next day. *Maybe he's with his uncle and family.*

Restlessness and unease began to set in. Galean's phone number at the bed-and-breakfast in Belfast was all she had. He'd said that as soon as he got settled in Ballykelly, he'd call her. That was supposed to be tonight. For some inexplicable reason, Casey went to the door, opened it and looked out into the dark. Possibly he'd decided to come home, she thought, and might be just now driving down the road. But only the black sky with some stars and a half-moon greeted her.

By nine o'clock she could not sit still. She didn't want to leave in case he called, thus she paced the living room till she began to feel silly. Turning on the radio, she whirled the dial, looking for music that might calm her. As she turned the dial she paused at a station reporting a special bulletin:

... the bombing took place in Ballykelly, Northern Ireland, just around the hour when British soldiers and townspeople were collecting at the pub for a special Christmas party. There have been fatalities and several injured, but we do not have details as yet.

Casey ran to the phone to call Claire. It rang just as she reached it. Grabbing the receiver, her voice shaking, she gasped, "Galean?"

"No, Casey, no. It's Claire. I just heard there's been a bombing in Ballykelly. Have you heard from Galean today?"

"No, Claire, I haven't." Casey felt a foreboding sense of doom; a feeling that started in her chest and spread into the palms of her hands.

"Have you tried to call him?"

"I can't. I don't have a number." Casey's voice began to break.

"Okay, I'm coming over," said Claire.

And Casey let the phone slip from her hand onto its cradle.

AT MIDNIGHT, THE TWO WOMEN SAT, STILL LISTENING TO THE radio. A special announcement in progress chilled them:

> *A bomb exploded in the Clyde Inn at Ballykelly,*
> *County Londonderry. No warning was given. The*
> *pub was crowded at the time with soldiers from the*
> *nearby army camp and civilians from the locality.*
> *The walls of the building were badly damaged and*
> *the roof collapsed. So far fourteen people have died,*
> *eleven of them soldiers and three civilians.*
> *In addition, sixty-six people have been injured.*
> *Forty of the injured are now being treated in hospi-*
> *tals in the immediate area and in Belfast. The Irish*
> *National Liberation Army has claimed responsibil-*
> *ity.*

"That's it," said Casey as she jumped up from the couch. "I can't sit here wondering if he's injured, dead or on his way back. I have to know."

Claire stood and wrapped her arms around Casey, gently guiding her back to the couch. "I'm going to make us some tea, and while I do that I want you to take this phone book," she said, pulling a thick telephone directory from her catch-all bag and handing it to Casey. "This will have the numbers of all the hospitals in Belfast and surrounding towns. I'd start with Belfast."

Out into the kitchen, Claire went around the corner where Casey could not see her. She bent her head, crossed herself and, straightening up, walked over to the kettle. By the time she returned with two mugs of tea, Casey was at her desk on the phone and furiously writing.

"Yes. Yes. No, I understand. Are you suggesting the best thing to do is come there? Yes. Yes, thank you." Putting the receiver down, Casey looked up, her eyes bright, fearful. Old memories, old terrors, flooded her body. "We have to go there," she told Claire. "We have to, there's no other way. The hospitals can't give me any information or any names over the phone."

Without hesitation, Casey ran into the bedroom, threw off her silk caftan and pulled on her jeans and heavy sweater. She dressed with the speed of fear. Back in the living room, she shoved bare feet into her winter boots. Tossing a jacket over her arm, she grabbed her car keys and threw them to Claire. "Let's take my car. Would you drive? I'm not sure I can."

Claire nodded as she caught the keys, and they ran from the house.

In the car, Casey held a flashlight over a map that Claire had magically produced.

"Here, Casey," she had said. "You navigate us there, and I'll make sure we arrive as fast as we can. There won't be traffic at this time of the morning, so it'll take us about five hours."

Most of the way, their conversation consisted of short, clipped directions. Claire spoke little, listening only to Casey's instructions.

"Turn right here. Then left."

Silences reigned while Casey figured out the best route as they drove. At one point she advised, "I think we have to go over to Kildare and on up to the border from there."

Claire, staring straight ahead at the road, took a deep breath, "You do know that we may be stopped at a British checkpoint. We'll be questioned, maybe even taken aside. Two women headin' north in the middle of the night might seem a bit suspicious in their eyes."

Casey said nothing for a moment. "If we do, would you let me explain?" For some irrational reason, Casey believed that if the British soldier heard her Canadian accent, he'd let them go on through without questioning.

And in fact, the soldier at the checkpoint who asked their intent on going into Northern Ireland, indeed seemed sympathetic. The woman wanting to get to her injured friend stirred some place in the soldier who had seen enough devastation during his short tour in Ireland.

TWO HOURS FROM THE CHECKPOINT, THE SKY STILL DIM, they drove into the parking lot of one of Belfast's main hospitals. Royal Victoria Hospital. Casey had been intent on going to this one first.

"I have a feeling," she said to Claire as they were getting out of the car, "that if Galean has been hurt, and he's conscious ..." Casey, knowing his history of head injury, felt a chilling dread. "And if he's conscious at all," she continued, "the doctor in him will ask to be taken to the Royal Victoria."

Trying to keep up with Casey, who was running now across the parking lot, Claire called to her, "Just go to the main desk in Emergency, and I'll catch up." Letting Casey go on in, Claire turned back to a group of ambulance drivers who were standing at the entrance to the emergency department. They seemed to be waiting for something.

"Excuse me," said Claire. "Have you brought any people here from the bombing in Ballykelly?"

"We all have, ma'am," said the driver closest to her. "It was a mess. Worst I've seen."

"Do you perchance know the names of any you brought

here last night?" Claire squeezed her hands into fists, digging her nails into the palms, so afraid that one of the names they'd say might be Galean's.

"'Fraid we can't give out that information, ma'am," said the driver. "But I'm sure if you go directly to Admissions, they'll help you." He pointed inside the doors where she could see Casey talking to the nurse at one of the desks.

Just as she spotted her, Claire saw Casey's hand rise, covering her mouth. The nurse talking with her ran from behind the counter and started to lead her down the hall. Claire could tell it was bad. She ran in to follow them. When she was at her side, she reached over and circled her arm around Casey's back.

Rounding a corner, the nurse led them into a small room. Two couches faced one another. A lamp glowed with a soft light on a table where clean cups and saucers sat alongside a pot of tea—balm for the grieving. The nurse spoke in a gentle voice. "One of the doctors will be right in," she said, directing her words to Claire.

Casey eased herself down onto the couch, holding herself straight, her hand grasping the fabric of the arm. "They brought Galean here. He was at the pub where it happened. As soon as I asked for Dr. Laihy, they knew right away. I lied and said I was his wife." Her words and sentences seemed disconnected and jerky, as though she were reaching to understand everything that had happened in the last few hours.

The door opened just as Claire sat down beside Casey. Neither stood as a young woman in a white coat walked in and, without hesitation, sat down opposite them. She leaned forward and reached for Casey's hands. "Mrs. Laihy, I'm Doctor Oliver, a neurosurgeon. I have been taking care of your husband since they brought him in late last night."

"He's alive?" Casey asked, grasping the doctor's hands as though hope lay in those fingers.

"He's had a serious head injury and that's why I was called in."

Casey looked at the doctor's eyes and for some reason felt better. She saw a soothing calm—or was that only what she wanted to see? The doctor's hand felt gentle against her grasp. Within minutes she was telling the doctor about Galean's previous head injury. She spoke clearly, calmly, as though she felt Galean depended on her to save his life.

Interrupting her, the doctor asked, "Would you like to see him? He's in intensive care and he's unconscious, but sometimes it's helpful, even if you can say a few words to him. Maybe somewhere in there he will hear you."

Just then, the doctor's beeper began to vibrate with a kind of insistence that, for Casey, sounded forbidding.

The doctor glanced down at her message and turned to both women. "Your husband is seizing. I need to go." She gestured to a nurse. "Could you bring Mrs. Laihy and her friend up to the intensive care unit, let them sit in the family room." And she ran down the hall into an elevator.

Later, Casey would not be able to recall those anguished moments clearly when the doctor came out of intensive care. She remembered Dr. Oliver's arms around her. She remembered how she whispered, "I'm so sorry."

From then on, for the rest of the day, all was a blur.

OF ALL THE TIMES SHE HAD WRITTEN ABOUT GRIEF AND LOSS, nothing prepared Casey for the slow, searing pain that entered her body. The required details kept her moving in and out of reality throughout the first few days. One of those details was Galean's belongings at the hospital. The nurse who had been caring for him brought his battered briefcase to Casey while she and Claire were still sitting in the family room, absorbing the awful news.

"I thought you might want to take his things now, before …" the nurse paused as she set Galean's briefcase on the floor beside Casey's feet. "I am so very sorry." Hardly a sound echoed as the nurse opened the door and went out to the hall.

Casey did not look up nor did she see the tears on the nurse's cheeks. The briefcase sat at her feet; Galean's worn bag, now covered with grey ash and granules from a broken ceiling. It was the one he carried everywhere for as long as she'd known him. It wasn't surprising that he'd taken it with him to the pub that night. Reaching down, Casey saw what looked like an envelope in the side pocket, her name written on the front. It was a letter. Galean, in his organized fashion, had written a letter to Casey. Everything was there in it. Everything. It was dated the morning he had left Clonakilty for Belfast. *Did he sense something?* she wondered.

Dearest Casey:

Leaving you today is going to be very difficult. But I am grateful you understand why I must go, why I must complete this journey. You and I have been there for one another through disappointments, through extraordinary moments and through ordinary every-day life.

If I have not told you in so many words, because I sometimes don't pay attention to the nuances of life, I will tell you now. Here in the shades of an early Irish dawn, you, my dear Casey, need to know you will be

*my friend and my love, forever. Took me a while to have
the courage to say all this to you—knowing that nothing
is forever, as you keep telling me. But may I differ here
this morning, because I believe we are, forever.*

*Now the hard part. I know you are worried about me
going into, as you call it, a war zone, but I will not be
stupid, yet who knows what life holds at any time. If
you are reading this letter, something has happened, a
possible something that will not allow me to come back
to you. So here is what I ask of you.*

*I want to be cremated, and I want it done soon. And
Casey, please scatter my ashes (even if you have to do
it in the dark of night) along that beautiful stretch of
beach where we have sat together, so many times. Any
other kind of memorial, I will leave to you.*

*Do let James Atwater know what a good friend he has
been. My lawyer knows what to do with my house. He
will sell it and the money from that sale will go to you.
I posted a letter to my lawyer before I left Toronto just
to be sure that my affairs were all in order.*

Casey let the letter sit in her lap for a moment, as she
imagined Galean making arrangements to "settle his affairs"
before he left upon his trip to Ireland.

*Just know this: you, Casey, have brought me home.
With love forever,
Galean*

––––––––––

CASEY, IN HER OWN STEADFAST WAY, HONORED EVERYTHING
that Galean had asked of her. And as she did, it felt in some
way as though he was there at her shoulder.

Casey, Claire and John walked the beach one night shortly after they brought Galean's ashes home from Belfast. As the sky dimmed and the stars became small lights here and there throughout the sky, the three friends took the lid off the simple wooden urn and scattered the ashes into the sand, covering them as they walked. Waves washing ashore touched the silence between each of them. When the last few ashes lay in the bottom of the urn, Casey, with John holding a flashlight, read what she'd written. It was the last line of their book:

Love and loss are the marrow of our human lives. They create the meaning we yearn for. They are the food of our personal history, the adventures we risk if we choose to be bold. Each day when we awake, we re-experience the grace of being alive. Be there, pay attention, if only for a moment. Invite the unexpected, do not hesitate.

"Thank you, Galean," said Casey. "For teaching me how to be alive and for urging me always not to hesitate. May the road rise up to meet you, my friend."

Casey then handed the wooden urn to John. He walked to the shore and, with a strong right arm, threw it far out into the ocean. It floated for a few minutes and then sank, out of sight.

CLAIRE STAYED AT THE COTTAGE WITH CASEY FOR TWO weeks. Any Christmas and New Year celebrations were muted, yet songs were sung some evenings at the pub and stories told.

One day Casey looked over at Claire and said, "I think it'll be all right for you to go home." But that night while the two were preparing vegetables for their supper soup, Casey slipped down almost gracefully to the floor in the kitchen and began to cry a deep heartbroken wail.

Claire did not leave her for another week. Near the end of that week, the phone rang, early in the evening.

Casey picked up the receiver. "Oh, Anne, it's so good to talk to you."

"Casey, I am so, so sorry," said Anne. "We all came back from Christmas break and that's when we found out. Can you tell me what happened, or is it too soon to talk about it?"

Casey walked over and pulled her leather chair up to the desk, winding the phone cord around her hand as she went. Sitting back in the chair, she closed her eyes, "Actually, Anne, it's time to talk about it." And she began to tell the story of how Galean was killed in a pub bombing. How he had begun to finally discover family and put his old story to rest, and how the two of them had come full circle to find home.

Anne was quiet for a few minutes before asking, "And what now for you, Casey?"

"Well, I have this letter from Andy Kingwood. I'd like to read it to you."

EPILOGUE

the stars began to burn
through the sheets of clouds,
and there was a new voice
which you slowly
recognized as your own.

—MARY OLIVER, "The Journey"

September 1983

A warm September morning lit the seminar room. Windows looked out upon a quadrangle of green lawns and flowered gardens. Queen's College Cork in Ireland, Casey's new academic home. She stood at a carved-oak lectern, which she would eventually move over to the side of the room while she chose a place to stand among her newly arrived graduate scholars.

These were her enthusiasts, students in her care, fresh from City University in Toronto. Teachers, psychology and philosophy majors, writers and one man with a brand new pre-med degree. All had scrambled to apply for the newly established post-graduate study-abroad program, for which Casey had been chosen as Program Director by the dean of graduate studies and the provost at Queen's College Cork, with some encouragement from one Doctor Andrew Kingwood.

Now this morning, the first day gathering together, she looked out at the men and women settling themselves into their chairs, all placed in the circle that Casey had asked for. They were quietly greeting one another, all new to the country and to this university. All like Casey, setting out upon a new adventure.

"Welcome, ladies and gentlemen," she greeted her students. "Welcome to this beautiful university here in Ireland." Lifting the book that rested on the lectern, she moved away and walked over to stand among them. Gazing out the window for a moment as though seeing something beyond, something others might not see, Casey began. "Before we start telling who we are and where we've traveled from, I'd like us to try something rather different for a group of academic graduate students." She turned her gaze toward them and away from the window. "I'd like us to become storytellers for a while. In fact, we might remain storytellers throughout this year we've chosen to spend together." She paused. "And I'd like your permission to begin with my story. May I?"

A few nodded. Some, now curious, leaned forward.

Casey opened the book she had brought from the lectern. "I want to read something to you." Holding the book in one hand, her other hand placed gently on the page, Casey spoke these words:

We are born vulnerable and exquisitely delicate.
We may live our days seeking a place of wholeness.
Feeling "less than," we may aspire to be loved in all
the wrong places, by all the wrong people, for all
the wrong reasons.
Until that day when we turn back to ourselves, feel

the strength of our own spirit, uncover our own stories and move into our lives.

"A good man wrote that. And he is here within these pages. So. Let's begin, ladies and gentlemen. Let's begin to uncover our stories."

Bibliography

Bass, John. 2016. Sister. *unpublished poem*. Portland Oregon.

Blixen,Karen. wikiquote https://en.wikiquote.org/wiki/Karen_Blixen.

Briggs, Patricia. 2008. Cry Wolf. An Ace Book published by arrangement with Hurog, Inc. (p.79).

Clare, Cassandra. 2014. *Clockwork Princess.* New York, NY. Simon & Schuster.

Dunn, Stephen. 2014. Formalities For the Long Road, in *Lines of Defense.* New York, NY. W.W. Norton.

Franklin, R.W., ed. 1999. Fr.# 515 in *The Poems of Emily Dickinson: Reading Edition.* Cambridge MA. The Belnap Press.

Goolrick, Robert. 2008. The End of the World as We Know It. In *Scenes from a Life.* Algonquin Books of Chapel Hill, N.C.

Green, John, Lauren Myracle & Maureen Johnson. 2009. *Let It Snow: Three Holiday Stories.* Speak. Reissue edition.

Herbert, Frank. 1965. Dune. *Ace 40th Anniversary ed. Edition* (2005).

Hoagland, Tony. 2015. *Message To a Former Friend.* in The Sun, August 2015, Issue 476.

Kingsolver, Barbara. 1995. High Tide in Tucson. *Essays From Now or Never.* New York, NY. Harper Collins.

L'Amour, Louis. 1986. *Lonely On the Mountain* New York, NY. Bantam Books.

Norris, Kathleen. *Answered Prayer* https://thevalueofspar-rows.com/2014/12/.../poetry-answered-prayer-by kathleennorris.

Oliver, Mary. 1986. The Journey in *Dream Work*. New York, NY. The Atlantic Monthly Press.

Oliver, Mary.1986. Wild Geese in *Dream Work*. New York, NY. The Atlantic Monthly Press.

Oliver, Mary 2006. The Uses of Sorrow in *Thirst*. Boston, MA., Beacon Press.

Oliver, Mary. 2009. Love Sorrow in *Red Bird*. Boston, MA.,Beacon Press

Oliver, Mary. 2009. Evidence. in *Evidence*. Boston, MA., Beacon Press.

Oliver, Mary. 2010. Don't Hesitate in *Swan: Poems and Prose Poems*. Boston, MA.,Beacon Press

Proust, Marcel. 2000. *Within a Budding Grove, Part 1*. Modern Library UK.

Rochefoucauld, Francois. 2010. Reflections; or Sentences and Moral Maxims. HardPress Publishing

Rumi. 1996. Childhood Friends. from *The Essential Rumi, Coleman Barks* New York. NY. Harper Collins.

Shakespeare, Wm.,Sonnet XXXIV By Wm. Shake-speare. At www.poetryfoundation.org/poems-and-poets/.../90049

Shakespeare, Wm. Troilus and Cressida *in Act 3 Scene 2.*

Shakespeare, Wm. A Midsummer Night's Dream *in Act 3, Scene 2.*

Shakespeare, Wm. A Midsummer Night's Dream *in Act 3, Scene 1.*

Shakespeare, Wm. Julius Caesar *in Act 5, Scene 1*

Scullard, H.H. 1981. *Festivals and ceremonies of the Roman Republic.* Janus. Ithaca, NY. Cornell University Press.

Shihab Nye, Naomi. 1994. Kindness in *The Words Under the Words.* The Eighth Mountain Press.

Thoreau, Henry David. Brainy Quote. Retrieved October 22, 2016 from Brainy Quote.com web site: http://www.brainyquote.com/quotes/quotes/h/henrydavid103847.html

Tolstoy, Leo. 1877. Anna Karenina *Translated by Constance Garnett Revised.* New York. Random House 1965.

Williams, Hugo. 2002. Tides. *Hugo Williams Collected Works.* London, UK. Faber & Faber.

Whyte, David. 2014. Touch. excerpted from *Consolations* Langley WA. Many Rivers Press.

Whyte, David. 2015 *Consolations: The Solace, Nourishment and Underlying Meaning of Everyday Words.* Many Rivers Press, Langley, Washington (p.102).

Acknowledgements

My gratitude:

To Irene Graham of The Creative Writers of Ireland, who listened with a writer's keen mind and ear, who read each draft with care, encouragement, and celebration. She inspired me to write from my deeper self and to discover the truth of my story. She is my coach, my editor, and my friend.

To my friends:

Heather Donaldson, who listened with care and delight when I gathered courage to read a few lines to her, who never doubted my writer's heart.

Annie Peace, who sent me emails, talked to me, appeared on my computer screen, enlivening, and inspiring me, whose inner wisdom shepherded the journey.

Laura Jeffrey, who was there with me in Ireland on Innes Mor Island, where Casey found her home. Laura gave me my song and cheered on my story.

Catherine Comuzzi, whose insights into the wounded soul gave me ground for the truth of Casey's experiences.

Carol Howitt, who makes me laugh at myself and who says, "Of course you can." And so I do. I write.

Elizabeth McAuliffe, who keeps me together body and soul, every step of the way.

Barbara Rennick, who is there, no matter what, friend extraordinaire. Who gave me my first foray into the world of publishing and introduced me to the wonder of unicorns.

To those who embolden the writer in me:

Lindsay Humphreys, who finds just the right word and understands my story.

Jane Kirkpatrick, writer and story teller whose wise counsel led me into a community of writers.

Pat Sands, who gave me time and wisdom, ferrying me into the world of independent publishing.

Tina Redd, a friend and a teacher of storytellers read my first drafts and encouraged me to tell Casey's story.

Kimberly Roy, what would I do without her gift, her readiness to gather in my stories, and make them come alive.

Patricia Marshall, Claire Flint, and Kim Harper-Kennedy at Luminare Press, for the care you took to send my book out into the world.

Jamie Passaro, who read and edited with artful eyes and insight.

Sandy McCormack and Pacific Northwest Writers for inspiration and laughter, the necessary ingredients.

How strange it might seem to thank my main character, Dr. Casey MacMillan, professor of philosophy and literature. Yet, her love of learning and her respect for her students reflects all those education professors who taught me the joy and value of living and exploring our inner lives. Casey represents those graduate professors with whom I've worked, who have inspired and encouraged me to see the poetry in our personal relationships, with others, and within ourselves. My colleague and friend Dr. Carmen Shields taught me well about telling our own story.

To my family in Ontario:

Kath, who read more than one draft, who loves my stories, and lets me bask in her belief in me.

Heather, who laughs with that joyous ring, who is wise and unflagging in her love and support.

Phil and Julie, who are ever patient and loving, there always, ready for the next book, never doubting.

To my family here in Oregon:

Tom, our love of words, language, and ideas is our shared bond.

Bob, Jen, and Carter, you brought me into the world of a family who inspire and care deeply. You open my creative soul.

John, Jenna, Claire, and Olivia. You are the poetry of family and the laughter of belonging, the rhythm and beauty of kinship.

Jerry, my personal wordsmith and ever-present story-teller.

To Janice, Alex, Jack, and Steve, my forever family, always and ever, whose adventures inspire me.